BREAK AWAY

The High Sierras – Book Seven

Diane Benefiel

PRAISE FOR DIANE BENEFIEL

Solitary Man

NATIONAL READERS' CHOICE AWARD WINNING NOVEL

"I am in love with this story. I devoured this book and didn't want it to end. The chemistry between the characters and the plot kept me wanting to read late into the night. This is my first read from Diane Benefiel but definitely not my last. I can't wait to read more from this amazing author. Thank you Diane Benefiel for getting me hooked on your books!" ~ CJ's Book Corner

"Ryder was exactly who Brenna needed in her life, and trust me when I say you will love him because yeah he really is that good of a guy. Solitary Man is my first book by this author and it will not be the last. I really think you all will enjoy this one as much as I did it is one I do recommend." ~ I'm A Sweet And Sassy Book Whore

"I really enjoyed this book and there were a few twists and turns that kept me completely involved in the story. This is the first time I have read this author and it definitely won't be my last!" ~ Sassy Southern Book Blog

HIGH SIERRAS SERIES

Flash Point

"Diane Benefiel takes us on a story filled with mystery, suspense, and action as we try to solve what is going on in the small town of Hangman's Loss. Flash Point is a story that will have you flipping the pages and wondering who is the behind the attacks against Hangman's newest resident and why." ~ Sarah Reads

*"**Flash Point** really surprised me. It's not what I was expecting but I really enjoyed reading it. It's a fun easy read that captured me from the start."* ~ Coffee Chat

Dead Giveaway

"Diane has written yet another winner in her High Sierra series. Murder witness and 'person of interest' Gwen flees with her godson to Cameron's uncle Eli. Gwen and Eli have no use for one another but come together for Cameron's sake and to find the true murderer...and in the process find their way to one another. My evening with Gwen and Eli couldn't have been more delightful, and I look forward to the next installment of the High Sierras." ~seniorphotog

*"I loved this second book in the High Sierras series. This is a story of two people who are attracted to each other, but reconnecting under the worst of circumstances. I discovered Ms. Benefiel's books and have loved the careful way she draws you in to the story with characters that make you feel as if you are reading about friends. I am really looking forward to the next High Sierras book, **Already Gone**."* ~paytonpuppy

Already Gone

"This series has only gotten better and better! Seriously, there's something that really speaks to my heart about Maddy and Logan, and Hangman's Loss FEELS like a small California town tucked away in the Sierras. They're such a power couple! I read this book in just a couple of days--totally sucked me in. It's that perfect blend of fun, sizzle, and suspense! I just want to live in Maddy's life forever but since I can't--I can't wait for the next book!" ~Katharine Montgomery

"A wonderful story about second chances. The minute you start reading, you will be instantly hooked. The author weaves a tale of drama and romance that keeps you enthralled and turning the pages. Maddie is feisty and Logan is her brooding and over protective suffering hero. The sparks fly every time they see each other.

Eventually they give in and realize that they are perfect for each other and have always been. This is a great story right up to the last word." ~Simatsu

Burnover in Rescued Anthology

"Sweet, Sexy stories featuring furbabies and helping to save lives, it's a win win for all." ~Kara's Books

"8 stories by 8 outstanding authors. In these stories, there is a tattoo artist, two firefighters, two sheriff deputies, a famous furniture maker, a veterinarian, and a country music singer, and I loved them all. Then add in that each story has a dog or puppy that is rescued, along with a story of love and romance, it is a winning combination." ~Susan D

Deadly Purpose

I loved everything about this book, and it made me want to check out the other books in the series! The immediate suspense drew me in, and the High Sierras setting was perfect, as was the mysterious stranger Meg finds in her cabin. This novel had a well-written, exciting, and descriptive narrative that kept me glued from start to finish. Without giving away spoilers, the author has crafted one exciting, romantic ride, full of twists and turns. I highly recommend this book and can't wait to see what the author comes up with next. ~Sebastian Moran

This book took me by surprise. I didn't expect to get so caught up in this book that my whole day was spent captured in its pages. It has been a long time since I couldn't put a book down but Deadly Purpose did this to me. I loved every page. ~WildfireJane

Clear Intent

"I'd been waiting on this one awhile!! I truly loved the story! I laughed, cried and got so frustrated I couldn't see straight! I'm now hoping there will be more from Hangman's Loss, I don't want to see this series end! Thank you for a very wonderful getaway!! I highly

recommend this complete series!!!! Wow! Just Wow!!" ~Linda Helms

"I've looked forward to every book in this series and have enjoyed each one, loving the characters as it feels you walk with them through exciting, scary situations and sigh as relationships become beautiful. This was an exciting story with almost nonstop action and heart stopping dangers. All of my favorite people in Hangman's Loss are together to help Jack, Dory, Adrian and the town through crisis." ~JLocke

JAMESONS U.S. MARSHALS SERIES

Hidden Betrayal

"As someone who never pre-orders ANYTHING, I put my order in a WEEK before it came out. Know why? Because I just didn't want to wait! Not to give away any spoilers but this is my favorite book from this author yet, in no small part because Mikayla is my favorite type of heroine. Right from the get-go, she's absolutely determined to meet everything on her terms. I loved the dialogue between her and Linc--with her saying, "I didn't stay back because *I* was handling it." Yes, he's a hottie with a protective streak, but she's certainly no little woman. It really WORKS. In the end, 10/10. Can't wait to pre-order the next one too!" ~Amelia

"An exciting, romantic read with a sexy hero and a determined heroine who is hell-bent on doing things her own way. The romance heats up as the plot thickens. Linc and Mikayla need to work together to survive, but along the way, the sparks start flying. You need to read this!" ~danube eichinger

www.BOROUGHSPUBLISHINGGROUP.com

BREAK AWAY
Copyright © 2019 Diane Benefiel

ISBN 978-1-951055-38-7

To my parents, Charles and Dagmar Benefiel, who took their girls on family vacations that always included adventures in the great outdoors. They instilled in all of us an enduring love for the wildness of nature.

BREAK AWAY

Chapter One

Levi took the turn onto the dirt driveway, the morning sun sending sharp shafts of light into his eyes. He squinted and shifted in his seat to stretch his back. Exhaustion made the last ten miles feel like a hundred, and he was sure his ass had permanently molded to the seat of the Suburban. He scrubbed a hand over his face, the scruff on his chin reminding him he hadn't shaved in over a week. The caffeine boost from the coffee he'd consumed the first three hours of his drive had worn off, and he'd refrained from getting more when he'd stopped for gas. He'd never had trouble sleeping before, but hey, another new thing in his life.

His destination finally in sight, a cabin his mom owned about fifty yards up the dirt-packed driveway. Renting it from her had been tricky. She'd refused to charge him, and he'd refused to stay there if he didn't pay. He'd won that skirmish only because his mom wanted him back home so damn bad she would've sold a kidney to make it happen.

He bumped along the pitted driveway, counting the minutes until he could fall face first onto the bed, and, if the gods were smiling, not surface again for twenty-four hours.

Levi noted the small home to the left, the other rental on the property, which sat under a grouping of tall pines. The structure was made of golden wood, its shutters and the deep porch painted a dark forest green. Wind chimes and some sort of coppery metal thing glinted in the light hanging from under the rafters. The cottage looked like it could belong to the queen fairy. An older model, dusty blue Prius sat parked in front.

He jerked, stomping on the brakes more out of instinct than awareness, bringing the Suburban to a skidding stop. His first thought was bear: big, black, and in the middle of the road.

Then the animal moved and he realized it was a big-ass dog nearly the size and shape of a bear. Black on its back, it had a white chest, and white with lighter brown markings on its face. It sat on its haunches in the middle of the driveway, not even twitching when the Suburban came within feet of flattening it. No matter how big the dog, it wasn't going to tangle with a car without major damage. Bear dog stared through the windscreen at Levi, then opened its huge mouth and gave a deep baying bark.

Levi pinched the bridge of his nose, sighed, and waited for it to move. The mountain of fur didn't appear ready to give up the middle of the road. He tapped the horn and eased the SUV forward. When the beast remained unfazed, he contemplated taking the Suburban off the driveway.

Figuring the trees were too close together for that, he parked and opened the car door to peel himself out of the seat with about as much dexterity as an octogenarian. A lungful of the pine-scented air had him stopping to take in his surroundings.

Large aspens, fresh air, and to the west, the granite peaks of the Eastern Sierras. Home. He'd left Oakland before dawn, and now it was midday. Not a bad ride, but given the turmoil of the past couple of weeks, he felt like he'd gone extra rounds with the champ and not come out the winner.

He glanced at the cottage, hoping to see the dog's owner. "Hey, bear dog," he called and held out a hand. No perked ears, no tail wag, not even an effort to sniff his fingers. Just a steady dog stare. Inspiration struck. He reached in the car to grab a bag from the center console. He ripped it open and reached inside. Black eyes followed the movement and Levi made sure the dog saw the chips before he stuffed them in his mouth.

Purposely, he dropped one on the ground. "You want that, bud?" Bear dog stared at the chip, then at Levi, then back at the chip. It glanced toward the cottage, a long string of drool landing at its feet. Then, with what seemed like a herculean effort, it rose to all fours and lumbered to get the dropped chip. Levi moved to the side of the road, dropping chips as he went. The dog followed, slobbering profusely as it used its massive tongue to snag each chip.

"Lucy, no." The sharp command rang out and the dog froze, its gaze locked on the last potato chip, drool now dripping like a leaky faucet.

"Busted. Sorry, bud."

A woman marched down the steps from the porch of the fairy cottage. Hmm. Compact and curvy and with a wild mass of dark curls piled on top of her head into a messy bun. Her jerky movements broadcast she was supremely pissed. Cute, but pissed.

"Time out," she pointed at the cottage. She and the dog had a stare-down. "Lucy, time out."

Levi wasn't sure if he'd name a bear dog Lucy. He thought maybe Ursula or Olympia, but the dog named Lucy dropped her head, heaved a big breath that sounded suspiciously like a sigh, and with a last longing look at the remaining chip, walked with dragging steps to the cottage.

"She acts like she's going to death row."

"Guilt trips are her best weapon." The woman turned flashing eyes on him. "Why would you feed my dog potato chips?"

"I'm not sure that's a dog." She glared at him and he shrugged. "She was in the middle of the road. I want to get by, tried honking and edging forward and she didn't move. Seemed like a good alternative."

"Do you know what potato chips do to dogs?" Her hands were on her hips in the classic *you're in deep shit, mister* pose.

"Make them happy?"

"How about give them diarrhea? A sudden dose of fat like that and she'll be a miserable mess."

The dog had climbed the steps and was regarding them with what could only be described as a woeful expression.

"That dog wants the chips bad."

"Well, she can't have them."

"Right." Because they were in his hand, Levi stuffed the remaining chips in his mouth and crunched as he checked out the woman. Flowy dress in bright tie-dye colors, a loose top with a wide neck, dangly earrings, plus about half a dozen bracelets on her left wrist. Add the fresh complexion without a hint of makeup, the Prius, the dog and potato chip lecture, and he had the type: earth mother.

The dose of fat from the chips must be doing him some good because Levi felt a spark of interest he wouldn't have thought possible ten minutes ago. The petite, curvy earth mother might be uptight about the dog, but she was hot.

"You got a body in there?"

"What?"

She pointed to his Suburban. "Big black monster. That thing looks like a hearse."

"Ah, no. No body."

He glanced at her Prius and figured she was judging. He couldn't help feeling a little defensive. Without doubt, the Suburban was a gas hog.

He stretched his back, glancing up the driveway where the cabin stood, shingled siding, metal roof, and with a bed that was waiting for him. Oh, so close.

He should've left the SUV in the driveway and walked around the dog and saved himself some grief. When he'd stopped for gas and called to give his brother an arrival time, Brad had asked him to check on the woman living in the cottage. Levi wasn't sure if he'd told him why he needed to check on her, but he might as well get the chore out of the way.

He wiped his hand on his shorts and stuck it out. "I'm—"

"I know who you are." She left his hand hanging. She turned and the midday sun lit her face. The side of her forehead had a healing scrape surrounded by mottled green of a fading bruise.

"Okay." He didn't like the look of that bruise or the deep purple one on her elbow.

She ran an assessing gaze over him. "Levi Gallagher of the locally prominent Gallagher family. Brother of Hangman's Loss police chief Bradley Gallagher, and related through blood and marriage to a couple dozen people scattered around this area."

Locally prominent? Bullshit. But the rest was true.

"You were also first baseman and team captain for Loss High's varsity baseball team the year they made it to the state championships. You got a full ride to University of the Pacific to play baseball." She ticked off his accomplishments on her fingers while he ran through his mental people files. Nothing pinged.

"You go to Loss High?"

She nodded, and Levi sighed.

"You going to tell me your name?"

"Big brother didn't pass along that little detail when he asked you to check on me?"

"He told me, but I don't remember. Why is my brother having me check on you?" When she didn't respond, he barely stopped an eye roll. "Cut me a break here."

For the first time, the woman seemed to really see him. He must have looked like any more verbal sparring would be the end of him. "Zoey Hardesty. I was two years behind you in high school."

He narrowed his eyes as the ping sounded inside his head. "Your hair was blue and you had a ring through your eyebrow."

"Yeah, that was me." She did a fluttering thing with her hands that came across as self-deprecating. "I'm not much for fitting in."

"You weren't the only kid who dyed their hair a weird color or pierced body parts."

"Those of us who did were rare enough to stand out."

Levi considered her. "You were also a brain. You may have been two years behind me, but you were still in my AP Bio class. You'd have been what, a freshman taking AP Bio?"

She shrugged. "We also had the same trig class. Listen, tell your brother I'm fine and not to worry." She turned back to her cottage, and Levi would've had to've been dead not to notice her rounded ass as she walked away. Or the limp.

***

Sharp knocking sounded at the door. Levi debated dragging himself out of bed to tell whoever was there to go away. Instead he pulled a pillow over his head to muffle the sound. The knocking stopped and he drifted back to sleep. The next time he surfaced was to find sunlight streaming through the window and the bedroom stuffy. Since the window faced west, the late afternoon sun was doing its job, and he bet he'd slept through most of the day. He got up to pull down the blind, figured he wasn't going to be able to get back to sleep, and wandered into the kitchen.

The cabin wasn't much. Just the basics, but good enough for him, and more importantly, it meant he hadn't had to move into his mother's place. Rentals were scarce during the summer vacation season, which would be picking up in a few weeks. He frowned at the vase of fresh flowers sitting on the little dining table. Next to the flowers sat a bowl containing several bananas and a couple of apples. They hadn't been there when he'd come in.

Opening the fridge, he spent a minute to take in the bounty. Milk, OJ, eggs, cheese: all good. But the best was a glass dish of something that looked intriguingly like home-cooked lasagna. He grabbed the OJ, shook the carton, then opened it to drink straight from the container. He went searching for his phone, found it in the bedroom, and brought it with him back to the kitchen.

He tapped a number from his favorites list, and with the phone tucked against his shoulder, pulled the lasagna from the fridge.

"That my baby?"

"I love you."

"Always the perfect thing to say when you call your mother."

"You brought me groceries and flowers." He opened cupboard doors until he found the plates.

"I did. I knocked, but when you didn't answer, I figured you were sleeping so I let myself in. There's French bread to go with the lasagna."

He found a spatula to scoop lasagna onto a plate, then put it in the microwave. "It looks amazing. Thanks, Mom."

"When are you coming over? Landon and I would like to see you."

He was still trying to get his head around the reality of his mom having a boyfriend. "Not today, but soon."

"Have you seen your neighbor, Zoey?"

"I have. She's got an oversize attitude, weeks-old injuries on her forehead and arm, and a limp. What's the deal?"

"She was in a nasty accident a week or so ago. She was crossing Main Street, at a crosswalk, mind you, and was hit by a car. The driver was speeding around the corner and didn't stop. The blow was glancing, thank goodness, but she was badly bruised. She's lucky she didn't end up with broken bones or worse."

"Jesus. No one saw it?"

"No. Your brother is fit to be tied."

"I bet. Brad likes his city all neat and orderly."

"Since he's police chief that makes sense. He does his best to keep us all safe, Levi."

"Yeah, I know. I'm not criticizing."

"Good." There was a long pause. "Rest up, come by anytime, but put Sunday on your calendar. Landon and I are having everyone over to my house and that includes you. Show up around noon. It will give you a chance to catch up with your family. We've missed you."

"I've missed you too. I'll be there. Bye, Mom."

Trish Gallagher had shown exceptional restraint during that conversation. Levi could all but feel her compulsion to ask him a million questions. Was he eating properly? Was he able to sleep, or was insomnia still kicking his ass? What were his plans now that he'd quit the force?

She'd held back, for which he was immensely relieved.

Levi found the bread, cut off a hunk, and since beer hadn't been among the groceries in his fridge, he made do with a glass of milk. The microwave dinged, and in less than a minute he was sitting at the dining table eating the lasagna, which was excellent despite the vegetables Trish had slipped into the dish. Staring at the bouquet of bright flowers, he reviewed his life for the ten thousandth time. His career was in the toilet, he hadn't had sex in four months, and the little stray dog that had adopted him had died two weeks ago. Now Levi harbored guilt wondering if feeding him potato chips had contributed to his demise. Sounded like a bad country western song.

But despite all that, he felt better than he had since his giant fuck-up.

Chapter Two

With the engine idling, Levi sat in the driver's seat staring at Lucy lying in the middle of the road. She was on her stomach in a patch of bright sunlight with her front legs stretched in front of her and her back legs splayed behind her, once again blocking his way. This time to an important step in his plan to get his shit together.

Driving home, he'd had the forethought to drape the cleaned and pressed chinos and shirt still in their plastic from the laundry service across the boxes. That had left his primary challenge of the morning locating his good shoes and the appropriate socks. He'd even donned a tie, and god knew he hated ties. A sport coat was draped over the passenger seat. He hoped Brad appreciated the effort.

His plan had been to hit his sister Maddy's café for coffee and a muffin before heading to the station for his job interview. Which he'd have time for if not for the dog doing a bear rug imitation and blocking the damn driveway.

He rolled down the window and leaned out. "Lucy, move it."

Lucy lifted her head, seemed to consider her options, then opened her mouth in a huge yawn.

He didn't have time for this.

A quick look behind and under the seats didn't turn up any bags of chips. He didn't care what the hot earth-chick said, he'd use chips as a bribe if it got the fur mountain to move. He opened the glove box. Score. No chips, but something even better.

Stepping out of the vehicle, he made sure the dog was watching when he peeled back the plastic. "Look what I have, big girl." He held it up so the dog could see the yellow and red wrapper. "Ever had one of these? What we have here is a Slim Jim, also known as pure American processed meat brilliance." He bit off a hunk, chewing slowly.

That got her attention. Lucy lifted her head, gaze steady on the meat stick in his hand.

He tore off a hunk and held it out, waving it about so the scent carried. Slowly, the dog rose to her feet, waterworks already started, a string of drool hanging from her jowls. Ears perked, she made her way over to him. He let her sniff the treat before tossing it. She caught it mid-air. "Swallowed it whole, good girl." He glanced at the cottage. "Want more before we both get in trouble?"

He took another bite before moving to the side of the driveway. Lucy followed and he fed her a piece of Slim Jim. By the time the screen door on the cottage slammed, he'd lured her far enough he could drive by.

"We're busted, Luce. Play it cool."

"What are you feeding my dog?"

Earth-chick was still hot. Spirals of curly black hair stuck out in odd directions, a wide band in bright orange around her head controlling some of it. It should have looked messy, but instead she hit the mark at sexy. And while he'd like to think the rosy flush of her cheeks was because she liked him, he might be mistaken about that. He held up the package in his hand. "Slim Jim. Lucy's into it." He bit off another piece. Not exactly what he'd wanted for breakfast, but it would do.

The horror on Zoey's face couldn't be faked. Slim Jims must be another no-no for the bear dog.

"You actually eat that?" She put a hand to her throat like she was trying not to gag. "Slim Jims aren't food, they're a processed product made of chemicals and god knows what. They're not fit for dogs, let alone human consumption."

Levi took another bite. "Yet they taste so good."

"Have you looked at the ingredients? Do you even know what you're eating?"

"This one is bacon flavored, so I'm guessing bacon."

"Read the ingredients list. I bet there's no bacon in it."

Levi shrugged, then held up the wrapper, squinting at the tiny print. "Ha, looky here. It says 'beef,' which is not bacon, but it's meat."

"Keep reading."

"Okay. Next is 'mechanically separated chicken.' I wonder what that means."

"It's chicken that's been pulverized and forced through a screen to make a kind of chicken sludge."

"So basically all the good stuff." He glanced at Zoey. "Hey, you feeling okay? You look a little green."

"That's because I'm going to throw up."

"Slim Jims are not for those with delicate digestion. I bet you're vegan."

"You'd lose. I love eggs and cheese, and will occasionally eat meat, depending on how it's raised and sourced. But mostly, I eat a plant-based diet."

He swallowed the last of the Slim Jim. "You're missing out on the benefits of a preservative-based diet."

"A sacrifice, I'm sure." He thought he caught a smirk to go with the eye roll. Progress. She gave the dog a stern look and pointed to the cottage. "Lucy, time out."

"She going to doggie jail again? It's not her fault she consumed the processed product made of chemicals and god knows what. I corrupted her."

"Yes, you did. She should resist your many temptations." Her gaze flew to his and he gave her a wide smile. "I didn't mean that how it sounds."

"Too bad."

"Anyway, Lucy is on time-out for blocking the driveway again. For some reason she likes this particular patch of sunlight."

"Who wouldn't?" He caught sight of the bruise on Zoey's forehead again and felt the humor slip away. "Heard you got hit by a car. How's the recovery going?"

"I'm alive with no broken bones. I'm good."

Since she did indeed look good, he nodded. "Now that bear dog has freed up the driveway, I need to get on."

He hopped into the Suburban and used the rearview mirror to watch her watching him as he drove away.

***

Levi stepped through the office door marked "Chief of Police, Bradley Gallagher." The man rising from the other side of the wide desk brought a familiar jumble of emotions to the fore. Admiration, pride, sometimes the feeling of never quite measuring up, but over everything else, love. His brother had always seemed smarter, stronger, and competently in charge. Levi was trying to get past the lifelong habit of feeling overshadowed.

He found himself engulfed in a hug. After a couple of slaps on the back, Brad stepped back, sharp green eyes giving him that familiar all-seeing assessment. "Glad you're back."

"Me too. It was the right move."

"You settled in at the cabin?"

"No. I still need to unpack the car. Mom came by with a bunch of groceries. That helped."

"Let her baby you a bit. She's glad you're back. Now that all her chicks are living in the same general area, she can hardly stand it. She's doing her best to hold back and not smother you." He motioned Levi to the padded chair in front of his desk. Brad turned to the coffeemaker on a table against the wall. He indicated the full pot with a raised brow.

Levi sat, nodding at the offer. "I'll stop by and see her later."

"Good." Brad handed Levi a steaming mug before taking his seat behind the desk.

"You look happy." Levi tapped his temple, then pointed. "A few gray hairs in there, brother. Other than that, I'd say being a family man and chief of police sits well on you."

"Three kids. Who the hell thought I'd have three kids? I don't know how our parents managed four."

"You need advice on birth control?"

"Shut up. I love my kids. The house is crazy sometimes, but Emmaline is like the calm in the middle of a whirlwind. She centers me."

"You hit the jackpot with her."

"I did." He gave Levi a level look. "You thinking to settle down?"

"I've got to get my life together before I can even begin thinking about it. And since I haven't been in a serious relationship in over a year, it's not looking likely." He sipped his coffee. Strong and dark the way he liked it.

"Over a year? That's plain sad." Brad shook his head. "Brace yourself because you're Mom's current project. She's already asked Emmaline and Maddy if they have friends they could introduce to you."

Levi closed his eyes, pinching the bridge of his nose. "Oh god. Shoot me now."

"Thought you might like a heads-up."

"Yeah, thanks."

Brad sipped his coffee. "Have you thought about our offer?"

"I have. The job appeals, but I don't want it because we're family."

"That's not why you're being offered the job. You're a decorated detective from a big city. If anything, you're overqualified. But to keep everything aboveboard, we had an independent panel review the applications with the names omitted to prevent any concerns over nepotism. Bottom line? You're the best candidate. You have the most experience, and it didn't hurt that you've earned commendations for your service."

Brad wasn't telling Levi anything he wasn't already aware of. He'd done a Skype interview with the panel, and had been up front about the incident that led to him quitting the Oakland PD. An incident that, if he'd handled it better, wouldn't have ended with his partner being shot, or a kid being killed. All the panel had been concerned about was that IA had deemed his use of force a "good shoot."

He'd been called with the job offer the day after the interview.

Moving back home had been step one of the getting-his-shit-together plan, accepting the job offer was step two. "Then I accept."

Brad grinned and stuck out his hand to shake Levi's. "When can you start? The city annexed the area west of the lake. We're stretched thin right now. You'll come in at the rank of captain, one of three we will have on the force, the others being Monica Valdez and Jack Morgan. With a baby girl and a ten-year-old at home, Jack will be happy if you take some of the load."

"Jack and Dory have a baby?" Brad nodded. "Huh. I have a lot of catching up to do. Okay then. I can start tomorrow."

"Good. Be here at seven, morning roll call is seven thirty." Brad leaned back in his chair. "You run into your neighbor, Zoey Hardesty?"

"Almost ran into that beast she calls a dog. Literally. It has a habit of taking naps in the middle of the road."

"Lucy. Cool dog. What did you think of Zoey?"

"In what sense? She's got the hot earth-chick vibe going, and is uptight about junk food, but otherwise seems okay."

"You know she was the victim of a hit-and-run."

"Yeah. She's got a couple of bruises and walks with a limp. How long ago was it?"

"Ten days." Brad set his coffee mug on the desk, the lines of his forehead settling into a frown. "She was crossing Main Street and going to the old Odd Fellows hall. It's being used as a yoga studio now. It was early evening, twilight. The streetlamps were on and they light that intersection well enough. She was using the crosswalk and was wearing a bright pink sweatshirt."

"You're saying the driver should have seen her." Levi knew the intersection a few dozen yards from his sister's café. "What did Zoey say? Did she see the vehicle coming? Give you a description?"

"She said it was an SUV or a truck with a shell over the bed, she wasn't clear which. Said the color was navy or black, and that it came around the corner fast, not giving her time to get out of the way."

"Did she notice anything about the driver? Passengers? Identifying marks on the vehicle?"

"No to all of that. She hasn't been what we'd consider cooperative."

"Why the hell not?"

"Not sure. That's what you're going to find out. Use your detective skills, brother. The case is now yours."

***

Levi stepped out his door and stood on the stoop for a minute, absorbing the last warmth of the day. He'd stopped at Maddy's café and had the lucky fortune of finding not only his mom there but both his sisters. Hard to believe that in addition to Brad, Maddy and Jenny were married with kids too. Maddy was only a year older than him, but farther down the road in the getting-her-life-together department. Their impromptu lunch filled a hole Levi hadn't even been aware had been dug into his heart. That's what this move home meant— being able to be a daily part of the lives of the people most important to him.

Snow on the high slopes of the mountains to the west gleamed as the sun began its descent behind the peaks. Closer around the cabin, aspens wore the bright green of their late spring colors. He filled his lungs with the pine-scented air he always associated with home. Summer, his favorite time of the year, was weeks away, but the warm days were already signaling its arrival.

He opened the back of the Suburban he'd borrowed from a coworker to haul his stuff home. He'd have to return it on the weekend and retrieve the motorcycle he'd left in the friend's garage. He thought of what Zoey said about the Suburban. Big, black with dark tinted windows, he guessed it kind of looked like a hearse.

He took in the haphazard mess in the back of the truck. Why the hell hadn't he packed with a little more finesse? Oh yeah. He'd wanted to get out of Oakland so bad he'd all but thrown his shit in the Suburban and took off like the wind. Since the cabin was furnished, he'd been able to get rid of most of his possessions, only keeping clothes, books, and some electronics. A pathetic showing for thirty-three years of life.

Something touched his leg and he found himself reaching for the weapon that was no longer in a holster at his shoulder. He cursed the instinctive response as Lucy stared at him, her head level with his belt. She wore a sturdy-looking orange and gray pack secured to her back with a harness around her chest. Large pouches bulged at her sides, and he guessed the hand strap in the middle was designed so you could grab the dog if there was a problem. But if that dog wanted to go, she'd be a one-hundred-pound bulldozer and he didn't think anything, including Zoey, would stop her. He wondered who weighed more, the dog or her owner.

He reached out a hand. "Hey, Luce. You being put to work?"

Lucy planted her nose on his leg again as he stroked her head, leaving a wet spot on his jeans. She had long, fine fur that had to be a bitch to keep brushed. He stopped petting, and she nudged his hand with her nose. "Got it, don't stop, right?" He gave her a vigorous rub on her side, and she let out a throaty groan.

He kept stroking, and in seconds, despite her doggie backpack, she was on her back, paws in the air, swishing her tail in the pine needles. He went down on a knee to scratch her belly. "We're not going to get in trouble with the short one if you get dirty, are we?"

"The short one?"

Shit. "Did I say short one? I meant mighty one." He glanced up. The hot earth chick now looked more like nature girl and, like the dog, carried a backpack over her shoulders. She had switched up her hippie-dippie clothing to shorts that showed toned legs perfectly proportioned to her small stature, and a sleeveless top, which hugged her small breasts. The mass of dark curls was pulled back in a ponytail, and sunglasses covered her eyes, hiding their color. If he remembered right, they were dark.

"Nice recovery. The national average height for women in the US is five foot four, so at five three, I'm almost average."

"I stand corrected." He rose to his feet and towered over her.

She took off her glasses to give him an exaggerated once-over. Her eyes were brown, a rich golden brown. "Not all of us can be all long legs and long body. What are you, six three?"

"About that." The dog scrambled up beside them, giving herself a shake that had fur flying and the side pouches of her pack snapping back and forth. "You guys heading out?"

"We're hiking up to Ruby Lake. It's only about three miles round-trip to the overlook. We'll get back before it's all the way dark."

"I know where it is. The trailhead is about a hundred yards up the road. Want company?" The question was out of his mouth before he could think it through. A short hike with her might be an opportunity to find out what was up with her lack of cooperation over the hit-and-run. Then there was that hot earth-chick vibe.

Still, she hadn't been exactly friendly. He almost hoped she'd turn him down.

"Ah, sure. If you like."

Chapter Three

Why had she accepted his offer of company? Levi Gallagher was the last person Zoey should be going on sunset hikes with, yet here he was, walking with her on the trail, all tall, dark, and irritatingly sexy in a scruffy, easygoing kind of way.

There were many guys who'd been plenty cute in high school who had grown out of their looks. But not Levi. The Gallagher family DNA came in a variety of color combinations, and Levi's worked exceptionally well together. He shared his brother's rich, dark brown hair, and his sister Maddy's bold blue eyes that contrasted strikingly with his tanned complexion. Kind of like the super hottie Bradley Cooper, who was Zoey's one and only celebrity crush.

But her high school infatuation with the youngest Gallagher sibling was long over and done with. Back then she'd been a defiant misfit. The one with the little brother with autism, the one who dyed her hair weird colors, and the one and only girl to play drums in the marching band. When the cute girls were straightening their hair, she embraced her curls. If crop tops were in fashion, she was all about the long and loose fitting. Back then, she hadn't stood a prayer of gaining the attention of star first baseman and popular cool kid Levi Gallagher.

Yet here they were, hiking along like they were buddies. Lucy tugged on her harness and Zoey let her go. The dog took the trail at a run, charging up the switchbacks like the mountain dog she was.

"What breed is she?"

"Bernese Mountain dog. They're from Switzerland."

"Cool. She won't run off?"

"No, she stops every now and then to let me catch up, but then she's off again. She's got a lot of pent-up energy and I let her burn it out. She's friendly and won't bother other hikers."

"What about you, should you be doing this?"

"Doing what?"

"Hiking. You have a limp from the accident."

"I'm fine. Make sure you pass that along to your brother." Or she would be fine.

The steady upslope grade made her bruised thigh muscle ache, but not so much that she couldn't do it. She hated people worrying about her. No way was she telling Levi this hike was a test. Her job depended on being able to go a lot farther than three miles and over much more difficult terrain than this.

The trail gained in elevation and they didn't talk much. Zoey could admit to herself that it wasn't so bad going on a hike with another person. She didn't need a companion and her job often meant trekking on her own, but still, it was kind of nice to share the evening.

The trail leveled out, cutting around the mountain. They followed the curve and reached the view that made the hike worth it.

The jagged peaks of the Minarets gleamed in the distance, the setting sun casting purple light that gave everything a monochromatic gleam, the little gem of a lake reflecting back the twilight sky. A meadow dotted with yellow and purple flowers spread before them, and in the shade of a grouping of trees, Lucy found the snowy remnant of a spring storm.

The dog bounded through the drift, then began digging furiously, snow flying behind her.

"This is why I came back home." Levi spread his arms and tipped back his head with his eyes closed, the utter peace on his face making Zoey feel like he was sharing a private moment with her.

He made her remember how she'd felt when she'd finally made her way back to the little mountain town of Hangman's Loss, which had been her home for three short years when she'd been a teenager.

"It's not your family that brought you back to Hangman's Loss?"

He dropped his arms and opened his eyes to look at her. "They were a huge part of it, but I got to see them occasionally when I lived in Oakland. I visited them here. They visited me at my condo. But I was never happy there. In the past six months shit happened and I wanted to break away from my life there. The need to come home to this perfect corner of the world became huge."

He shook his head as if clearing it, then gestured to the scene before them. "You know the John Muir quote, 'The mountains are calling and I must go'? That pretty much sums it up for me. I think I lost myself when I was living in the city."

She swallowed an uncomfortable lump in her throat. She felt strange they had something so elemental in common.

"It's the same for you, isn't it?"

His gaze snagged hers, but she shrugged before turning away. She wanted to say yes, it was the same for her. She wanted to ask him what "shit" had happened in Oakland, but couldn't bring herself to pry.

Taking a step back was safer. She didn't do vulnerability.

Lucy, done with her digging, launched herself into the snow, bellying down, then flipped onto her back. Zoey let the dog play until finally giving a shrill whistle that brought her bounding up to them, shaking, which sent snow flying. Her new pack was snow encrusted but was supposed to be watertight. Guess they'd see about that.

Zoey turned her head to Levi. "We better head back before the light is totally gone."

They set out, Lucy again charging ahead.

Levi asked, "What have you been doing since high school?"

"Really? We're sharing our history like we were besties back then?" She stifled an inner groan. That was rude. He was making an effort to be friendly, and she should do the same. It took her a while to warm up to people, which was why she had a few good friends rather than a wide circle. She knew herself well enough to understand her reserve was often a protective shield.

The clear, deep timbre of his voice brought back memories of high school when she'd been so aware of him. He had presented a project in their bio class and she'd been surprised when he'd fumbled nervously. He'd always seemed so confident, but his obvious nerves had made him even more likeable. She'd been able to really look at him, instead of pretending not to see him in the halls, by his locker, in the parking lot. His voice had sounded wonderfully deep and grown-up. That he was now walking with her as the blush of the sky deepened with the setting sun was unexpected and maybe even a little exciting. But she didn't want to like him that way again.

"What, we're on a hike together but can't have a conversation? If you didn't want to talk with me, why did you agree to me coming?"

The trail widened enough for them to walk side by side. She glanced up at him. Blue eyes gleamed from under the bill of his ball cap.

"It was a crazy impulse."

"Which you're now regretting."

"I didn't say that."

"Good. So let's hear it. You were two years behind me at Loss High. What did you do after graduation? Work, college, travel through Europe with a backpack?"

"Europe? I wish. But I didn't graduate from Loss High."

"You didn't graduate from high school?"

"I did, but not from Loss High. I transferred midway through my senior year to a high school in Fresno."

"Why the hell would you do that?"

"To stay clothed and fed. Mom was moving to Fresno. She realized it was a crappy time for me, but she did what she had to do."

"You couldn't have stayed here with friends so you could graduate from Loss High?"

She shook her head. "There was stuff going on. Plus, my brother needed me, and I didn't want to be separated from him and my mom. So I went with them."

"Why did your mom want to leave the Loss?"

Talking about herself made Zoey itchy, but his point that she'd invited him on this trek was valid. She'd answer his questions but hold back on crucial details. He didn't need to know everything.

"Mom broke up with the guy who'd been living with us. Kicked him out. She had a job lined up in Fresno. Having me when she was eighteen had crushed any chance of college, and by the time I was in high school she was still young. In her early thirties. I'm almost that age now. That's weird to think about."

Zoey went on, wanting to finish it. "Mom wanted to do more with her life than wait tables, and she wanted to set a good example for Charlie and me. Her new job was at the community college in Fresno where she was planning to take classes, and there was a program at the university that would help Charlie. Really, it was no big deal."

"Hangman's Loss must have felt like home for you too since you eventually made it back here."

"I'm not sentimental. Hangman's Loss is only another town. The scenery is pretty, but other towns have pretty scenery, too."

"It's not sentimental to want home."

"Well, not all of us had an idyllic childhood with a big, loving family they can come back to."

"Ouch."

Would she ever shut it with the snide comments? Once again she'd been rude, but she checked the impulse to apologize. Distance was better where Levi Gallagher was concerned. He made her feel too emotionally exposed. She'd have to be dead not to have noticed that flare of interest in his eyes when she'd been chewing him out about giving Lucy potato chips. Better to pull that weed up by the root than to let it grow and blossom.

"So if it wasn't the people or pretty scenery of Hangman's Loss that brought you back, what was it?"

"Work. I was transferred to this area about a year and a half ago."

"What do you do?"

"I'm a wildlife biologist."

"No shit? You must have really liked that AP biology class we had together. What do you do? Count the number of fish eggs in the creek, or how many flies land on a lily pad in an hour?"

"Ha. My project is studying the impact of climate change on the pika in the higher elevations of the Sierra Nevada range."

The grin he flashed gave her a jolt she felt all the way to her toes.

"You sounded all kinds of professional." He paused as if in deep thought. "I'm trying to recall what I know about pika and all I've got is they're a small mammal. They like a rat?"

"No. They're related to rabbits and are crazy cute. They're not good temperature regulators and live exclusively in talus slopes where they burrow under the rocks to keep cool."

"Okay. What's a talus slope?"

Zoey pointed to a spot across the valley. "You see the broken rock piled at the base of the granite face? That's talus."

"So there are pika living in there?"

"Possibly. They like a little higher elevation than that, but it's possible."

They hiked down a long slope, Zoey answering Levi's questions, more than a little surprised at how easy it was to talk to him. The trail took them to the road that went in front of their homes. She snapped on Lucy's leash. A car went by too fast, headlights blazing in the dusk, and Zoey made an instinctive movement away from the road, jerking Lucy after her.

"Hey, it's okay."

"You can't assume someone sees you, especially when it's getting dark like this." She couldn't control her sharp tone.

"You were hit at this time of day." His move to stand between her and the street didn't go unnoticed.

"Yes." They rounded the bend in the road, and she was relieved to see the glow in the window of her cottage.

Trying for a return to normal after her overreaction, she asked, "What do you do, Levi Gallagher? Do you have a job here in Hangman's Loss?"

He cast her a sidelong look. "I start my new job tomorrow."

"Which is?"

"Hangman's Loss PD. I'm a cop."

He walked a few steps before turning back to see she'd stopped in her tracks. "Cop? You're a cop?"

"Yeah. That surprise you?"

"Yes, it surprises me. You're all charming and affable, not cop-like at all."

"Are we going for stereotypes? I'm supposed to be surly and have a shaved head? Sport a flabby gut from too many donuts?"

"There are commonalities among police officers that aren't necessarily stereotypes. Like profiling, or closing ranks to protect their own, even if they've done something wrong."

"You're making overgeneralizations. The press hasn't necessarily been even-handed when dealing with police issues."

"There's a reason for the bad press and mistrust. Too many police abuse their authority and have gotten away with it."

"Interesting, because the cops I know believe in justice and fair play." The snap of temper was there, barely beneath the surface.

"I hope so."

"Believe it." They turned up the driveway to their homes, stopping where it forked. The little globe lights she'd strung across her front porch shone warmly in the gathering darkness. Lucy parked her butt and did her leaning thing against Zoey, a hundred pounds of weight that had her bracing herself. Levi faced her, hands on hips.

"I've been assigned your case."

"What?" The easygoing bro was gone, and in his place was this new Levi, all cop and all business.

"Your case, it's mine now. Word is you haven't been particularly helpful with the investigation."

"Oh geez. I haven't been unhelpful."

"You know that isn't the same as helpful, right? Someone hit you, caused bodily injury, and left the scene without identifying him- or herself or rendering aid. That behavior would most likely be charged as a felony."

"I told the police what I remembered. I'm not sure how I could be more helpful."

"Did you lose consciousness?"

"Briefly."

"See? That wasn't in the report. Captain Morgan asked for a copy of your medical report, which you didn't give him. Why is that?"

"I forgot. Look," she blew out a breath, "it was an accident. The person must not have seen me. They might not have even noticed they hit someone. Or they could have been under the influence, or in the country illegally, so they didn't stop, and being charged could really mess up their life. I'm willing to let it go."

His voice snapped with sharp incredulity. "You've got to be kidding me. Whoever it was hurt you, badly, and you don't want to *mess up their life*? You know that sounds crazy, right?"

"It's not crazy. I've seen what getting caught up in the justice system can do to people. They can lose their jobs, marriages fall apart, and some become homeless. I don't want that to happen to anyone because of a moment of distraction. I was hurt, but I'll be fine."

"What if it wasn't an accident? Ever think of that?"

"Don't be absurd. Of course it was an accident."

"You don't know that. That's why we do investigations, Zoey, to get information. Not to ruin lives."

She nudged Lucy off her leg. "Investigate all you want, but don't expect me to help you." She walked Lucy toward her cottage, all but burned by the irritation radiating from Levi.

She was pretty sure whatever flicker of interest he'd felt for her was now cold.

Chapter Four

Zoey pulled the toasted baguette slices from the oven, arranged them on a platter, and began putting together the crostini with various toppings—tomato and basil, goat cheese with caramelized walnuts, warm Brie and cranberries. A knock sounded at the front door, followed by Lucy's loud bark.

"Come in," she called as she drizzled honey over the walnuts and goat cheese.

The door opened, followed by kissy noises as Zoey's BFF Eva showered Lucy with love. Zoey and Eva had only known each other a year, and had become fast friends, which was new for Zoey. She'd never had a best friend, or a group of friends like the one that came with Eva. She did now, and she intended to enjoy them.

Eva entered the kitchen, a bottle of wine cradled in one arm. Two men followed her. Dark-haired and dimpled Diego held an aluminum baking tray covered by a checkered dish towel, while Justin, a baseball cap over his red curls, brought a plastic dessert carrier.

"Diego said our pizza would be better if we cooked it here." Eva dipped her head. "Is the oven free?"

"Sure is," Zoey replied.

Diego turned on the oven and pulled off the towel, holding out the pizza for Zoey to see. "Behold, perfection."

Olives, mushrooms, peppers, and artichoke hearts: absolute perfection. "You're right. You should use my pizza stone. It's on top of the fridge. You need to preheat it."

"Hey, I brought something amazing, too." Justin flipped up the lid of his dish.

"Crème brûlée. You made crème brûlée?" Zoey reached out a finger, but Justin pulled it out of her reach.

"Don't touch."

"I want a taste."

"You can have a taste later."

"I love you, Justin. I might be willing to give sexual favors in return for an immediate taste of crème brûlée."

"If anyone could un-gay me, it would be you, darling, but your offer of sexual favors doesn't even tempt me." He set the dish on the counter and gave her a warning look. "Don't touch."

"No one offered me sexual favors for bringing my perfect pizza," Diego complained.

"That's because your wife," Zoey pointed to Eva, "would stab me with a spoon if I did."

"Sure I would, but it wouldn't be personal. I love your skirt, by the way."

"Me too. I got it from that shop that opened a couple of weeks ago across from the Mexican restaurant on Main." Zoey had paired the swishy multicolored skirt with a sleeveless peasant blouse of deep garnet and several beaded bracelets of the same color. She handed a stack of plates with cloth napkins and utensils stacked on top to Justin. "Take these out front. It's too warm to eat inside. We'll stuff our faces on the porch."

"Got it."

"Out." Zoey pointed to Lucy, who made the already crowded space more crowded. "Out of the kitchen." Head hanging in dejection, the big dog moved to the dining area and sprawled belly down in front of the fireplace.

Diego slid the pizza onto the prewarmed stone, then into the oven. Eva grabbed wine glasses while Zoey uncorked the bottle.

In minutes they were sitting on the porch in mismatched chairs and loveseats, the tray of crostini on the little table she'd found at a yard sale set in the middle of their circle.

Eva bit into her crostini choice and groaned. "This is wonderful. You make the best bruschetta in the world."

Justin popped an entire appetizer in his mouth, then leaned back in the loveseat he shared with Zoey, the bottle of the beer he preferred over wine resting on his knee. Given the angle of her house, she could barely make out Levi opening the back of his Suburban.

Justin nudged her shoulder. "Who's *that*? He's hot."

"My neighbor, Levi."

"Straight or gay?"

"Hmm, he hasn't said, but I'm getting a straight vibe."

"Oh my god, Levi." Eva set down her wineglass before bolting down the steps. "Levi," she yelled, running to where he stood by his monster vehicle, throwing her arms around him. Zoey watched Levi gather Eva to him in a warm embrace.

"Good thing they're related," Diego grumbled.

Eva was tugging Levi's hand to lead him up the steps to the porch. He glanced up and caught Zoey's eye. They hadn't spoken since their conversation on the hike the day before, and she thought she detected reluctance in his posture, but there weren't many who could resist Eva.

"Zoey, did you know your neighbor is my cousin?"

"I kind of figured that out since Maddy and Brad are also your cousins, and he's their brother."

Diego rose to shake Levi's hand. "Good to see you, bro."

"And this is our good friend, Justin," Eva motioned to Justin. "He's a firefighter and is on the same crew as Diego."

Levi leaned over to shake with Justin. "Cool."

"Join us for dinner." Eva handed him a plate. "We've got these amazing crostini Zoey made, and Diego is baking a pizza as we speak."

"Damn, my pizza." Diego ran for the door.

Justin rose to follow Diego. "You want beer or wine, Levi?"

"Ah." Levi locked eyes with Zoey, and she knew he was waiting for a signal. They hadn't parted on particularly amicable terms, and he was letting her decide if she wanted to him crash her party.

Zoey hesitated. Despite his chosen profession, she liked him. Maybe she should get to know him as a man, and not the fantasy she'd built from her high school crush on a teenage boy. His expression closed like he was sure she was going to make an excuse and give him the boot. Instead, she made herself smile. "Please stay, Levi."

He glanced at Justin. "Then I'll have beer. Thanks."

Eva pulled up another chair to widen their circle, Levi tugging the cushioned wicker wingback chair closer to Zoey's end of the loveseat. He selected a crostini, white teeth showing when he bit into the appetizer.

He swallowed, wiping goat cheese from his lip with his thumb. "Hmm, good. What are these again?"

"Crostini. A simple and tasty appetizer." She watched as he demolished another topped with creamy Brie and jellied cranberries. She found herself staring at his long, squared-off fingers. He'd pushed up the sleeves of his casual shirt, revealing forearms corded with muscles that went with the long and lean build. The whole package was too uncomfortably appealing, and noticing all that wasn't a good start to moving past her teenage crush.

"What? You're staring."

She was *not* going to tell him where her mind had wandered. "I'm surprised, that's all. I wasn't sure if you ate anything that didn't come wrapped in plastic."

He gave her a wolfish grin. "There's a lot you don't know about me." Those bold blue eyes locked on hers and her stomach did a slow somersault. When he spoke, his voice was a low growl. "I'd like to talk to you when you have a minute. Alone."

"Ah, sure." She would *not* read anything into that request. "You can hang around when the others leave, if you like."

She wasn't fooling herself that he wanted to talk with her about anything personal. He was a cop who had been assigned the hit-and-run investigation. Zoey caught Eva's speculative gaze and gave her friend a quick headshake. She'd have to find a way to discourage Eva from thinking what that look said she was thinking.

With the appetizers consumed and the pizza cooling between them, Zoey leaned back against the cushion, the sweater she'd pulled on keeping the evening chill at bay. This was one of the nicest evenings she'd had since her move back to Hangman's Loss a year ago. She loved the relaxed casualness of getting together with the friends she'd made, the easy talk and laughter. Maybe she liked that Levi had joined them a little too much, but she'd cut herself some slack. She couldn't fault her teenage self for knowing a good thing when she'd seen it.

"Levi, word is you joined the Loss police department," Diego said around a bite of pizza. "Small-town cop job is going to be a hell of a lot different than big-city cop job."

"I'm hoping it will be a good difference. Today was my first day."

"How was it?" Diego asked.

Levi shrugged. "Good. Drove around a lot to get reacquainted with the area. There's been development on the other side of the lake I hadn't seen before."

"Ooh," Eva exclaimed. "Levi is a really good baseball player. We know what that means."

"What does it mean?" Levi's longneck bottle dangled loosely between those all-too-appealing fingers.

"These guys," Eva pointed at the other two men, "have been bragging about how they are going to crush the Guns this year."

"Crush the guns?" Levi looked confused.

"How good is good?" Justin interrupted.

"The Guns are the police department's softball team, and the fire department's team are the Hoses," Eva explained. "Diego, Justin, and the other firefighters have been practicing for months. The Guns and Hoses play in an annual charity softball game with proceeds going to local kids' programs."

"How good?" Justin asked more insistently.

"Levi is awesome." Eva batted her eyes at her cousin. "He played first base in high school and college. He's got a great bat and is awesome on the field. He was even scouted by the big leagues."

"Really?" Zoey asked him. "What happened with that?"

Levi shrugged. "I was good enough to play in the minors, but probably not good enough to go farther than that. I didn't want to spend year after year chasing a break into the majors that might never come."

"The Guns also have Jack Morgan," Eva added. "The guy can hit home runs like he's swatting flies."

"Hey, who's side are you on? Besides, we've got Tank," Diego interjected. He glanced around the group. "He's Tank because he's built like a tank. He's our power hitter."

"True, we do have Tank," Justin muttered. "Dude," he motioned to Levi while talking to Diego, "they're going to draft you to play in the Guns and Hoses game. There's no way they won't. We won last year, but barely." He pointed at Diego. "We've got to start practicing every night."

"When is the game?" Levi asked Eva.

"A couple of weeks."

"Would you play if asked?" Zoey sat forward and started stacking plates.

"Hell yeah."

"Damn," Justin muttered.

Darkness had fallen, and the globe lights gave the gathering a sweet, cozy feel. Zoey rose to gather up the stacked plates, putting out a hand when Justin would have risen. "You all stay seated. I'll bring out the crème brûlée."

"No dipping in your finger," Justin called as she crossed the porch.

"Awesome," Eva said, and Zoey caught her snuggling in next to Diego on their loveseat.

Zoey carried dishes to the cabin door, not realizing Levi had followed her until he reached around her to push it open. The door opened a scant inch before it was blocked on the inside.

"Lucy, move."

A groan sounded from the other side of the door.

Zoey put her shoulder into it and pushed harder. The door gave abruptly and Levi dropped an arm around her shoulder to steady her.

"Bear dog lies against the door?"

"There's no logic to where Lucy sleeps. The only thing you can count on is that it's not likely to be her bed, unless it's bedtime or she's not feeling well, then that's the only place she wants to be."

"Huh. Funny dog."

Bright headlights speared through the darkness as a car turned onto the driveway.

"Expecting more company?"

Zoey was more than aware of Levi's arm still draped around her shoulders. "No, are you?"

"Nope."

"I'll go see who it is," Diego said, rising from his seat.

Zoey and Levi stood in the glare of the headlights as Diego approached the driver's window. Before he could reach the car, it bulleted in reverse back onto the street before tearing off in the direction from which it had come.

"What the hell?" Levi leapt off the porch and across the driveway to the street, where he stood staring in the direction the car had gone. He walked back to Zoey's house and met up with Diego on the steps.

"You recognize the car or driver?"

"No. It was a small SUV, light colored. Could be anywhere between gray and white. That's what we get for not having streetlights out here. I couldn't see through the windows. So basically, I got nothing."

"Surely that was someone turning around. Why are you so concerned?" But Zoey felt suddenly cold and gathered her sweater around her.

"Whoever it was seemed anxious not to let me get close enough to see who was driving," Diego observed.

In the shadowed light of the porch, the planes of Levi's face tightened. "Zoey, did the vehicle look familiar to you?"

"No. I don't get many unannounced visitors. We're far enough from town that most people will call first to make sure I'm home before making the drive out here. Maybe the visitor was yours."

Levi shook his head. "Same deal as you. I'm not likely to get casual visitors here, and since I only moved in a couple of days ago, not many people know I'm back home or where I live."

Eva bustled by with dirty dishes stacked in her hands. Zoey followed her into the cabin and returned a few moments later, carrying Justin's crème brûlée. Enjoying the creamy dessert, she tried to ignore the uneasy feeling brought by the arrival of the car that sped off into the night.

The brulee was gone. As in, no leftover finger swipes. Justin got high praise from everyone. Her guests helped to tidy the porch, and after hugs and promises to do it again soon, Zoey waved as they drove away.

Levi stood beside her on the steps, Lucy leaning against his leg. Zoey rubbed her arms against the evening chill. "Well, that was fun."

"Yeah."

Zoey angled him a look. "Is that you sounding surprised that you enjoyed yourself? I have nice friends, plus it's obvious your cousin loves you."

"My surprise has more to do with you letting her invite me."

"It's hard to say no to Eva, as I'm sure you're aware." She looked down as she stroked Lucy's head. "I might have gone a little overboard yesterday about the hit-and-run."

"A little?"

"Yes, a little. I like to be up front with people, so I'll tell you I have an inclination to resist authority if I think that authority is being heavy-handed."

"In what way have the Loss police, or me for that matter, been heavy-handed?"

"You haven't been, hence the apology."

"What apology?"

"The one where I said I might have gone a little overboard yesterday."

"See, I was a detective in Oakland. I heard that part, but somehow did not detect an apology."

She gave a throaty little laugh. "It was implied."

"Ah."

"Did you know Diego when we were in high school? He'd have been a freshman when you were a junior."

"No. There's a lot of my junior year that's a blur."

"Oh, jeez, that's right. Your dad died that year."

"He did." The warm glow from the globe lights reflected the closed expression on his face that didn't invite additional comment.

"Anyway, I'm glad you joined us, Levi."

"Me too." He seemed to make an effort to shake off the mood brought on by her careless comment. "I have a couple of questions about the hit-and-run."

Not what she wanted to talk about, but Zoey guessed she wasn't going to be able to put him off. She nodded and returned to the loveseat, pulling her feet up onto the cushion and covering her legs with her skirt. Lucy sat on the floor and rested her head on the cushion of the little sofa.

"I heard you when you said that you're not interested in pursuing prosecution if hitting you was an accident." Levi took the wingback chair and turned it so he was facing her. "I don't agree, but I understand. Kind of. But what if it was intentional?" He held up a hand when she opened her mouth to speak. "Hear me out. I'm pursuing the investigation and I'd like your cooperation. Main reason is because if it was intentional, you could be targeted again. If it was an accident, then there's a seriously deficient driver out there who shouldn't be on the road. The next person might not be as lucky as you. This isn't police heavy-handedness, Zoey, it's public safety."

She pulled a scrunchie out of her pocket and wrangled her hair back into a ponytail. He had a point, and she really didn't want to get into another argument with him. "Okay, but if it turns out that it was accidental, my cooperation ends."

She nudged her dog. "C'mon, Lucy. It's too cold to stay out here." She rose to her feet and held the door open for the dog before directing her next comment to Levi. "I need to clean the kitchen. You can ask your questions inside."

Chapter Five

Levi followed the irascible woman and lumbering dog into the cottage. Zoey switched on a lamp that cast a cheery light over the living room. She'd used lots of textures and colors in the rugs, furniture, and knickknacks, giving the room a welcoming feel. His family owned this cottage, and as a teenager he'd spent too many hours painting and doing repairs. He remembered complaining and swearing about having to spend what had seemed like his entire summer after graduating high school painting every damn room in the place, only to have Brad chew his ass while doing it.

Levi stopped at the bar separating the kitchen from the living room. All available counter space was covered with cutting boards, dirty dishes, food scraps, and pans in need of scrubbing. "Holy crap."

There was that laugh again. "Don't judge. Every time I start making something I tell myself to clean as I go, but I get too busy and then my kitchen ends up looking like this."

"Is there any dish you didn't use?"

She took off her many bracelets and set them on the windowsill above the sink. With the water running, she began rinsing dishes and stacking them on the tile counter. "I'm pleading the fifth on that question." She gave him that side look that he was starting to think was downright sexy. "Make yourself useful. You can feed Lucy."

He followed her instructions, scooping what seemed like an enormous quantity of kibble into a large metal bowl.

"There are some carrots in the fridge. Throw a couple in with the kibble."

"You give your dog carrots?" He opened the fridge and found the bag. Lucy's gaze tracked his movements, drool wetting the rug where she sat.

"Carrots are good for dogs. They've got vitamins A and K, and help keep her teeth clean."

Levi set the dog dish to where Zoey directed him. "Sorry, Luce, I'm out of Slim Jims. I'll pick up some later. Until then, it's carrots for you."

He heard a muffled laugh over the sound of water running into a basin. "You will *not* pick her up Slim Jims. I want Lucy to live a good long life, not one hampered by preventable heart disease or diabetes."

"You're pretty strict, Miz Hardesty," Levi drawled.

"With you around, I have to be."

Lucy pulled herself to a sitting position, the wet patch on the rug at her feet growing. Her eyes were fixed on the bowl of food, but she didn't make a move toward it. "Your dog wants it but she's not eating."

Zoey glanced over. "Crickets."

Lucy surged forward, burying her face in the bowl.

"She doesn't eat unless you say 'crickets'?"

"That's the theory. Apparently her training doesn't stand up against potato chips or Slim Jims. We're going to work on that." She glanced at him. "What questions do you have, Levi?"

He thought for a minute, then shook his head. "Where's a clean dish towel to dry with?"

"You're going to help me with the dishes?"

"Yeah, I'll help. I ate but didn't contribute anything, so it's the least I can do. We'll get to the questions after."

He liked the way her smile lit the gold in her eyes before turning up the corners of her mouth. He was starting to think that there were quite a few things he liked about Zoey Hardesty, and maybe she was getting past being constantly pissed at him.

She bumped her hip in the direction of a drawer. "Towels are in there."

Towel in hand, he dried, stacking dishes and utensils on the counter for her to put away. Since he liked the sound of her voice and wanted to hear more of it, he decided to ask a non-investigation-related question. "What's your brother doing these days?"

"College. He's going to Cal State Fresno and majoring in computer science. Computers are Charlie's thing. He's interested in going into cyber security."

Levi had a vague recollection of an awkward, skinny kid with round Harry Potter glasses that made him look like an owl. Exactly the type of kid to be picked on in high school and hazed in college. "He doing okay there?"

"His first year was rough. Making friends is hard for him, but he managed to find a couple. He's in his second year now and seems to be doing better. He made the giant step of joining what he calls a geek club and found other kids interested in computers and gaming, and now he's got a group to hang out with."

"Hey, that's great."

"Yes, it is. It's made all the difference. I finally feel like he's going to be okay."

"And your mom?"

"She got her degree and is working as a special ed teacher. She learned a lot being Charlie's mom."

They worked side by side until Levi wiped the last dish and added it to the stack. He wondered if having a brother who needed so much attention had meant her needs were too often pushed aside. It was something to ask her, maybe when she was a little easier with him.

Once everything was put away and Zoey had hung the damp towel to dry on the handle of the stove, he motioned to the front room. "Can we sit?"

She nodded, moved into the living room and sat in a cushioned chair angled toward the fireplace. She was putting on the bracelets, and the beads were making little sounds as they clicked together. He followed her and took a seat in a sofa covered by a flowered slipcover.

"You don't have a TV."

"I'd intended to get one, but never got around to it. I found I didn't watch enough TV to bother. I use my iPad if there's a movie I want to watch, which isn't often."

"I'm guessing you're not a sports fan; otherwise, you wouldn't be able to forego the TV. Little screens don't work for a ball game."

"True, I don't watch sports."

"That's just sad."

Zoey drew up her feet to tuck beneath her. "What are your questions, Levi?"

"Not so many questions, but more of an exercise. I'd like to take you through a process that might help you remember some details from the time you were hit. That okay?"

"Brad and Jack both questioned me. I already told them everything I remember."

"And now I'm doing the investigation. I want to try this my way and see if it shakes something loose. Humor me. Close your eyes, bring up a mental image of what you were seeing and hearing before the car hit you."

She closed her eyes. Her long, dark lashes fanning her cheeks.

He forced himself to ignore the pull of attraction. "Once you're there in your head, visualizing the scene, pay attention to impressions—images, sounds, smells—they're all important if they give us a clue."

She'd opened her eyes as he'd spoken. "Try it. Close your eyes and concentrate. Think about getting out of your car, walking toward the intersection."

"Fine." This time, she tipped her head back against the cushion as she closed her eyes. "If I fall asleep, give me a nudge to wake me, okay?"

Her tone said she was doing as he'd asked to placate him. He shook his head. "Put yourself there that evening. You were going to a yoga class?"

"Yep."

"What were you wearing?"

"Stretchy exercise pants, t-shirt, sweatshirt, Uggs."

"Were you carrying anything?"

"I was carrying my yoga mat in my big hobo bag. Everything in my bag went flying across the intersection when the car hit me." She opened her eyes to look at him. "It knocked my shoes off."

He'd seen the police photos. Zoey, sitting on a gurney, scraped and bruised. The dazed look on her face, her things strewn across the pavement. Anger twisted in his gut. The memories couldn't be fun for her, either. "Eyes closed."

He caught the eye roll before she closed them, and held back his chuckle.

"Where had you parked?"

"In the parking lot behind your sister's café. It's not open in the evening, and Maddy doesn't mind."

"Visualize the scene. Was there anyone on the sidewalk, coming in or out of any of the shops? Were there other cars in the café parking lot or on the street that you recognized?"

Her brows dipped and he was relieved she was trying.

"No, I don't recall seeing anyone, and I don't remember anything in particular about cars in the area."

"What about the shops near the intersection? Did any have their lights on like they were still open?"

"No. That late in the evening and before the summer season, most close early."

He pushed back against the frustration. "Okay, think about when you were crossing the street. Give me all the sensory images. What you saw, heard, felt, and smelled."

"Okay." She blew out a breath. "I was using the crosswalk. I'd waited for the 'walk' sign even though there was no traffic. But honestly? I was kind of on autopilot. Wait for the light to turn, look both ways, start walking. I was irritated."

"Irritated, why?"

"There's this woman in the yoga class. She's competitive, passive-aggressive, and targets me with her attitude. It's a damned yoga class. Yoga is supposed to relieve tension, but she's all about showing that she can do these crazy poses that I don't even know how to pronounce. I mean, good grief, it's a beginners' class."

"Had you seen her outside of the yoga class?"

"No." Her eyelids snapped open. "But she was obnoxious enough that I had debated not going. That's why I was irritated. I'd seriously considered not going to the class I'd paid for and would otherwise enjoy because of her snide attitude."

"What's this woman's name?"

"I'm not sure. We introduced ourselves the first day of class and she said her name is Karma, which I hope bites her on the ass. I'm pretty sure Karma isn't her legal name."

He bit back a smile. He'd figure out who Karma was and ask her a few questions, too. "Eyes closed again. Think past being irritated. What other impressions do you have?"

"There's a truck or SUV coming up Pine, parallel to the crosswalk I'm in. Headlights are on. I can hear the engine. It was coming kind of fast and I thought it was going to go straight. By the time I realized it was turning it was too late to get out of the way, and bam, it hits me. You read the report, right? I gave the vehicle description." Her fingers had knotted in her lap.

Levi had read the report. Older model light-colored smallish pickup or SUV. That was it.

"Did you hear anything besides the sound of the motor?"

She breathed deeply as if to calm herself, the motion lifting her breasts.

"Music."

"Music? Coming from the truck?"

"Yeah, the window must have been down. Something with lots of electric guitars and heavy bass. Could have been metal, though I'm not positive about that. And weed. There was a whiff of weed. I hadn't remembered that before."

"Smoking marijuana could be an incentive for the driver not to stick around. They didn't want to face DUI charges."

"It's possible. Being high would also have impeded their reaction time."

"Anything else you can add?"

She shook her head, eyes opened and on his. The sound of Lucy snoring vibrated the air.

"Okay. You've given more for me to think about. Thanks."

"You're not bad for a cop, Levi."

He gave a brief laugh. "Isn't that what they call being damned by faint praise?"

Her smile lit her entire face. "I guess so. But it's better than 'I hate all cops.'"

"There's that." He smiled. "I'm going now. Thanks for this evening. Good night, Zoey."

***

Charissa sat in the car in the darkest shadows of the already dark street. She'd given it a half hour and then carefully driven back, no headlights this time, to take up her spot for observation. It had been a mistake to come up to the driveway like that. She'd hadn't expected that there would be people outside. Gathering on the porch, socializing, having fun.

She tugged on her hair until it hurt, using the pain to focus. Now that Levi was back home where he belonged, things would get better. Only she hadn't counted on him moving into the little cabin.

Trish would have wanted him home, and he was a good boy, a loving son, and that's where he should have gone. But that would have been temporary anyway, she thought, because after they were married they'd buy their own home. There was a beautiful log cabin home for sale on the other side of the lake she had her eye on. It had a three-car garage and a pool. She'd even gone to the realtor's open house to check it out and found it perfect for a family. She'd waited long enough, and wasn't getting any younger. She wanted a husband, a house, and a couple of children who looked just like their daddy. Dark hair and blue eyes was such an attractive combination.

But when the headlights of her car had shone across that tableau on the porch, she'd been infuriated seeing Levi with his arm around that hippie woman. Resentment burned like acid in her stomach. Charissa opened her pill bottle and swallowed one of the little white tablets with a sip from the coffee in the cup holder. She followed the white pill with two of the chalky antacids, popping them in her mouth and chewing slowly.

Levi was hers, and she didn't share. She'd have to formulate a plan. It would have been more appropriate if Bradley had reciprocated her interest in him. He was the right age for her, and it bothered her some that she was older than Levi. She remembered the father's funeral all those years ago. She'd hit on Bradley then, but he'd looked right through her like she didn't exist. Then she'd offered the shell-shocked youngest son a hug that was a little more than a hug, but he'd withdrawn, his movements mechanical, as if going through the motions.

Since Bradley was better suited, she'd done her best to make him notice her. She'd made sure to patronize Maddy's café because big brother frequently dropped in. She loved how the family supported each other. It had burned, oh, how it had burned, when that bitch Emmaline Kincaid had shown up out of the blue, and stupid Bradley Lucas Gallagher had fallen like a blithering idiot at her feet.

She wasn't even that pretty. The fake damsel in distress act had worked though. It had nearly gotten Bradley killed. But when it should have been her at his bedside, nursing him after he'd been shot, making him love her, Emma had usurped that spot.

Now they were married and Emma had given birth to those beautiful babies, who should have been Charissa's by rights. She'd thought of getting rid of Emma and the children, causing an accident of some sort, then she'd be there to console Bradley. But in the end she had deemed it too risky. So she'd turned her attention to Levi.

When he'd been a cop in Oakland, she'd even gone there that one time and "accidentally" bumped into him at his gym. She'd overheard Maddy talking about where he worked out and that'd given Charissa the idea. That café had its uses.

She'd planned it so carefully and then he'd passed right by her without so much as a hint of recognition. She'd gotten a day pass and ended up having to tap him on the shoulder to say, "Remember me?" His vague "Oh, hey" had been a bruise to her ego. She'd ended up stalking him for several days. Long enough to be certain he didn't have a girlfriend.

Occasionally he came home to Hangman's Loss, and she always made sure she was where he was.

When he was in town, he'd spend evenings shooting pool at Hangman's Brew Pub, so she'd made a point of being there. If the Gallaghers had a family gathering at the park, she'd be at the park, too. She always got her coffee from Maddy's café, making a point to chat with her future sister-in-law.

Charissa knew everything about the Gallaghers. Theirs was the kind of family she'd always craved. She'd been an only child of an alcoholic single mother, but when she married Levi, the Gallagher family would be hers. She'd have a brother and two sisters, and Trish Gallagher, who had once been so kind to her, would be her mother-in-law. Charissa wondered if she would call Trish "Mom."

Now was the time to act. Hangman's Loss was Levi's home and he'd finally returned. They would get married, and this time the beautiful babies would be hers, hers and Levi's.

She watched the lighted window of the cottage, relieved beyond measure when the door opened and Levi walked out. He and Zoey had been together inside her house for too long, but Charissa was thankful he'd had better sense than to spend the night with the hippie woman. Maybe Zoey needed a warning not to overstep the boundaries. And if she didn't pay attention to the warning and kept throwing herself at Levi, well then, more direct action would be taken.

Chapter Six

Levi locked the door of the cabin and walked to his vehicle. He was enjoying working for the HLPD. Reconnecting with the community, learning what changes had come over the past ten years, what had stayed the same, was all good. Big drawback? The uniform. As a detective in Oakland he'd been able to wear whatever the hell he'd wanted, but now here he was in a navy shirt, name and badge on his chest, captain's bars on his lapel. It would take some getting used to. Extra-big drawback? The body armor under the shirt. Necessary, but hotter than hell.

At least the morning air was cool, and then there was the call of a red-tailed hawk echoing through the trees. Gotta like that. The coffee he sipped from his travel mug gave him his first hit of caffeine. It wasn't as good as Maddy's, but he'd get a refill at the café later.

He tried not to burn his fingers on the recently nuked Jimmy Dean egg and sausage breakfast sandwich. He blew on it, took a bite, and deemed it not bad. This morning was his last with the Suburban. He had the weekend off, and one more chore to handle. He was driving the hearse back to Oakland and retrieving his motorcycle.

Settling behind the wheel, he started the engine and made the three-point turn to head for the road. Hitting the brakes had coffee sloshing in the mug. Bear dog sat in the patch of sunlight wearing her dog backpack, face turned up and eyes closed like she was worshipping the sun goddess. He edged forward a few more feet, and when she didn't move, he lowered the window and whistled. Her eyes opened, ears perked up, and he tossed a chunk of sandwich onto the side of the road. Bear dog heaved herself onto all fours and sauntered to give the sandwich a sniff, before turning to face Levi.

"What, now you won't eat without the magic word?"

He wasn't fooled by the nonchalant act. That dog was drooling enough to fill a kiddie pool. "Crickets." Like a switch had flipped, the dog leapt on the sandwich, and Levi drove past her with a grin.

***

Thirteen hours later he returned from work in not nearly as good a mood. For one, Charissa what's-her-name had run into him at the café. Literally. He'd gone to Maddy's for that refill and he'd ended up with coffee dumped on his pants. The smell had stayed with him all damn day.

Charissa had always been a bit weird, and the coffee spill wouldn't have been a big deal, except it hadn't felt like an accident. Then he and another officer had responded to a late afternoon call to Hangman's Brew Pub where a couple of bros were following up their morning fishing venture with liquid refreshments of the alcoholic variety. What the hell would lead friends to duke it out over who tied the best fly-fishing lure? Levi had a suspicion that a fight over the lures was more a fight over the size of their dicks. Even that wouldn't have messed with his mood, but the domestic violence call that followed had. As they always did. Especially when kids were involved.

Seeing the blue Prius coming from the other direction when he turned into his driveway was a nice distraction, particularly when it followed him. He parked, then walked to where Zoey stood next to the open door of her little car.

He had to admire her effort to tame the hot earth-chick look for work. The khaki and green Forest Service uniform camouflaged her curves, the beaded bracelets were absent from her wrist, and she'd tried to subjugate the wild curls into a braid down her back.

"C'mon, Lucy. Out."

Levi dipped his head to peer into the backseat. "Big dog, little car. I'm surprised she fits." Bear dog sat on a thick mat that covered the seat and wore her doggy backpack. The seatbelt had a strap thing that looked like it attached to the sturdy karabiner ring on the pack. Sitting up, Lucy's head brushed the headliner of the roof. She ignored him, staring straight forward.

Zoey bent down, her head next to Levi's.

"She doesn't want to come out?"

"No, she loves going to work with me, which is what she did today. We did a survey of pika in a talus near Obsidian Dome. She thinks if she stays in the car her excellent day won't end." Lucy looked at them, then returned to gaze out the windshield. Levi felt

Zoey's frustrated sigh against his cheek. She moved closer and sniffed. "Did you have a donut with that coffee?"

"Ha. Do you think I haven't heard every cop joke out there?"

"I couldn't resist, but you do smell like coffee." She reached in and grabbed Lucy's collar. "Come on, Lucy. Out."

Lucy braced her feet and didn't move so much as an inch.

"You need a Slim Jim to bribe her."

The minute "Slim Jim" was out of his mouth, Lucy whipped her head around so fast drool splattered the windows.

He caught the shaming look from Zoey.

"A Jimmy Dean biscuit sandwich worked this morning. And it's a good thing I know the magic word."

"You're poisoning my dog."

"She looks healthy to me. Want a Slim Jim, big girl? I restocked."

Lucy scrambled out of the car, pushing past Zoey. She trotted to the Suburban, going up on her hind legs to place her paws on the driver's door and shove her wet nose against the window.

"Levi Gallagher, I don't want you feeding her junk food."

"She's out, isn't she?" He laughed at Zoey's exasperated look. "Okay, okay. She's your dog, but I have to give her one this time. I can't lure her out of the car with the promise of a Slim Jim and not deliver."

"Fine, but then it's agreed no more garbage, which includes any made by your friend Jimmy."

"Right." Levi got the Slim Jim, peeled back the wrapper, and tossed a chunk to the expectant Lucy. He glanced at Zoey and, gauging his target, took a bite for himself before directing his comment to the dog. "We've got to share, big girl. This is my dinner."

Zoey didn't disappoint. "A processed meat product is your dinner? You've got to be kidding. No one can subsist on Slim Jims and potato chips."

"I need to pick up potato chips from the mini-mart. Tonight it's either the Slim Jim or another microwave sandwich." He paused for effect. "What are you having?"

She narrowed her eyes. "Homemade kale and quinoa burgers."

He could feel his face fall.

"Gotcha," she said.

"That's plain mean. Take out the kale and the quinoa, and the homemade burgers part sounds good."

"I'm not making you dinner for the second night running, Levi."

"Technically, you didn't make me dinner last night. You made the appetizers, which were excellent. The dinner part was pizza, and Diego made that. Too bad there's none left over. But," he said, holding up a hand to forestall comment, "you did host the dinner, so that counts for something."

"Oh, does it?" Her tone was utterly bland.

"Yeah. Come out with me. We'll go to the Brew Pub, which has a full menu that includes vegetarian options, plus, and even more importantly, Hangman's Best Ale on tap."

She studied him, and he hadn't thought it was that big of a deal until she was so obviously weighing her decision, and he found he really wanted her to say yes to spending time with him.

"Okay, but this isn't a date. We get separate checks."

"You sure you don't want this to be a date? Could be fun."

"Absolutely." Her adamant assurance stung. "I could never date a cop."

***

Zoey crossed the parking lot beside Levi. He wore a black, button-down shirt tucked into dark khaki pants. He looked good. Date good. But as she'd put on a colorful skirt with a blousy top that sparkled with tiny beads, she had to admit she looked date good, too.

But it didn't mean this was a date.

Levi opened the door and she walked in ahead of him. Despite living in town for over a year, she'd only ever been to the popular Hangman's Brew Pub a few times. The sound of tuning guitars and the clank of glasses greeted them. A big-screen TV with a baseball game on mute hung over a long bar that dominated the far side of the room. To the right, a band was setting up on a small stage in front of a pocket-size dance floor. Tables were scattered about on both sides and booths lined the walls.

"There's a table." Levi began to lead her to the side opposite from where the band would be playing. She recognized two men leaning against the bar. One of them elbowed the other, and they both straightened and headed across the room to intercept them.

Logan Ross, ridiculously handsome and with a fast grin, caught Levi in a hug.

"Glad you're back, man." With a hand still clapped on Levi's shoulder, he asked, tone serious, "You good?"

"Yeah. Better," Levi said. "Zoey, do you know Logan Ross?"

Zoey wondered at the undercurrents between the two men, and Logan's question made her speculate if there was more to Levi leaving Oakland than he had revealed. She nodded to Logan. "Sure, I've helped Eva babysit the twins a couple of times. Nice to see you again, Logan."

Levi turned to the other man and shook hands. Jack Morgan had to be nearly six and a half feet tall and had shoulders that looked wide enough to stop a freight train. When he'd interviewed her following the hit-and-run, he'd been steady and compassionate.

Jack dipped his head. "Hey there, Zoey. How's that dog of yours?"

"Lucy seems to be getting over the puppy stage and finally settling down."

"I haven't met Lucy," Logan commented. "How old and what breed?"

"Two, and she's a Bernese Mountain dog. Levi has been trying to corrupt her with junk food."

Logan rolled his eyes. "Sounds about right. Junk food king here."

"Hey, I don't eat *only* junk food. It just happens to be convenient."

"I don't think I've ever seen you eat anything that isn't wrapped in plastic," Logan responded.

"See." Zoey turned to Levi. "That's exactly what I said. And plastic is bad for the environment. It's made from oil and is killing the ocean."

"Plastic keeps my Slim Jims fresh."

She knew he was baiting her but couldn't keep herself from responding. "I think Slim Jims would survive a nuclear apocalypse."

Zoey caught the speculative gleam in Logan's eyes at the exchange and thought, *uh-oh*. First Eva, now Logan. She did *not* want rumors starting about her and Levi.

"Watch out," Jack said. "Dory told me I can't put my sandwich for lunch in a plastic bag anymore, I have to use waxed paper. And now I'm not supposed to use paper towels, either. I can't keep up."

"Good for her, she sounds smart and aware."

Jack pulled out his phone and checked the time. "I promised my smart and aware wife I'd be back in time to give the ten-month-old a bath, and this guy has twin terrors to get home to."

Logan's eyes crinkled with a smile. "Here's a warning for you, Zoey, in case you think Uncle Levi is daddy material: twins run in families."

Levi smirked. "Did Maddy ever tell you about our grandmother? She and her sister were one of two sets of twins in that family. That could be you, man. Twins times two."

"Good god, don't even say something like that out loud." He shook his head as if he were trying to get the thought out of his head. "Anyway, we're going. Great to see you both."

Jack and Logan left the bar, and Levi put his hand to Zoey's lower back as they walked to a booth.

After they sat, a waiter approached their table and took their orders, Levi insisting they share onion rings as an appetizer.

"You won't regret it, I guarantee it. Best onion rings in the world." Before she could respond, he changed subject. "So, how did you end up with a Bernese Mountain dog?"

"The usual way. My ex-boyfriend brought me flowers, a puppy, and a spa weekend, all as 'just-because' gifts. Since I'm smart and aware, it made me suspicious. I dug a little and discovered he'd cheated on me with our neighbor."

"Crap. So Lucy was a sorry-I'm-an-asshole gift, huh?"

"Yep. She was a super-cute puppy, so I kept her, and told him to keep his flowers and spa weekend, and to get out."

"He deserved it."

"Boy, did he."

The waiter placed foam-topped glasses of beer on the table, settling the platter of onion rings between them.

"Do onion rings qualify as junk food?" Levi asked.

"Probably, but I'm eating them anyway. They look amazing."

Zoey dipped a golden ring into a small bowl of ranch dressing, bit in, and chewed. "Oh my god." She dipped again. "These are fantastic. I could make a meal of just the onion rings."

Levi tried his own. "Better than a Slim Jim. I'd forgotten how good they are."

Zoey ate another onion ring, closing her eyes to better savor the flavor. When she opened them, she found Levi looking at her with an intense expression.

"What? Do I have ranch on my chin or something?"

"As a matter of fact." He reached out his thumb to swipe along her chin, then took it to his own mouth. "Yum."

Zoey lowered her brows. "Are you flirting with me? That felt like flirting."

"Who, me?" His innocent expression wasn't particularly persuasive. "I can't flirt. This isn't a date. Remember? And while we're on the subject, tell me why you can't date a cop."

"Remember that anti-authority streak I told you about?"

He scratched his chin. He'd shaved the scruff, and the shadow of his beard made a rasping sound. "I remember that you don't like authority when it's heavy-handed. What makes you think I'd be heavy-handed?"

"Cops in general have a tendency to throw around their authority. It's not personal."

"Cops in general have a tendency to want to keep people safe, and sometimes have to exert their authority to do that. But let's be personal, since generalizations and stereotypes suck."

The lick of temper was there under his words. She studied him. "Maybe you're right. I'm sure some cops aren't like that."

His expression had her rolling her eyes.

Levi sipped his beer before choosing another onion ring. He dipped it in a different bowl. "This one is honey mustard sauce, which doesn't sound like it would be good, but is." He handed it to her.

She took it from him and crunched. "Yum, it's almost as good as the ranch." She returned her gaze to his. "I can't help how I feel about cops. It comes from personal experience."

"Why don't we try this? Talk to me about that experience. Maybe it will help."

That meant opening up to him, something she wasn't usually willing to do with anyone but her closest friends, but for some reason she wanted him to understand. She traced a finger through the condensation on her glass, considering her words. "You sure? It's not pretty."

He picked up her hand, turning it over in his to rub a thumb across her palm in a gesture that had the blood singing up her arm. "Yeah, Zoey, I'm sure, 'cause the other thing that sucks is you won't date cops. Help me to understand."

She pulled back, closing her hand in a fist. Then she started telling him. "We were homeless for a while. Charlie's dad left us. He couldn't take the stress of being a parent of a child with autism. That wouldn't have been so bad, but Mom didn't have a job because taking care of Charlie was a full-time commitment. He was five, and he'd have tantrums. Mom homeschooled him so he wouldn't get picked on. Ted, that's Charlie's dad, had a daughter who came on the weekends, and there were times things were pretty chaotic."

His blue gaze didn't waver as she continued. "Ted decided he couldn't do it anymore, which apparently included being a dad in any way, at least to Charlie. He stopped paying child support, and didn't want to see his son. The consequence was that we were evicted from our house within a couple of months."

"Shit. I've known a couple guys who have done that. Maybe they pay child support, but they totally check out of their kids' lives. They're selfish bastards."

"Ted certainly was. There was a lot more that went into it, but in the end, Mom decided we'd live in our van. We had one of those VW Vanagon campers. Mom got the night shift waiting tables at Denny's. She'd park the van in the back, and Charlie and I would sleep there while she worked. The manager was cool with it, and she'd feed us breakfast in the morning. But we'd have to take off during the day." Zoey realized she was gripping the edge of the table and forced herself to relax her hold.

"That had to be tough."

"Yep. We had a lot of sponge baths and washed our hair in the sink. Charlie had to go to regular school. I was in middle school. Mom would drop us off, then find a place to park so she could sleep."

"What happened to change things?"

"There was this cop, Officer Barille, who was one of Mom's regulars at Denny's. One morning he hung around until she got off shift and followed her to the van. He'd figured out it was her vehicle and thought it was a perfect setup so they could hook up. They'd have a quickie, and he'd be on his way. He didn't like 'no,' so he started to get grabby, Mom was fighting him off, and then Charlie was screaming and I was coming out of the van to help my mom. It wasn't quite how that asshole thought things would turn out."

"Fucking bastard should never have been a cop."

"No, he shouldn't. He called for backup, and soon there were cops all over. The end result was that child services were called. They came pretty close to putting Charlie and me into foster care, but we ended up at a shelter instead."

"Other cops at the scene must have known Barille was up to something with your mom."

"They did. I heard another cop say something like he needed to stop messing with women. So they knew what he was there for. Luckily, Mom wasn't arrested. She filed a complaint, but nothing came of it. Don't cross the blue line, right? Cops don't rat on cops."

"That's true sometimes. But like I said, there are a lot of cops who believe their job is to serve and protect, even if that means protecting citizens from bad cops."

The waiter brought the burgers they'd ordered, and Zoey was glad for the reprieve from the conversation. She bit into her veggie burger, washing it down with a sip of beer.

"How long did you stay in a shelter?"

"Four months. Mom got a lawyer who agreed to take the case pro bono, and went after Ted for child support. She got an office job, and things were better. Then a friend of hers who'd moved to Hangman's Loss and opened a business offered her a job, so we moved up here."

"What about your dad? Did he support you?"

"Somewhat. My bio father was the local pastor's son. They met when Mom was seventeen and he was home from college for the summer. She got pregnant and he acted like she'd managed that all by herself.

"His parents freaked. How could their good Christian son get a girl from the poor side of town pregnant? They wanted her to get an abortion." She laughed at Levi's surprised expression. "Ironic, right? They were hypocrites, through and through. Mom refused and told anyone that'd listen who the father was. His family fought child support until they could get a DNA test, which proved he was the daddy. After that, he paid, or at least his parents did. I never met him."

Levi leaned back against the seat. "You've had it rough. People have let you down your entire life. What about your grandparents, your mom's parents? Did they support her?"

"The best they could. Grampa was a long-haul trucker and money was tight. Mom was the oldest of six kids, so she dealt with a lot on her own." Zoey cleared her throat. "And that's more than I've shared with anyone in forever. Enough about me. Why don't you tell me what made you leave Oakland?"

He hitched a shoulder in a shrug and his gaze traveled around the room. "I told you, I missed my family. My nieces and nephews are growing up and I want them to know me."

"Good reasons, to be sure. That's what pulled you back home, but my guess is there was something that pushed you out of your previous job."

There was that shrug again. "Sure there was, but it's behind me." He paused. "How are the pika doing?"

Chapter Seven

Zoey steered her Prius through the dark, Levi sitting beside her in the passenger seat. She took her eyes from the road to glance at him. The hollowed-out look he'd worn when she'd first seen him standing in her driveway his first day home had eased a bit. He'd been friendly, but she had the feeling that underneath all that affability something had made him seriously unhappy. Who'd have thought he'd be such a good listener?

"You know all that stuff I told you? Despite what it might look like from the outside, my childhood was mostly good. Mom, Charlie, me, we persevered."

"Perseverance is good. I hope there was some fun and laughter in there as well."

"Absolutely. I think Mom wanted us to avoid the mistakes she'd made. One thing Dawn Hardesty instilled in her kids was that you set your goals and then work harder than anyone else to achieve them. She led by example and graduated with her bachelor's degree, and now she has the job she's always wanted. Charlie's done the same and he's in college."

In the shadowy interior of the car, Levi appeared thoughtful.

"I don't want you thinking my life was pathetic. It wasn't."

"Okay."

"Now it's my turn. What's it like being a Gallagher in a town where the Gallagher family is like local royalty?"

"That's bullshit. You have a skewed view of the Gallagher family."

"Oh, come on. Everyone loves the Gallaghers. You guys aren't snooty about it, but it's true. Your mom has that nonprofit and does important work for people who are struggling. Then there's Brad. You'd think he wears a superhero cape. People here believe he can solve any problem. He's so diplomatic and levelheaded. The community loves him. And Maddy is the reigning sweetheart princess. People go to her café to bask in a little of her sunny personality. Her cheerfulness gives a boost to their day."

She pulled to a stop in front of the cottage.

"You could be right about Brad, but Maddy had a few rough years." He broke off, staring intently at the front of her house. "Are the lights on your porch on a timer?"

"No, why?"

"Because they were on when we left but aren't now."

She peered through the windscreen as he was doing. "You're right. Maybe they shorted out or something." Then she heard it, the mournful howling coming from inside her home. "Something's wrong with Lucy. She's always been fine when I've left her alone before."

Zoey had her seatbelt undone and was reaching for the door handle when Levi grabbed her arm.

"Wait."

"Why? Lucy is upset."

"Something's not right." The bright moon gave enough light that she could see his easy mood of the evening had shifted, his expression taking on what she could only describe as cop face. Intent, focused, serious. "Drive to my cabin."

"Why? I want to—"

"Zoey, do it."

A chill skittered up her spine, and she followed his direction without further argument. She started the car and drove slowly up the driveway to park next to the Suburban.

"Give me your keys, lock the doors when I get out, and stay put." He must have sensed her opposition even before she said anything. "I mean it, Zoey. I'm going to check it out. I've got my phone, but if you see anything that doesn't look right, call nine-one-one. And don't get out of the car."

He took the keys from her and was out in a flash, shutting the door with barely a sound. She thought he'd go straight to her cottage, but instead he slipped into his cabin. She had only a moment to wonder at his intention before he reappeared, moonlight glinting dully off the gun in his hand.

Lucy's howling had anxiety twisting in Zoey's belly. She turned in the seat to keep Levi in her field of vision, but within seconds he was out of sight.

She'd never been good at waiting patiently, having to sit with nothing to *do*. She went over the reasons she should do as Levi had ordered and stay in the car. He was a cop. He was trained to do exactly what he was doing. She, on the other hand, was a wildlife biologist. Want to know about deer migration? She was your girl. Helping a cop? She'd never even taken a self-defense class in her life, which now seemed like a gross oversight. She'd be smart and do what the cop said.

She turned in her seat again, peering through the back window. The moon shone enough light that the trees cast faint shadows. She strained her eyes but could not detect any movement. Lucy's crying stopped. Damnit. She wanted to be out there to know what was going on with her baby. Her hand was at the door handle, but she stopped herself from opening it. She'd told Levi she'd stay put. Crap. Waiting sucked.

She retrieved her phone from her purse, tapped on the screen, and looked up "what to do if someone has broken into your house." First thing on the list, call the police. Done, kind of. Second, take pictures. She hoped there was nothing to take pictures of. That somehow the lights had gone out on their own, and Lucy had been barking at shadows. Rapping against the car window had her jolting and sucking in a wheezy breath. Levi. The flashlight from his phone shone bright against the darkness as she opened the door and was greeted by a happy dog.

Relief washed through her. "Oh baby, you're okay." She dodged the sloppy tongue and rubbed Lucy's face. Comfort for Lucy meant all one hundred plus pounds of her sitting on Zoey's lap. "Oof, off girl." Zoey shoved, and Levi pulled back on the leash so she could get out of the car. "What happened? What did you find?"

"I'm not sure. Your things on the porch are scattered everywhere. Maybe you had a bear." There was a thread of doubt in his tone.

"It didn't get inside?"

"No. Whatever it was upset Lucy, and stuff was knocked around, but that's about it."

They walked up the driveway, and Lucy, pleased with her outing, pranced as much as she ever pranced at the end of the leash. Zoey rubbed her arms against the nighttime temperature that had to have dropped down into the forties. Levi passed his light over the bear-proof trashcan enclosures. They were intact, with no evidence of bear tampering.

They reached her porch, where Levi had already turned on the light by the door. She looked around with growing despair. Everything was a mess—a clay pot shattered, wind chimes pulled from their hooks, the fairy lights ripped down, the glass from smashed bulbs littering the floor.

"Here, hold Lucy, I want to get pictures before the scene is compromised." He handed Zoey the leash and took out his phone.

Zoey looped the leash securely around her hand. Lucy wanted to sniff around and do her own investigation. "Lucy, sit."

She sat with a huffing sound, obviously not pleased. Zoey took in the overturned chairs, the pitcher of wildflowers she'd had on a little side table, the flowers crushed on the wood floor. "This doesn't make sense."

"What?"

"The flowers being crushed like that. It looks like they've been stepped on and purposefully mashed. That's not typical bear behavior."

"How about the cushions being pulled off the furniture, the table overturned. Would a bear do that?"

"Maybe. If a bear comes up to a house like this, he's thinking of one thing. Food. He'll go for the trashcans first. But if he sees something that looks like food through a window? He'll go through the window. But smashing light bulbs, and pulling down wind chimes? Bears like to play, but that seems off to me."

Levi nodded, then held his phone to his ear. "Brad, it's me. Zoey's house has been vandalized." He paused, then said, "Between seven and ten tonight. Zoey says it's not likely a bear. I've taken pictures. I'll send them to you."

He waited, gaze on Zoey, then replied to his brother. "I'll look into it. By the way, I'm out of town tomorrow, coming back Sunday early enough to make Mom's thing. I want extra patrols keeping an eye on Zoey's place."

"Now wait a minute, I—"

He raised a hand to cut her off, listening, then responding to Brad. "I'm on it." He slipped his phone in his pocket. "Let's get this straightened up."

"Hold on. What do you mean, 'you're on it'? What are you on?" There wasn't much that put her back up like someone trying to manage her.

"The job. I'll be looking into whether this is related to the hit-and-run."

The job. Right, he was a cop, and Brad had assigned him to her case. The whole thing made her itchy. "Stuff gets thrown around on my porch, how can that be related to a hit-and-run?"

"That's what I'm going to find out."

Zoey secured Lucy's leash to a post, not willing to risk letting her off leash and having to round her up in the dark if she took off.

Levi righted a table, then tossed cushions back onto the loveseat. "What are you doing tomorrow?"

She shrugged. "Saturday things."

His gaze was expectant, and when she didn't elaborate, he raised an eyebrow. "Come on, Zoey. Give me more than that."

"Why are you asking?"

"Isn't that obvious? You've recently been the victim of two crimes. If they're related, I need to find out who's targeting you."

"Remember that authoritarian cop thing I don't like? You're doing that."

"Asking what you're doing tomorrow is me being an authoritarian cop?"

"Yes."

"My job is to serve and protect. That's what I'm doing."

"I am not your responsibility, and what I do on a Saturday is my business."

Even in the shadows cast by the porch light, she could see the flash of temper. He straightened, hands on hips, none of the easygoing, junk-food-loving guy she'd had dinner with earlier. This version of Levi was all serious business.

"The hell with that. I'm doing my job, and I need your cooperation. See this?" He motioned to the destruction on her porch. "When someone is targeted, the perpetrator usually starts small, but when that doesn't satisfy them, they escalate."

"Then it doesn't make sense that this is related to my accident. That had a lot more impact, no pun intended, than throwing around cushions and ruining a bunch of flowers."

Levi speared a hand through his hair, exasperation evident in the gesture. "Is there anywhere you and Lucy can spend tomorrow night?"

"Yep. Right here in my own little cottage." She gave him a fake sweet smile as she moved past him to pick up the strand of broken lights. Setting them carefully aside, she went through her front door that Levi had left slightly ajar. Flipping lights on inside, she crossed to the kitchen to retrieve the broom and dustpan. When she stepped onto the porch again, she gave Levi a feigned look of surprise. "Still here?"

He ignored her snarky tone. "What about Eva and Diego? I'll call Eva and see if you can spend tomorrow night with them."

"Don't you dare." She pointed a finger at him. "I am not going to impose on Eva and Diego, in no small part, another pun for you, because me spending the night means Lucy spending the night. And beyond that, I don't want to go anywhere. Someone throwing things around on my porch, while it hits the odd scale, is hardly life threatening. This is my home, and I'm staying." While she spoke, she swept broken glass into a pile.

"You being hit by a car is life threatening. You're damn lucky your injuries weren't a lot more serious. If this," he indicated the porch with his hand, "is connected, then I don't want you here by yourself when I'm not nearby."

She tried for a patient tone. "I appreciate your concern, Levi. I won't be alone because I'll have Lucy, and we'll be fine. Amazingly, I managed to live here quite happily before you moved in, what? A week ago?" The patient tone didn't make it quite to the end of her statement.

"Will you be reasonable?"

"Reasonable? What exactly is that? Men use 'reasonable' to suggest that women are emotional and not capable of making rational decisions. For you, me being 'reasonable' means to do what you want me to do."

"Fuck that. My mother would kick my ass if she thought I didn't respect women or their intellect."

"Well, my mother would kick *my* ass if she thought I didn't stand up for myself and for what I believe in."

"Now you're being difficult."

"You want to see difficult? How about this?" This time her finger pointed to the steps. "Why don't you get off my porch, Levi Gallagher? And while you're at it, why don't you take your reasonableness and shove it up your ass?"

***

Levi throttled up the drive to the cabin a solid twelve hours after he'd left, set the kickstand, and cut the engine. He sat there, letting the silence roll over him. Riding through Yosemite and over the Tioga Pass made for some beautiful scenery, but five-plus hours on a motorcycle added on top of five-plus hours in the Suburban and he was feeling a bit rough. He eased off the bike and stretched.

He had to check on Zoey.

Her Prius was parked out front, and there was a light on inside the cottage. He hoped she was home and everything was okay. He'd confirm that, then figure out what he had in his fridge for dinner before hitting the sack. He'd also have to apologize. He had two sisters and knew how this worked. It didn't matter that he'd been right last night; his approach might have come off as a little heavy-handed, and god knew Zoey didn't like heavy-handedness.

He pulled the helmet off his head as he climbed the steps to her porch, stopping in his tracks when he spied her through the front window. She was in the living room, on her phone, talking animatedly with her hands the way she sometimes did. She wore one of those flowy skirts, and her curly hair formed spirals around her head. Her all-in laugh carried through the window and shot him through with an unexpected clutch of lust.

Lucy's bark announced him as he raised a fist to knock on the door. A moment later it opened. Zoey stood there, and his heart took a solid jolt he felt deep down to his bones. She gave a half smile. There was still hesitancy in her expression, but he'd count the smile as a win.

"Hey."

"Hey, Levi." Zoey's gaze ran over him as Lucy pushed past her and began busily sniffing his pants. "Why are you dressed like that?"

He pulled off the leather jacket, then the Velcro straps that secured the body armor so he could pull it over his head. "Protection from road rash."

She frowned. "You have a motorcycle?"

"Yeah. I borrowed the Suburban from a friend for the move. I returned it today and picked up my motorcycle."

"I made rude comments about the Suburban and it wasn't even yours."

"Do I look like the kind of guy who'd drive a hearse?"

There was that smile again that hit him square in the solar plexus. "Motorcycles are dangerous. I'm putting that out there."

"Hence the helmet and body armor." He dumped both onto the loveseat with the jacket and peeled off black leather gloves. "But they're also fuel efficient and easy to maneuver through Bay Area traffic. Not good for winter in the Sierras, but I have a couple of months before that becomes an issue to figure out what I'm going to drive." Lucy gave up sniffing his jeans and wandered out onto the porch.

"So you drove all the way to Oakland and back today? Did you just get back?"

He nodded. "Everything okay here? No unexpected visitors?"

Watchfulness returned to her eyes. "Nope. Only me and Lucy, best buds hanging out." She hesitated, then seemed to come to a decision. "Do you want to come in? I made chili for dinner if you'd like some." She gave him a sideways glance. "It's made from scratch, not from a can, so it may not be what you're used to."

He held her gaze, not answering, and she finally asked, "What's wrong?"

"Hell if I know. You were mad at me, and now you're not. At least I don't think you are. I haven't even apologized, and I was ready to do that."

She cocked her head. "Apologize for what? Wanting to keep me safe?"

He narrowed his eyes. "There's got to be a trap here somewhere. I have a mom. I have two sisters. This isn't how they operate. When we argue, even if I'm right, I'm made to suffer before I'm forgiven."

"You weren't right, but I don't hold a grudge because you thought, however misguided, that you were doing the right thing. Have you eaten? Do you want that chili?"

"No, I haven't eaten, and yeah, chili sounds perfect."

"Then you can come in and tell me how your drive was. The cornbread is almost ready to come out of the oven."

Levi followed her into the house. Lucy trudged behind him and gave a groan as she did her bear-rug sprawl in front of the fireplace. "I feel you, Lucy," he muttered. Zoey's couch with its brightly patterned slipcover looked inviting, making him think he could be like the dog and stretch out.

Zoey confused him, no doubt, but he could deal with being confused. A woman who was hitting all the sexy marks for him had invited him to dinner. He had chili and cornbread in his near future, and he couldn't think of anywhere he'd rather be.

An hour later, Levi carried bowls to the sink. For not having meat, the chili had been amazing, and he couldn't remember the last time he'd eaten homemade cornbread. When she reached around him to run water over the dishes, he held up a hand. "If you put the leftovers away, I'll wash the dishes."

"You don't have to do that."

"You fed me a fantastic meal. I'm doing the cleanup." He began filling the plastic basin with hot water. "And next time I see Brad, I'm talking to him about installing a dishwasher in here."

"No, you're not. I don't mind washing dishes, and I don't want to give up the cabinet space. You don't have to manage things for me, Levi. If I wanted a dishwasher, I'd ask Brad myself."

"Right," he grunted. She had a point. She was capable and could deal with her own affairs. He had to check the impulse to assume he always had to take care of people.

He scrubbed dishes, then rinsed, and placed them on the drainer. He guessed the task wasn't so bad, particularly since an interesting woman was sitting at the table sipping from a mug of tea, golden brown eyes watching him as he worked.

"Didn't you tell Brad you were coming back tomorrow?"

He paused, suds on his hands, then resumed washing. She did use an inordinate number of pots and pans for what was basically two food items. "I did. I changed my mind and decided to make the trip in one day."

"And how was that?"

"Traffic around Oakland was a bitch, per usual, but the drive around the Yosemite Valley never disappoints."

He caught her speculative look.

"I see. Did your decision to make the trip in one day have anything to do with me not leaving my home after someone messed with my stuff last night?"

He shrugged. "It saved me from having to find a place to sleep tonight."

"I'm sure you have friends who would have lent you their couch."

He didn't disagree, and continued to rinse the dishes.

Zoey came up beside him, a dishtowel in her hand. She pulled on his shoulder as she went up onto her tiptoes. He caught a whiff of fresh flowers and wondered if it was from her shampoo. Then she was brushing his cheek with her lips in a gesture that was both friendly and seductive.

"You're looking out for me. It's unnecessary, but thank you."

He turned to face her, and the air between them heated. Gaze intent on hers, he took the towel and dried his hands, placing it on the counter before settling them on her hips. "Want to try that again?"

Her smile faded, eyes reflecting the same inner conflict he was experiencing: need, want, and a healthy dose of caution all bound together in a messy knot.

The heat between them flamed brighter, then she was fisting a hand in his shirt to pull him to her. The earlier jolt was nothing compared to the hot blast when her lips touched his. He pulled her closer until her curvy body fit snugly against his and he dove into the kiss.

Vague warning notes sounded in the back of his head, but he ignored them. He skimmed a hand under the loose cotton top she wore, stroking her from hip to back, his hunger stoked by the feel of warm, taut skin. Her mouth opened and her tongue slid against his while he traced his fingers up the indentation of her spine. It took all his willpower not to unhook the back strap of her bra and enjoy the results.

He wasn't the only one digging it. Zoey released her hold on his shirt and slipped her hands under the fabric to rub over the muscles of his stomach, making what were most decidedly turned-on noises. Her fingers moved to his abs and the thought that she might reach lower had him harder than he had been and full-on ready. Then she hesitated, her hands going still, and he knew she'd heeded the warning signs.

She backed up a step, holding her hands up in front of her like he was a prowling bear ready to attack. He battled back the need until he had it strapped and under control. He could appreciate her wariness because he felt the same.

Breathing slowly and with deliberate care, he worked to steady the rhythm of his heart. He didn't need complications in his life right now, and he had a feeling Zoey Hardesty represented one exceptionally big complication.

She licked her top lip and his heart rate kicked up again, and he backed up another step. "That was a mistake."

Right. Maybe it was a mistake, but he wasn't sure he liked her saying so. "I should go."

"I think you should."

She walked him out onto the porch where he retrieved his gear. He crossed to the steps, then stopped and turned around. She stood under the porch light, and he didn't think any woman had ever stirred him as she did.

"It may have been a mistake, Zoey, but you can't deny we both liked how it felt."

Chapter Eight

Sunday afternoon, Zoey passed the driveway full of cars and looked for a place to park on the street. Gallagher events were sprawling affairs. Family members extended invitations to their friends and those friends sometimes passed on invitations to others, and pretty soon there were dozens of people showing up. She found a spot on the street, gauged it to be long enough, and squeezed her Prius in between two larger vehicles.

Hitching her hobo bag over her shoulder and with a large, flat container in her hands, she weaved her way through the cars on the long driveway and told herself she wasn't looking for Levi's motorcycle. He wouldn't miss his mother's barbecue, so she was sure to see him. But she wanted time to mentally prepare herself.

When she'd opened the door to his knock last evening, she'd had to force back the lick of lust at the image he'd presented. The helmet had left his dark hair sticking up at odd angles, and when matched with the shadow of beard along his jaw, he'd hit smokin' hot. Then there was all that black leather and motorcycle gear he'd started pulling off. That would have gotten any woman hot and bothered.

Ending the evening with a kiss that had nearly blown the top off her head, and had left her feeling more than a little off balance. Since there were no motorcycles parked anywhere she could see, she figured she'd arrived ahead of Levi and breathed a sigh of relief at the reprieve.

The sounds of the gathering came from the back, so she let herself in through the side gate. When she reached the edge of the back deck, she stopped to survey the scene. A net had been rigged across a flat area of the sloping lawn, and several kids were playing volleyball. She recognized Cameron MacElvoy, longer and leaner than when she'd last seen him, with Christy and Robby Cutter from the Broken Arrow ranch. Jack Morgan's stepson, Adrian, launched the ball high and wide to bounce on the deck between two large barbecues. The smell of grilling meat carried in the breeze. Brad Gallagher, a spatula in one hand, caught the ball in the other and winged it back. "Keep the ball off the deck," he yelled.

"Zoey, look, I'm making a giant bubble."

She turned her attention to where Levi and Brad's sister Maddy stood in the center of what looked like half a dozen preschool kids with a wide tray set on a small table. A couple of the kids held plastic hoops, and Maddy's daughter Keeley dipped hers into the tray, then ran with it across the grass, a giant, shimmering bubble billowing behind her.

"That's a good one," Zoey called. Keeley passed off her hoop to her twin, Mason, who dipped it in the soapy water and twirled in circles to make his bubbles. Zoey waved to Maddy and turned when she heard Eva's voice.

"There you are." Eva came down the steps from the deck with a clatter of footsteps. "What'd you bring?"

"Vegetarian kabobs for the grill."

"Ooh, what's on them?"

"Marinated mushrooms, onion, peppers, zucchini, some extra-firm tofu, and pineapple. We'll see how they hold up on the grill. I made a pineapple teriyaki sauce to go with it."

"That sounds yum. Aunt Trish has those basket things you can put them in to barbecue. They work pretty well with vegetables. Let's get this inside."

She followed her friend onto the deck, then nearly tripped when she recognized the couple sitting on a long bench. Meg and Declan Murphy sat with their little girl. She wore cute pink shorts and a t-shirt with a big rainbow-colored heart, and was taking tiny bites from a huge slice of watermelon her mother was holding for her.

Zoey liked to read, and she'd read Dex Michaels books even before knowing the author's real name was Declan Murphy and that he was local. Then she learned Declan's wife was Meghan Bennett, whose *Darkening of Ardenstal* fantasy world had grabbed Zoey and hadn't let go until she'd read every book in the series, and she was feeling a little starstruck. Acknowledging Meghan's wave with a little one of her own, Zoey weaved through chairs to the door.

Eva held open the screen door for Trish, who was carrying a platter of hamburger patties. She was dressed for summer with white shorts and a sleeveless denim shirt, her strappy silver sandals providing a nice contrast to the deep red toenail polish. When she grew up, Zoey wanted to be as well put together and poised as Trish Gallagher.

From Eva, Zoey had learned how Trish had taken over the family's rental properties after her husband had died, invested wisely, and now not only supported herself, but had established a nonprofit to help single parents struggling to make ends meet. Beyond being a smart and successful businesswoman, she'd raised four amazing children who adored her.

Trish handed off the patties to Brad, then turned to greet her guest. "I'm so glad you came." After a quick hug, she reached for the container Zoey carried. "What do we have here?"

"Vegetarian kabobs. Once Brad is done with the barbecue, I can grill them."

Trish pried up a corner to peer inside the container. "Oh, this is perfect. Thank you. Current evidence aside," she waved at the meat on the grill, "I've told Landon we're going to be cutting back on our meat consumption. It's better for our health, and better for the planet. You'd have thought I'd suggested selling my house and moving to Bolivia."

"What's this about moving to Bolivia? I hear they raise a lot of beef in Bolivia." Despite his generally serious expression, the spark in Landon Halloway's eyes coupled with the hand at Trish's waist when he peered over her shoulder made it clear she was the center of his world.

Trish kissed his cheek. "Enjoy your meat today, my love, because going forward, moderation will be the name of the game." She turned to Zoey. "There are pitchers of water, lemonade, and iced tea, and we're using glasses instead of plastic cups, which I hope I don't regret. Help yourself, or head over to Jack who's making margaritas as we speak. I'll let you know when the grill is clear for you to put on your kabobs. It won't be long, and then we'll be ready to eat."

After grabbing a glass of lemonade, Zoey was standing at the barbecue with her kabobs in one of the basket things Eva had recommended when Levi came up the steps from the side gate. God, he was gorgeous, all tousled dark hair, bold blue eyes, and that lean, tough body.

His jeans were ripped at the knee and he wore a simple dark green t-shirt that hugged the muscles of his chest. Trish, stacking paper plates and napkins on the long table that would be used as a buffet, spied her youngest son and set everything down to walk into his open arms. Levi wrapped up his mother, rested his cheek on the top of her head, and closed his eyes. Zoey swallowed past a tightness in her throat.

Trish wiped her eyes when she pulled back. "I'm so damn glad you're home, Levi James."

"Me too, Mom."

She scrutinized him with a look Zoey recognized. "You look better. Are you sleeping?"

"Yeah, Mom. I'm sleeping. I'm fine."

Trish must have been satisfied, because she said, "Good," and resumed setting up the buffet. Levi scanned the crowd until his gaze snapped on Zoey like a rare earth magnet. He took a step in her direction before being intercepted by a small whirlwind.

"Uncle Levi, Uncle Levi!" Keeley ran onto the deck, adorable in her yellow shorts overalls, and missing one sandal. Levi swung her up into his arms and had the little girl shrieking with laughter when he pretended to gobble her neck. "Save me, Daddy!"

Logan paused in his conversation with rancher Eli MacElvoy. He crossed the deck to pluck his daughter from Levi's arms and she clambered up until she sat on her father's shoulders.

"Uncle Levi can't get me up here. My daddy will protect me."

"Hey, I'm the favorite uncle. Why's he need to protect you?"

Keeley wrapped her arms around Logan's head. "My daddy is my favorite mister person."

Logan's smile was smug. "Hear that? I'm the favorite mister person. Get your own fan club."

"Mister person? When did she learn to talk so much?"

"This kid was born talking. She's almost four and asks me a thousand questions a day. She's got a better vocabulary than I do."

Keeley thumped her bare foot against her father's chest. "I lost my sandal."

Logan cocked his head to look up at her. "Where'd you lose it?"

"I don't know. I think Mason stole it."

"Right off your foot?"

"He's sneaky."

"That he is. Let's go look for it." Logan trotted off with Keeley bouncing on his shoulders.

Watching Levi's interaction with his family reinforced Zoey's understanding of the pull that had brought him back to Hangman's Loss. She loved her mother and brother, but with only the three of them the family dynamics were different from what the extended Gallagher clan shared. She wasn't envious, though maybe a little wistful.

She removed the grilling basket from the heat, opening it to place the veggie kabobs on a platter. The skin on her neck tingled and she knew Levi had come up behind her, which frustrated her. She couldn't seem *not* to be aware of him.

He peered suspiciously at the kabobs. "Aren't these missing something?"

"If you're looking for hunks of meat, then yes, they are missing something."

"I heard some people put those little canned sausages on a skewer and barbecue them. Bet those are tasty."

"I'll get right on that." She turned off the gas to the barbecue and picked up the platter, and when she turned, nearly plowed the platter into Levi's chest. He steadied her with his hands on her elbows.

"You look nice."

She'd chosen a sleeveless white summer dress with tiny red flowers. She liked it because it showed off her toned arms stacked with her bracelets, and it was short enough to display some leg, but not so much that it didn't cover the bruise on her thigh from the accident. The elbow bruise had faded enough not to feel vain about it.

"Thank you." Why did it feel like little sparks snapped on her skin where he touched her?

"Where's Lucy? You could have brought her."

"Ah, no. She'd have spent the afternoon trying to herd small children. She's fine in the cottage for a few hours."

"Too bad, the kids would have loved her. Next time." He looked down at the loaded platter. "You want me to take this somewhere?"

"I've got it. Would you mind bringing in the grilling basket?"

Levi followed her to the buffet table where she placed her kabobs amongst the bounty. There were burgers and hot dogs, plates with deviled eggs, bowls of potato salad, and enough sliced watermelon to feed a small army. She took the basket from him and went into the kitchen, retuning in seconds with a little bowl of dipping sauce that she set next to the kabobs.

Trish turned to address the crowd. "Grab a plate folks, and enjoy, then come back for seconds. I don't want a bunch of leftovers."

Since she was already there, Zoey took a paper plate and began loading it with a little bit of everything. Levi right behind her. "Oh look. Quinoa salad with cherry tomatoes."

"I'll take some of that." He scooped some onto his plate, then laughed at her skeptical expression. "Just because I appreciate food of the processed variety doesn't mean I don't also eat healthy food. I try to balance it out."

"I don't think that's what is meant by a balanced diet."

"Sure it is. Slim Jims and an apple make for a balanced meal."

She gave him a sideway glare. "There's nothing I can say to that."

Picnic tables had been set up under a grouping of aspens that blocked the late afternoon sun. With her plate full, she hesitated, not sure where to sit. Levi moved around her to set his overloaded plate on a table. He took hers and placed it next to his. "This good?" At her nod, he flashed his smile. "Be back in a sec."

How, in the past week, had she spend more time socially with Levi Gallagher than anyone else? She'd wanted to get to know him, to move beyond her high school crush, but it wasn't working. He gave that wicked smile and her heart tripped over in her chest. She didn't like this feeling of being off balance whenever he was near.

True to his word, he returned in seconds with glass tumblers full to the brim with a frosty red slush. He held one out to her. "Jack's strawberry margarita. You want?"

"Oh, that looks delicious. Thank you."

"Hey, where'd you get that?" Diego set his plate down across from Zoey. He must've arrived straight from work, wearing the navy pants and trim shirt of the Hangman's Loss Fire Department.

"Jack's got the blender going in the kitchen." Levi told him. "You better get yours because he said he wants food and is quitting soon."

"Damn, I'll have to pass." He patted the firefighter's badge on his chest. "Can't drink while in uniform."

Eva settled herself next to Diego. She speared a roasted zucchini from her plate and raised her gaze to Zoey. "Mm, the sauce for the grilled veggies is yummy."

"Moving on to the important stuff, what's for dessert?" Levi asked his cousin.

"You just sat down to eat and you're already thinking about dessert?"

"I need to know how much room to save."

"You always have room in your stomach, but I'll tell you anyway. Maddy was whipping up peach blueberry tarts at the café this morning, and Landon is making homemade ice cream to go with them."

"Oh man, am I glad I'm home."

Chapter Nine

Conversation and laughter drifted from the tables. Levi felt himself relax, some of the weight he'd carried back to Hangman's Loss easing. He'd been honest with his mother that he was sleeping better, but better was a relative term. The nightmare about the shooting had woken him twice since his return home. Much better than the nightly occurrence it had been a month ago.

He glanced around. The people he cared about most in the world were here. And sitting next to Zoey suited him. He was tipping back his glass to get the last of the margarita when a flash of light from across the arroyo caught his attention. He stared at the spot it had come from. His mom's house backed up to a deep gully filled with native brush that stretched about a third of a mile across. The far side was forest service land with pines growing up to the edge of the bluff. He narrowed his gaze, waiting to see if the flash repeated. It had looked like sunlight reflecting off glass or a mirror.

Keeping an eye out, he scooped up the last bite of quinoa salad from his plate. He'd put it on his plate to get a reaction from Zoey, then been surprised to find it wasn't too bad. Trish rose to her feet, tapping the side of a glass with a spoon. Landon rose to stand beside her.

"Attention, everyone," his mother called out.

Conversation eased off, even the little kids quieting.

Landon touched her arm, leaning down to say something in her ear. At her nod, Landon took her hand in his and interlaced their fingers. The stab of panic lasted only a split second. Levi tensed, then forced himself to let it go. Maddy had given him a heads-up so he wasn't caught off guard.

"Thank you all for joining our gathering of family and friends." Landon spoke in his deliberate, quiet way. "You are the people who are most important to us." He leaned into his mom. "Four years ago, after my wife passed away, I moved to Hangman's Loss. I guess I was looking for a new beginning, and I wanted to live in a place I have loved visiting since my parents brought me to stay at Walt Kincaid's cabins back when I was a boy."

Levi caught Emma tilting her head to Brad's shoulder at the mention of her grandfather and the resort she had inherited from him.

"I never expected to meet the second love of my life." He brought her hand up and pressed a kiss her knuckles. "It took some convincing, but I got Trish to go out with me." He glanced at her and the adoration was hard to miss. "I guess we've been inseparable ever since. This afternoon, I have the pleasure of announcing that I have asked Trish to marry me, and she has accepted. She's agreed to become my wife and I'm the luckiest man in the world." He dipped his head and kissed his fiancée.

Whoops and calls of congratulations filled the air. Levi rose to his feet and crossed the lawn, Brad directly behind him. Levi shook Landon's hand. "Mom can take care of herself, but she's happier with you. Welcome to the family."

"Thank you, Levi."

He turned and kissed her cheek. "Congratulations, Mom. I'm happy for you."

She placed her hands on either side of his face, her brows lowered in a slight frown. "I hope so, Levi. I always thought you took you father's death the hardest. I never want you to feel that marrying Landon means I didn't love your father with everything that was in me. I did, and the memories of him are always in my heart."

He pushed the twist of sadness aside. "I know. I want you to be happy. You deserve a good man, and Landon strikes me as a good man."

"He is. I love him in a different way than I loved your dad, but it's strong just the same. I never expected to find another love, and I feel blessed." She patted Levi's cheek, and her voice turned husky. "Sometimes I see you and catch my breath. You look so much like your father."

Levi swallowed the lump in his throat. He dipped his head and kissed her again, and she let him go.

He returned to his seat next to Zoey, whose dark eyes were full of emotion. She didn't say anything, but she leaned a little so her shoulder was nestled against his. The simple gesture helped ease the tightness in his chest.

Maddy climbed to the top step of the deck. "In celebration, we have champagne on the buffet table for the adults and ginger ale for the kids. Be sure to pick up a peach tart with a scoop of Landon's homemade ice cream for dessert. Come and get it."

Levi rose with Zoey and they crossed the deck to get in line. Landon was dishing out ice cream in bowls for the little kids, while Maddy cut the tarts into smaller pieces they could manage. A flash caught his attention once again, and Levi scanned the arroyo.

With an uneasy feeling, he returned to the table with Zoey at his side. The tart was amazing, as was anything Maddy made, and the ice cream was the best he'd ever had. He glanced to where his mother sat with Landon and caught the shared look between them. He didn't like things to change, but he really wanted his mother to be happy.

Justin Trainer, also in his fire department uniform, joined their table with a huge scoop of ice cream on top of his peach tart. He sat beside Eva and, with Diego, entertained the group with the story from that morning. A call had come into 9-1-1, and the crew had been sent out when the dispatcher heard heavy breathing, but the caller seemed unable to speak. When pressed, the caller had emitted a high-pitched keening cry and seemed to be hyperventilating. They'd arrived on scene and quickly realized a woman was frightened speechless by the rattlesnake she'd found curled behind the toilet in her bathroom.

"She was sixty-three years old and dressed in short shorts and a tank top, so more power to her. All she could do was point to the bathroom," Justin said. "Then this guy," he clapped Diego on the back, "walks in with the snake grabber and gets the rattler in one try."

Diego smiled. "I bagged the snake. That woman about passed out when I brought it out. She kept pointing at the bag and wheezing."

"We did a health check and once the snake was out she recovered pretty quickly."

"She probably won't sleep in that house until she figures out how a snake got in," Eva commented.

"You relocated the snake, right?" Zoey asked.

"Yes, Ms. Wildlife Biologist," Diego assured her. "We released him well away from town so he can live out his snake life in the wilderness."

Brad came up behind Levi and clapped a hand on his shoulder. He bent his head and spoke in a low voice. "Come into the house with me."

Levi nodded and rose, figuring he had a good idea what Brad wanted. After a quick word to Zoey, he followed his brother into the house. In the kitchen, Jack leaned back against the counter, while Logan slouched on a bar stool chewing the kernels off an ear of corn.

"I'll be back in a second," Brad said, continuing through the house and out the front door.

"This about whoever's watching us from across the arroyo?" Levi asked.

"You caught that, too?" Jack muttered as he peered through the window.

"There's someone over there with binoculars," Logan said, tossing the corncob into the trash.

Brad returned with department-issue binoculars he must have had in his car. He put the lenses to his eyes and focused across the arroyo.

"There's a dirt road that dead-ends about where I saw the reflection off glass," Logan stated. "This is your mom's deal." He pointed to Brad and Levi. "You two should stay. Jack and I will go check it out."

Brad lowered the binoculars. "I don't see anyone. I think whoever it was is gone, but I still want you to go see what you can see."

Jack gave a nod and Logan raised his hand in a half salute as they left. Levi turned to his brother. "What the hell's going on around here? First Zoey gets hit by a car, then her place is trashed. And now someone is watching us having a party at Mom's house."

"That's what we're going to figure out. Who the hell knows why someone would be across the arroyo with binoculars? Could be a bird-watcher, or a hiker, or nothing. Makes the hair stand up on my neck, though."

"Yeah, mine too."

Brad eyed him. "Since I have you for a minute, you know Mom's selling this place when she and Landon get married?"

Another twist to his gut. Levi looked around at the house where he'd grown up. "No, I didn't. Guess it's too big for two people."

"Yeah, two people who are getting older. Landon's place is single story and smaller."

The considering expression on Brad's face annoyed him and Levi scowled. "Why are you looking at me like that?"

"You were always attached to this place, more than Jenny, Maddy, or me." Brad shrugged. "I don't want you upset when Mom puts it on the market."

"You make me sound like a wuss."

"Not a wuss, but you feel more deeply about some things than the rest of us, and I worry that you hold on too tight."

"What the hell are you talking about? First Mom tells me she thinks Dad's death hit me the hardest, when I damn well know him dropping dead from a heart attack took every one of us out at the knees. And now you're telling me I'm more attached to this house than anyone else. I'm not some emotionally fragile douche."

Ignoring the comment, Brad asked, "Do you remember the summer after Dad died?"

Levi shrugged. "Everything was a blur, so not so much."

"You wouldn't get out of bed unless I dragged you out. You must have read fifty books that summer, and that was pure escape. If you weren't reading, you were playing video games. And you were so pissed at me we bloodied each other's noses more than once. Remember any of that?"

Levi thought back. He felt like he was pushing through clouds of grief to remember. "You rode my ass. That's why you ended up with a bloody nose."

"I wasn't the only one with a bloody nose, pal. But yeah, I rode your ass. Got you to help with the rentals. Dad hadn't been feeling well for a while before the heart attack, and he'd let things go. I was worried Mom was going to lose the rental properties to the banks."

Levi shook his head. "I didn't know. Must have been tough on you, though. You were in college and took a semester off."

"I took a year and a half off."

"A year and a half, really?" It hadn't seemed that long at the time, but when he thought back, he realized Brad had been there for him in more ways than Levi had ever realized. "I never really thought about how bad it must have been for you. Or why you rode my ass."

"You were a teenager, and you needed someone to ride you. You resented me for taking over Dad's job, but someone had to do it. Mom was pulling herself together, but then Maddy got pregnant with Lily, and Lily was born sick. Maddy needed Mom. Jenny had Derek, so she was okay. You seemed to get lost in all that."

The memories tumbled back, but now with a different perspective. Maybe coming home meant he was done running from the emotions that for so long had felt like they would rip him apart. "I guess maybe I did need you." Levi rolled his shoulders. "I'm okay now, and I'm glad Mom is with Landon. She deserves to be happy, even if that means selling this house."

"Right. She deserves our support. Landon's a good guy."

Levi gave a short laugh when he caught something in Brad's expression. "You ran a background check on him."

Brad didn't look even a little sorry. "Damn straight I did. I never got any bad vibes about him, but no way was I going to let some loser take advantage of my mother."

"Then you probably got the same result I did. I ran my check after hearing they were dating. He's never been in legal trouble and is financially secure."

"And we better keep this between us or we'll both get our asses chewed." Brad clapped his brother on the back. "On another topic, we've got an important ballgame coming up. You in?"

"I heard about that. Yeah, I'm in. Who do you have playing first?"

"You. I want the Guns to win this one, and we need your bat and your glove. Be at the sports park for practice six o'clock tomorrow evening. We're getting pizza after."

Brad's phone buzzed, and he pulled it out of his pocket. "That's Jack." He put the phone to his ear. A minute later he was slipping it into his pocket. "Fresh tire tracks on the forest service road. There's a trailhead there with scuffed footprints in amongst a lot of other footprints, so nothing clear. They found a plastic disc that looks like it could be a binocular lens cover. Logan bagged it and we'll try to recover prints from that."

"Well, shit."

"Exactly."

***

Charissa peered through the binoculars, focusing on one face, then moving onto the next. She took pride in knowing about every person at the gathering in the backyard. She turned the lenses to where a long table stood piled with food. She was hungry, and the feast made her mouth water. She could have brought a sandwich, but making it would have delayed her leaving her home and she hadn't wanted to risk missing anything.

She wondered what she would bring once she was part of the family. Maybe her strawberry Jell-O and Cool Whip dessert. It was one of her favorites. That's what people did at such events. Everyone brought something special to share with others. She dropped the binoculars from the strap around her neck to take out her phone and zoom in to take photos.

When she'd been growing up, getting together with her own family had meant she and her mom going to her Aunt Judy's place on the other side of the lake, which also meant being careful never to be alone with Uncle Gary and his wandering hands. In a house that reeked of stale cigarette smoke and dirty cat litter box, Maryanne, Judy, and Gary would play cards, smoke, and drink until late into the night. For a while, when she was little, Charissa would have fun. Granddad had been alive then. He'd sit in his recliner with the tube in his nose that connected to the oxygen cylinder, and he'd talk to her and her cousin Trina about growing up in the Sierras. As a boy, he'd ditched school to ride his horse into the hills and hunt deer and elk with his pappy.

After Granddad's death, Charissa would hang out with Trina. They'd play Barbies and talk about school. They'd go out back behind the garage and smoke the cigarettes Trina had pilfered from her parents. Trina, who was four years older, had become more interested in texting to friends than spending time with her cousin. The minute Trina had turned eighteen she'd taken off, leaving behind the young adolescent girl with nothing to do and no one to talk to.

The Gallaghers weren't like that. The family supported each other.

Charissa had been so thrilled to run into Levi at Maddy's café. She'd *literally* run into him. She hadn't meant to make him spill his coffee, but he'd been ready to walk out and hadn't noticed her and she'd had to do something. Accidentally on purpose bumping against him had worked out perfectly except that he'd sloshed coffee onto his uniform pants. She'd felt bad, and the coffee had to burn, but still he'd been protective of her. He'd touched her, actually reached out a hand to her shoulder and steadied her. She had relived that moment hundreds of times since, and held the gesture close to her heart. A little something she and Levi would reminisce about when they were together.

She continued watching through the binoculars, pausing every now and then to raise her phone and snap another picture. The distance was too far to get good shots, but she liked taking photos of the Gallaghers. She'd taken several of Levi without him noticing before she'd bumped into him that day at the café, and now his face was the wallpaper on her phone.

Watching the party, she liked how the kids played together, and that the parents sometimes joined in. "Ooh, someone's not happy," she crooned when she saw a little girl in a blue romper take a tumble.

Trish helped the toddler to her feet and wiped the tears. She was a caring grandmother. When the game at the net switched from volleyball to badminton, Logan Ross held up his little boy, a racket in his tiny hand, and helped him hit the birdie. She could imagine the sound of the boy's laughter. Levi arrived and even through the lenses Charissa could appreciate all that deliciously thick hair. She thought she could make out the deep blue of his eyes even with the distance. Her heart swelled when he swept his niece up in his arms. He was a good uncle, and he'd be a good father.

Charissa gave a start when she spied that hippie woman who lived in the little house the Gallaghers owned. Digging through city records, she'd discovered her name was Zoey Hardesty. Charissa had been careful not to get caught, of course, as she didn't want to risk her job. Zoey Hardesty wasn't related to the Gallaghers. Why had she been invited?

Charissa had to stifle the urge to scream when Levi, *her* Levi, stood by the grill talking with that woman with all those beads. They moved to the food table, and Zoey turned her head to laugh up at Levi. It was so obvious the slut was making a play for him. Charissa felt like a knife was turning in her chest when Levi led Zoey to sit beside him at a table where they were joined by others.

Trish and Landon Halloway stood together and Landon said something that had everyone's attention turning to them. Charissa wished she could hear what he said. Whatever it was sent Levi to his mother for hugs. Such a good son.

Charissa continued to watch, moving into the shadow of a tree when she found Brad looking in her direction. Diego arrived with another fireman, one with red hair. It bothered her that she didn't recognize him. Probably someone Diego had invited from the fire station. She'd have to use her city job again to access information and find out who he was. It was always best to know all the players.

The two firemen talked like they were telling a story and had the others laughing. Anger over being excluded from the group at that table, the envy of wanting to be one of the beautiful people, talking, laughing, having fun, boiled over into rage so fast and so strong it nearly choked her.

She sat down on that dusty spot, pulling at her hair to redirect her emotions. When she got so mad, that's when the anger won. She couldn't let the anger win this time. Control was crucial, because if she lost control, she risked failure. Working toward her goal meant staying focused, not getting sidetracked. She wasn't about to let a slut like Zoey Hardesty get in her way.

Dusting off the seat of her pants, Charissa focused next on the children who would be her nieces and nephews, some of them only babies. They were so *adorable.* She couldn't wait until her own babies were there playing with their cousins.

She scanned across the entire group, then back over them again, her breath catching in her throat. Where were they? The men who were in law enforcement were no longer on the deck or at the tables under the tree. *Oh god, had they seen her?*

Fear had her scrambling up the trail to her car, panic biting at the back of her neck with razor-sharp teeth. She threw the binoculars into the backseat as sweat beaded on her forehead and acid churned in her stomach.

How would she explain herself if she were caught? People didn't understand her kind of devotion. The starter in her car made a grinding noise as it had been doing recently. *Please start.* She turned the key again, sweat slicking her hand. This time the engine turned over and she gunned the engine to make sure it caught.

She executed a hurried three-point turn, tires slipping and spinning on the soft shoulder. Then the front tire gained purchase and the car shot forward on the dirt road and she was racing away, a cloud of dust billowing behind her.

***

Levi turned his motorcycle into the driveway. He didn't want to go back to the cabin where he'd stew over his conversation with Brad. He didn't like to think that he'd been so self-absorbed after their dad had died that he'd totally missed what his brother had sacrificed. He'd never thought through the ramifications of Maddy needing their mom when her daughter had been so sick, or that Brad had taken time from college specifically to be there for Levi. That he'd resented his brother and acted like a shit didn't sit well all these years later.

Zoey's Prius was in its spot in front of her cottage. Going with the impulse, he stopped next to her car and leaned over to remove the extra helmet he'd hooked under the seat of the motorcycle, hoping she'd come for a ride with him. He climbed the steps to the porch, and once again Lucy announced him before he could knock.

The door swung open, framing the woman who had started occupying an inordinate amount of his attention lately. Zoey still wore the dress, but he didn't think that was what hit him like a sucker punch. The whole deal. The dark eyes, the mass of hair that seemed to go every which way, and the curvy little body he wanted to get his hands on in the worst way.

She didn't seem surprised to see him.

"Levi."

"Zoey." She gazed at him and he didn't have a clue what she was thinking. He knew what *he* was thinking. How she made him feel more like himself when he was with her, that simply seeing her made his day better, and how he could get used to that.

"Want to come for a ride with me?"

Lucy nosed around Zoey to sniff his jeans, then lean her not insubstantial weight against his leg.

Zoey lowered her brows and, call him crazy, but he found her instant suspicion a turn-on. "On your motorcycle?"

"Yeah, on my motorcycle." He motioned to the sky. "You see that?"

She looked past him. "What?"

He snagged her hand and walked her to the edge of the porch, Lucy following them. From there they could see the wide canvas of the western sky aglow with vibrant shades of pink and lavender, the granite peaks of the Sierras showing in an uneven silhouette.

"Come with me. We'll ride around the lake." He held up the helmet, eyebrow cocked.

She looked from the sky to Levi, then a smile bloomed. "Let me change into pants and a jacket. But, to make sure we're clear, this isn't a date."

Chapter Ten

"Here, you're wearing this on our non-date." Levi held out a bulky jacket. His words were light, but he seemed to be trying to shake off a mood. Since Zoey was feeling a bit preoccupied, too, maybe an evening ride would do them good.

In jeans and a jacket, she locked Lucy into the cottage. Levi returned from a quick trip to his cabin wearing black boots and pants with a leather coat over the body armor he'd worn before. Bad-boy sexy, and she appreciated the view.

"I'm wearing my denim jacket."

"This one is reinforced with impact protectors. See?" He opened it to show her how protective plates were sewn into the garment. "It'll be big on you but gives a lot more protection than what you're wearing."

She shed her jacket, dropping it on the loveseat, and donned the reinforced one. Before she could zip it, he held it open. "See these?" He held up a strap. "This strap goes around the belt loop on your jeans. They'll need to be cinched down since the jacket will be way too long on you."

"What's the point of the straps?"

"If you do hit the pavement, it keeps the jacket from pulling up and exposing your skin to the asphalt."

"Oh, that's smart." She attached the strap to a belt loop on the front of her jeans, then Levi moved behind her to attach the ones in the rear. Warm fingers brushed against the skin of her back, then she felt him go still until he traced a finger above the waistband of her jeans. "There's the top edge of a tattoo here."

"Everyone does something dumb when they're young."

"Getting the tattoo was dumb? Does it have an ex's name or something?"

"God no. Not that dumb. The tattoo is okay, but I guess I've outgrown it. I'm glad I stopped at one."

"You going to let me see the entire design?"

She pulled the jacket more securely over her hips and turned to face him. "Is this the modern version of I'll show you mine if you show me yours?"

His grin was quick. "Could be."

"I don't think so, handsome. At least not right now. Besides, the sun's going down and we're going to miss the window for our ride."

"Right." He handed her a helmet. "Put this on."

He put on his helmet, then pulled on thick black gloves. "Ever been on a motorcycle before?"

"Does a moped count?"

He snorted. "No, it does not. Motorcycles are in an entirely different class. A couple of pointers: Don't be shy about wrapping your arms around me, that's how you'll stay on the bike. Lean into the turns. If I lean, you lean. Keep the face shield down unless you want a bug or rock in the face. Last thing, my helmet is Bluetooth enabled, yours is not, so if there's an emergency, get my attention by tapping my shoulder. We won't be able to talk once we're moving."

"Got it."

They settled onto the seat and in seconds the rumble of the bike filled the air as they rolled down the driveway and onto the road. With her heart in her throat, Zoey rested her cheek against Levi's leather jacket and wrapped her arms around his waist. She hadn't anticipated the rush of acceleration. She didn't think they were going any faster than they would have in a car, perhaps slower, but the sensation was wicked fast movement.

They zipped down the winding road toward Hangman's Loss. Levi pulled to a stop at the highway that turned into Main Street once in town. He raised his visor and shouted, "Loosen up. You're stiff."

He flipped down the visor and took off. Zoey needed to stop worrying they were going to end up smeared on the road and embrace the adventure. Hugging Levi felt natural, and when she did as he'd told her and leaned with him into the curves, the movement of the bike felt less scary.

Hangman's Loss whizzed by in a blur. Once outside town, he flexed his hands on the grips and they zoomed onto the road with the wind whistling by.

Once past Hangman's Lake, Levi took the fork that brought them up and over a rise, and then down into the valley where they zipped past meadows bordered by dark pines, dotted by grazing cattle.

The day had turned to dusk and the sky darkened to deep purple. The bridge over the creek rumbled as they crossed, and they sped past the campground at the end of the valley. The highway snaked into the mountains, and she'd learned to anticipate the movement of the bike so she and Levi were responding as a unit.

Wrapped around him, she could feel his sinewy strength as he controlled the big bike. She tried to ignore the pull of attraction and reminded herself this wasn't a date, and they were not *going there*.

She loved the freedom of riding and being so close to nature. The bike slowed as they neared the top, then Levi pulled into a turnout.

The single headlight sliced through the vast semidarkness as he rolled to the guardrail of a lookout. He set the kickstand and she loosened her hold, and following Levi's motion, she swung her leg over the seat, then took off the helmet and shook out her hair.

Levi secured the helmets to the bike, then held his hand out. "Come."

Entwining her fingers with his seemed like habit, and it took a moment before she considered what they were doing. She tried to free her hand. "We can't hold hands. That would make this a date."

"A date involves dinner."

"We ate together at your mom's place."

"Being at Mom's place in the company of my entire family makes this most definitely a non-date. Holding hands can't change that reality. Besides, you like holding my hand."

"Oh, really."

"Really. Because I'm a hot guy and you kind of dig me. That's okay. I'm digging you too." Despite his teasing, she detected undercurrents she couldn't identify.

"Were you born cocky?"

He chuckled. "Seems like." He led her along a stone walkway, and when they rounded the curve of the hillside, quiet enfolded them. Gone was the occasional sound of a passing vehicle, now all she heard was the wind through the pines and the twitters of birds settling for the night.

Even though it wasn't completely dark, Levi took out his phone and turned on the flashlight. A few steps farther and they came to an alcove hollowed into the hillside. An intricately carved bench that looked as if it could have grown there was nestled into the protective embrace of the earth.

Zoey ran her fingers over the grain of the wood. "This is beautiful. I had no idea it was here."

Levi shone the light on a small brass plaque. She leaned over to see it, reading the words out loud. "In loving memory of Ben Gallagher. We lived and loved, and you are missed every day. Love, Trish." Emotion brought tightness to her throat. "Your mom had this bench placed here for your dad."

"Yeah. My motorcycle was his. He would take Mom for rides up here. This was one of their favorite spots." When he spoke, his voice was a little rougher than usual. He pulled her to sit beside him on the bench.

She gazed out at the incredible view. The lights of Hangman's Loss glimmered across the dark expanse of the lake. The businesses on Main Street glowed brightly while warmer lights from the homes nestled into the forest gleamed like jewels.

In the eastern sky a faint scattering of the brightest stars were visible. The altitude combined with night's arrival made the temperature drop rapidly, and she was glad for the heavy motorcycle jacket. Levi stretched an arm around her shoulders to bring her closer to him. "This make it too date-ish?"

She leaned into him. "Maybe, but it's nice." She wouldn't let herself think about just how right it felt to be here with him. There was a bare whisper of sound and the shadowy form of an owl glided past them.

"Everything looks so pretty from up here."

"You've never been here before?"

She shook her head. "I've driven by the turnout probably a hundred times, but never stopped. I'm glad you brought me." She turned her gaze from the view to focus on the man beside her. Despite her vulnerability issues, and the fear of growing too close to Levi, she sensed he had something on his mind and figured she'd be friendly and ask. "You going to tell me what's bothering you?"

He stilled for a moment and was quiet. She didn't think he was going to answer. Better that way, really. She didn't want to be privy to his inner thoughts. Knowing him, he'd expect her to reciprocate, and that wasn't going to happen.

When she felt certain he was letting it slide, he surprised her by answering in a low tone. "I've come to the realization I've been running away for the past decade. Maybe I was running when I left Oakland PD."

She shouldn't ask. She asked, "How so?"

"As I go through it, I'm only beginning to understand. Like, I could've come home after college, and instead went into the police academy and joined the force in Oakland." She felt his shrug against her shoulder. "I did good work there so it wasn't a bad decision."

"Why do you think that was running away?"

He loosened his grip on her hand but still held it in his, staring out at the view as he rubbed his thumb across her palm. She should've pulled her hand away, broken the intimacy, but was pretty sure he was caught up in the memories and wasn't aware of what he was doing.

"Because being home reminded me of my dad. I didn't want to be in a place where every time I turned around there was someone telling me how sorry they were, or what a good guy Ben Gallagher was."

He sighed. "Then there was Brad. It felt like I couldn't breathe without him getting on my case." He shook his head. "I was a selfish bastard. When Dad died, I was so caught up in my own head, I didn't care or pay attention to how hard it was for everyone else. Mom moved to LA to help Maddy after Lily was born. They'd both lost Dad too, then they were dealing with a sick baby. That was hard. As hard as it gets. I didn't make it any easier on anyone."

"Weren't Maddy and Logan going together?"

"They'd broken up, and he went into the military. He didn't know about Lily. Maddy made us swear not to tell him. Lily died, and it seemed like we'd just buried Dad, and then we were putting another family member in the ground."

Her heart hurt for him. For all of them. "You were a teenager. At the time, you think you're all grown up, but really you were still a kid. You're being too hard on yourself. Your family was going through an extremely difficult time. But from what I saw today, you supported one another as best you could, and have come out the other side pretty damn well."

He brought her hand up, pressing his lips to her knuckles, sending warmth rolling through her. "I wish I'd been more of a help than a burden. I was such an idiot. I never thought about how much Brad sacrificed. He left college to be home with me when Mom moved to LA."

"He loves you, and my bet, he's proud of you."

"I might not have made it if it wasn't for him."

"I think you would have, but maybe it would've been a rougher ride along the way." His expression was grim as he gave a curt nod. Despite the raw emotion he'd revealed, she thought there was more. She'd seen the shadows drop over his eyes, seen how sometimes he seemed to be elsewhere even when she was only feet away from him.

That she wanted to help alleviate his pain made her an idiot. Talk like this only deepened their relationship, and she was pretty sure she didn't want that with him. Yet, as if her mouth wasn't connected to her brain, she asked, "What made you decide to leave the Oakland PD?"

His grim expression turned into a mask of stone. "It's complicated."

She frowned. "I'd read about a questionable officer-involved shooting in Oakland several months ago. A cop shot an unarmed black man. Were you involved in that?"

"Let's not ruin our evening. Best to agree to disagree."

She nodded while wondering how big a violation of trust it would be to do an Internet search for "Levi Gallagher" and "officer-involved shooting."

She opened her mouth, but Levi held up a hand, head cocked. There was a rustling nearby, like something brushing against dry leaves, and a moment later a small shape emerged from the low brush at the edge of the clearing. Levi brought up his phone's flashlight to reveal the tawny coat and pointed ears of a feline. "That's a bobcat. A young one," Zoey whispered. "He's beautiful."

She watched, their hands still linked, as the wildcat saw them, froze, then darted back into the darkness.

Keeping their hands clasped, Levi stood and pulled her up. Silently, they returned to the motorcycle and were soon winding their way down the mountain.

As she laid her head against his back, Zoey felt the night cocoon them. Wrapped in their own world, they seemed to move as one through the curves and turns until they slowed to pass through

Hangman's Loss where the shops and restaurants were brightly lit. The road from the highway took them home, and Levi rolled slowly up their driveway, stopping next to her Prius. He steadied her with a hand to her arm as she swung her leg over the bike.

They stood next to the motorcycle and she pulled off her helmet, handed it to him, then unzipped and unsnapped the jacket and held it out for him to take.

She wasn't sure if he was feeling the heightened intimacy between them. Probably it was all in her head, and for him this was exactly what she'd told him she wanted, a non-date.

When she glanced up and caught the intense look he shot her, she knew he was feeling it too.

She couldn't invite him in. The impulse to do it was on the tip of her tongue, but she liked him too much, and the evening ride had been too magical. And really, sitting on the bench his mother had dedicated with love to his father while Levi had opened up about the time after his dad had died? Zoey was feeling a little too connected to him, and too vulnerable.

If he came inside, they'd end up in bed, and it wouldn't be a hookup.

Lucy woofed her welcome-home bark, and Zoey never loved her dog more than in that moment.

"Thanks for the evening, Levi."

He didn't say anything, but his penetrating gaze had heat coiling in her belly. He didn't act on that look. He gave her an abrupt nod then turned to her porch.

"Where are you going?"

"To make sure nothing's been messed with, that everything's okay with your house."

She trailed him up the steps to where her furniture and the fresh flowers she'd picked to replace the others were as she had left them.

"Keys?" She raised a brow when Levi held out a hand. "Humor me."

She dug out her keys from her pocket and dropped them onto his outstretched palm. He took them and unlocked the door. Lucy remembered her manners for once and sat while they entered the house.

"We're fine. Everything looks as it should be."

"Yeah. Guess Bear Dog wouldn't be this relaxed if anyone had broken in." He set her keys on the end table and gave Lucy a quick pet before turning to the door. "Good night, Zoey."

Chapter Eleven

Zoey leaned back on the pillows piled against the headboard of her bed. Lucy lay in her own bed, which took up nearly a quarter of the floor space of the small bedroom. The phone on the nightstand chimed with an incoming text. Zoey chided herself for feeling disappointed when she saw the message was from Eva.

E: *Don't check your LookBook status.*

Z: *Why?*

E: *Trust me. It'll be down soon.*

Eva's warning was like bait.

Zoey opened her tablet and tapped on the LB icon. Her family and social circle were small. Usually, she didn't have many notifications. The little bell dinged and "9+" came up. The drop-down tab showed a list mostly from people she knew: Eva, Maddy, Diego, Trish, as well as some names she didn't recognize. They had commented on a post from the Hangman's Loss community page.

She tapped the screen and opened the page. A post by "Slut Patrol" popped up. She squinted to make sure she was seeing what she thought she was seeing, then tapped on the image to make it larger. A woman wearing only a red thong and impossibly high heels, her naked breasts larger than Zoey could ever hope for, had one leg wrapped around a metal pole. Zoey's face was plastered onto whoever's body.

Her first response was to laugh. The photo editing wasn't badly done, but it was obvious the image had been altered. Then she read the accompanying text: *Zoey Hardesty is a slut and a whore, and moonlights as a hooker.*

Every post was an angry response from Zoey's friends.

Her phone rang with Eva's ringtone. "You looked, didn't you?"

"How could I not? But wow, me as a pole dancer. Not in my wildest dreams have I ever had boobs that big."

"I'm so sorry. Brad called the mayor to find out who administers the page and said they better take the post down. He said he'll file a complaint with the site."

"Okay." Zoey refused to be embarrassed, but her initial urge to laugh was chased away by burgeoning anger. She pressed a couple of buttons. "I took a screenshot. This is really weird. Obviously, someone has anger issues. I don't expect everyone to like me, but there's a lot of mean in this post. It feels like high school bullying. I can't think of anyone I've ticked off who would take it to this level."

"I just got a text from Brad. Refresh your screen."

Zoey did, and the image disappeared. She let out a breath she hadn't been aware she was holding.

A loud rapping sounded from her front door followed by Lucy scrambling to her feet.

"The post is gone. I have to go. There's someone at the door." She pushed herself up from the bed.

"Don't answer it!"

"Why not?" Eva's panicked response had Zoey hesitating.

She'd never felt nervous in her home before, even after her porch had been vandalized, but now caution had her hanging back. She walked into her darkened living room, phone in hand, then paused, staring at the door. She was glad she'd pulled the curtains shut, something she didn't always remember to do.

"Zoey, you still there?"

"I'm here."

"Don't open the door. It could be the crazy person who put up that post. Call Levi."

"I don't have his number."

A voice called out from the other side of the door, one she recognized. "Zoey, open up. It's me."

"It's Levi. I'm fine, Eva, but thanks for being there for me."

"That's what BFFs do. Promise me you'll be careful."

Zoey reached for the knob on the front door. "I'll be careful. Gotta go."

She pulled open the door. Levi stood on the other side, two-day beard, mussed hair, blue eyes blazing. Damn hot and sexy.

Despite the cool nighttime temperature, he wore only dark sweatpants and a white t-shirt that clung to his pecs, none of which detracted from the face of one pissed-off male.

"Can I come in?"

She stepped back, pushing Lucy out of the way, then shut the door after Levi.

"You saw the post?" His cop face was intimidating: sharp, focused eyes, lowered brows, and lips turned down at the corners.

"I did. Eva texted me. It's been taken down."

"Anything like that ever happen before?"

Zoey shook her head. "I keep a low profile on social media. Whoever posted it must be from Hangman's Loss." She shrugged, feeling a little self-conscious in the tank top and short shorts she wore to sleep. "I've been here nearly two years, and I can't think of anyone I've made angry enough for this."

"It could be someone from town, but it could also be someone from your past who knows you're living here now." He speared fingers through his hair, the first break in his cop demeanor. "Look, I'm on duty at seven tomorrow morning. I have to be at the station for morning roll call, but after that I want you to come in so I can ask you some questions formally. I'll be recording the conversation. I'm adding this post to my investigation of the hit-and-run and the porch vandalism."

She shook her head. "I have to go to work. I'll be in the field all day."

"What does that mean exactly?"

"I get a Forest Service truck and drive out to Virginia Lakes, and from there hike to a couple of different talus slopes and continue my study of the pika."

"You do this solo?"

"Usually, but not all the time. Some days I have another wildlife biologist with me. But I always take Lucy. Since the forecast said it'll get into the eighties, I'm planning on an early start to get ahead of the heat."

"What time will you be back?"

"No later than two or three."

"Come to the station when you get off."

When she nodded, Levi reached for the door, then paused. "Do you have my phone number?"

She shook her head, then unlocked her phone's screen and opened her contact list. She typed in his name and gave him her phone so he could add his number. He tapped, then swiped and tapped again before handing it back.

"I put in my personal number and my department cell number. I carry both phones with me. I also sent your number to my phone." His gaze sharpened. "I've already talked to Brad. The cottage is going to be wired with an alarm system. He'll be in touch to work out when it will be installed."

"That's going to be expensive. I wish you had talked to me first."

"You're a tenant. You should expect your landlord to take reasonable precautions to keep you safe."

"Right. Okay. I guess that makes sense."

"*I* want you safe, Zoey. We'll figure out what's going on, but anything that looks off, trust your instincts and call nine-one-one, then call me. Don't talk yourself into thinking it's nothing."

She nodded. He stared. She sighed. He left.

After she closed the door, dread formed an uneasy knot in her stomach. The nasty post was unsettling, no doubt. But talking to Levi made her wonder if he was right in thinking there could be a connection between that and the other things that had happened to her.

She turned the deadbolt then went to the kitchen and made sure that door was also securely locked.

When she finally settled back into bed, she found herself listening for any sound from outside. Knowing that Levi was in his cabin only a short distance away helped ease some of her anxiety. Plus, Lucy was an excellent alarm system and deterrent.

Still, it took a long time for Zoey to settle enough to fall asleep.

***

With a yellow legal pad in front of him, Levi propped up an iPad, tapped the screen, then adjusted the angle.

"Camera app is open, but I'm not recording yet."

"Is it really necessary to record this? I feel like I'm a suspect being interrogated."

"You're not a suspect in anything. Recording this interview is the best way to make sure I have an accurate record of everything you say, and it can help me formulate follow-up questions later."

"Right." She tapped her fingers on the table.

They were both in uniform: Levi's a dark navy blue, hers the dark green pants and khaki of the Forest Service. She was glad she didn't have to wear a bulletproof vest under her shirt.

"Do you want something to drink? Coffee, soda, water?"

"No, I'm good. Let's get this done."

"Okay, I'm hitting record now."

Zoey shifted and tried not to stare at the iPad.

"Tell me about the woman who goes by the name Karma. Her real name is Wanda Patterson by the way."

"Ha." Zoey gathered her thoughts. "I already told you all I know about her. I think she focused on me to pick on because I was new in town and didn't know anyone else in the class. Classic bullying crap."

"And you never saw her outside of the yoga class? Grocery store, bank, post office?"

She shook her head. "She behaves like a high school mean girl, and the LookBook post certainly had a mean girl element, but a hit-and-run is a huge step up from that."

"Agreed."

Levi pressed her, asking several more questions about Wanda Patterson, aka Karma, but in the end, there was nothing more that Zoey could add.

"Is she a suspect?"

"Not at this time. I spoke to her this morning. She's a piece of work. Denied the bullying, said you were too thin-skinned if you went to the police about anything she said. Didn't have any explanation for her behavior."

"I think most bullies don't understand their motivations."

"I believe it. About the post, the settings for the city page allows anyone to post, which is incredibly stupid and will be changed."

"That's one of those things that people figure are no big deal until they are."

"We're working on tracing who put it up. It appears to be someone who made up a profile within the last week." Levi tapped his pen on the table. "Let's try a different angle. Think back to high school. Did anything happen while you lived here that made you feel like you were being targeted?"

"You think this goes back to high school?"

"I'm looking at all the possibilities. Anyone come to mind?"

She tried to keep her expression neutral. "No. Kids pretty much left me alone."

He narrowed his gaze. "What about guys. Anyone come on to you that you rejected?"

"Geez, no."

"Any bad breakups?"

"No."

"How about breakups period?"

"I didn't have boyfriends when I was in high school. I went out with a few guys, but nothing came of it."

"I'll need their names."

"Really?" She raised her hand before he could respond. "Never mind. There was a guy I went to the movies with a couple of times." Her brow furrowed. "Honestly, I don't remember his name. Jason something, or maybe it was Josh. Oh." She smiled. "I did go out with Diego."

"Wait. You went out with Diego?"

"Yeah. He didn't seem to mind the funky hair or the eyebrow piercing."

"Diego Jones? You went out with Diego Jones?" Levi's shocked expression was almost comical.

"Yep, Diego Jones. You remember him, don't you? He's married to your cousin Eva. I don't know why you're so surprised. We were in the same year, and he was cute. Still is. We went to prom together junior year." Part of the reason she and Diego had never developed anything deeper was Zoey had been hung up on Levi, even though he'd left for college. She certainly wasn't sharing that little tidbit.

"So you did have a boyfriend."

"No, we never got to that point. We shared a few kisses, then decided we liked each other better as friends. That's all there was between us."

"Huh." Levi was staring at the notepad where he'd made a few notes. "Okay." He appeared to have to make an effort to mentally gather himself. "Was there anyone who paid you particular attention? Teachers, coaches, neighbors?"

Zoey hesitated, then shook her head.

"No one?"

"Nope."

Expression thoughtful, Levi leaned back in his seat, gaze steady on hers. "The only way this will work is if you tell me everything, even if it makes you uncomfortable."

She closed her eyes for a brief moment. Trust Levi to pick up on that split second of hesitation. "It's not relevant."

"At this point, everything is relevant."

Counseling had helped her deal with her past, but that didn't mean she wanted to unlock those memories where she'd stashed them away.

"Would you prefer someone else asking the questions? I could get Monica if you want a woman."

She shook her head. "You're the only person I'll talk to."

"You can trust me, but you can also trust anyone in this department."

"Cops always say you can trust them. But that's not always true."

He tapped the iPad screen. "I stopped the recording. Let's get this out there. I'm not only a cop, Zoey. We're friends, and I'll be honest, I'd like to be more than friends. Either way, I'll do everything I can to protect you."

His admission gave her a jolt and had warmth stealing up her cheeks. "Um, okay."

"You want to tell me what you're holding back?"

She chewed her lip, then took a steadying breath. "I don't want this part recorded."

He nodded, then pushed back from the table. "I'll be right back."

He left the room, returning a moment later with two chilled water bottles, and set one on the table in front of her.

"Thanks." She twisted the lid off and took a sip, glad for the brief reprieve before carefully screwing the lid back on. Levi sat back down across the table from her. "I'll tell you, and I figure once I do, you'll want to investigate." She shrugged. "I guess I'll have to live with that."

"Tell me, then we'll decide."

She took another steadying breath and began, choosing her words carefully. "Remember when I told you that I left the Loss halfway through my senior year?" He nodded, and she went on. "There was more to it than Mom getting a job in Fresno."

Zoey hated feeling vulnerable, and that's how talking about this made her feel. She forced herself to press on. "Mom's boyfriend had been living with us for several months. His name was Paul. At first he seemed cool. He'd take us out for pizza, or we'd go out on the lake in his boat. He taught Charlie how to fish. He knew computers, and he and Charlie would build them together. I think Mom liked that Charlie had a male role model who seemed to really care about him." She sipped from the bottle again and let the cool water ease the tightness in her throat before continuing.

"Paul mostly ignored me, which was fine. I guess I'd never really warmed up to him, and I'd caught him watching me a couple of times in a way that made me uneasy. Anyway, we were alone one night. It was before Christmas break. I was baking cookies for a class party and he'd been sitting at the dining table doing something on his computer, which was unusual because he didn't normally sit there. Most of the time he closed himself in the bedroom he shared with my mom and sat on the bed with his laptop."

Zoey realized she'd been peeling the label of the water bottle as she'd been talking. She pushed the bottle away and glanced across the table to find Levi's gaze steady on her, compassion evident, as if he guessed what was coming.

"We were each doing our thing, then it was like he'd come to a decision. He shut the lid on the laptop, got up from the table, and said he wanted a blowjob."

The tightening of his jaw belied the impassive expression on Levi's face.

"I remember I'd just taken a tray of cookies out of the oven. I stood there like an idiot, staring at him. The tray was starting to burn my hands through the oven mitts, but I couldn't seem to move." She reached for the water bottle and drank before carefully screwing the lid on once again. "He walked into the kitchen and told me to put the tray down and get on my knees."

"Christ. What did you do?"

"I hurled the tray at him and bolted for the back door. He caught me by the hair. He went nuts. He was screaming that I'd pay for what I'd done. He hadn't been expecting it and the tray hit him in the face. It must've burned. He had chocolate chip cookies stuck all over him. To this day, the smell of baking chocolate chip cookies makes me sick to my stomach. I can't eat them."

"I can imagine." Levi leaned forward, forearms resting on the table. "I was drinking a Coke in the den when Mom came in to tell me Dad had died. I haven't had a Coke since." He waited, and she thought his personal comment was his way of giving her a little break. "What happened then?"

"Paul hauled me back into the kitchen by my hair. The knife block was there on the counter where it always was. I didn't think about it. I reached out and grabbed a knife and stabbed him in the hand. He screamed and let go. That's when Mom and Charlie walked in the house."

She squeezed her eyes shut at the memory. Another deep breath and she opened them again. "He tried to spin it, say that I'd gone crazy and attacked him. I'm standing there with a knife in my hand, and there's blood and chocolate chip cookies all over the floor. I must have nicked a small artery when I sliced him across his knuckles because there were even spots of blood on the ceiling. He kept yelling at me, told my mom that I'd snapped and went at him with a knife."

Her heart beat faster in her chest, and despite the air conditioning, sweat rolled down her neck. Even after all these years, talking about it made her sick to her stomach.

"What'd your mom do?"

"Turned to me calm as you please and asked what had happened. I told her. He denied it, but Mom was having none of it. I thought she was going to grab a knife herself and finish him off."

"Did she call the cops?"

"Yeah, she did. He stormed out of the house, saying he was done with us, that we were all a bunch of freaks."

"Did you press charges?"

"Tried to. But it was his word against mine. The cops didn't believe me."

"Fuck that. Did they at least look into his past to see if there were other allegations against him?"

"No. Remember what I said about the blue line? You see, he was a cop too."

"With the Hangman PD?"

"No. We lived outside the city limits so the sheriff's department had jurisdiction and they responded to the call. He worked for them."

"What's his name?"

She didn't know why even now she wanted to hold back. "Paul Clauson. His name is Paul Clauson."

Levi wrote the name on the pad in front of him, underlining it several times. It struck Zoey that he was left-handed. That had never registered before. "So Clauson was never charged."

"No. That night, Mom took all his stuff and dumped it on the street in front of our house. She was so angry with herself that she'd trusted him, and had allowed him into our home, let him near her children."

"Did he come back? Bother you any?"

"He harassed us some. He'd drive by the house in his sheriff's cruiser, going slow, or show up at school events. He pulled Mom over one night when she was driving home from work and scared her to death. Nothing happened, but it could have. That's when she decided we had to leave town."

"She should have filed a complaint."

"She did. The sheriff's department investigated. I think they must have found other misconduct, enough at least that even they couldn't completely ignore it. As far as I know, he was never charged or punished, but he resigned. By then we'd moved to Fresno."

"Son of a bitch. Is he still in the area?"

"Last I heard he'd been hired by a police department in Colorado and had moved somewhere near Denver."

Levi made more notes on the pad. "Have you had any contact with him since then?" When she shook her head, he said, "I'm going to locate him, find out where he is now. Not that he needs to live here for the cyber-bullying, but if the post is related to the vandalism at your place and the hit-and-run, and he's not in the area, then it's not likely he'll be our guy."

"Okay." Now that she was done, she was glad she'd told Levi. A little of the weight she'd carried lifted, and she found she didn't really care if Levi investigated Paul Clauson. She'd been a kid, and he was an asshole, and maybe a pedophile. She needed to let go of the embarrassment and the shame.

With the interview finally over, Levi walked Zoey to her car in the police parking lot. A breeze had picked up that helped to cool the warm afternoon.

"I appreciate you coming in. This is important."

She gave a short laugh. "I know what I said about the hit-and-run, Levi, about not wanting to prosecute if it was truly an accident. But after these latest instances, I'm feeling more than a little nervous. I want to know who's behind them."

He ran a hand down her bare arm. "Like I said last night, call me any time, no matter when, even if you think I'm busy."

She hated the feeling of vulnerability brought on by the harassment, which put her in the position of having to rely on others for protection. "Okay."

"Brad wants to know if Thursday works for the security company to install an alarm system. He wants cameras. They'll be doing your place and mine."

Zoey chewed on her bottom lip while she considered the logistics. "I'll take Lucy with me to work, but I don't want to leave my doors unlocked so the alarm crew can get in."

"You won't need to. Brad will give them a key."

She nodded, catching her breath when he snagged her hand and turned it over in his. He rubbed a thumb over her palm, much as he had the previous evening when they'd been sitting on a bench looking out over the town. "Would you go on another non-date with me?"

Her heart gave a strong thud. "Do you think it's a good idea?"

"Why, you afraid you'll start to like me?"

"No." *That ship sailed years ago.* "What do you have in mind?"

"The Guns have softball practice this evening at five thirty. It'll probably go for an hour and a half, then we're all going out for pizza. You could join us."

"So this is more of a group thing."

"Right. No way is it a date. I wouldn't want to challenge the 'no dating cops' rule. Pizza, beer, and a group of friends hanging out."

She didn't give herself time to overthink it. "Sounds like fun. Why don't you text me when you're done with practice and I'll meet you at the pizza place?"

"Sure."

He dipped his head, then seemed to catch himself. "Damn. If this was going to be a real date, I'd kiss you good-bye. Can't let that happen." He straightened and started for the back door to the station. "See you this evening, Zoey."

Chapter Twelve

Zoey stood in line at the post office. Three people were ahead of her, two looked like they had multiple packages to send. She wanted to get home, take a shower, then try to put a little effort into her appearance for her non-date with Levi. But she had a card to send her brother for his birthday, and she wanted to pick up the cool solar eclipse stamps that changed color with heat. He'd like that.

Levi was sneaky. He'd slipped the idea of a kiss into her head, and it had lodged there ever since.

Kissing Levi again would be disastrous. She knew exactly how hot a kiss between them could get, and from there it would be a slippery slope into more. She figured she was already on that slope by accepting his non-date invitations, but had she said no? Of course not.

She'd tried to stick to her date-no-cops rule. Cops were controlling, some too easily abused their authority, and, as she'd seen more than once, were too often willing to sacrifice the community they were supposed to serve to protect fellow officers.

Except Levi didn't fit the mold. He seemed honest and caring, and restrained in his interactions with others. Despite that, she'd seen him drop the laid-back persona and shift to cop mode in the blink of an eye. Maybe he had to do that for the job, but she had trouble trusting him not to revert to type. You never could tell.

He'd evaded answering her about what led to him leaving the Oakland PD, which had her wondering what he was hiding. She hadn't searched him on the Internet, and she wasn't sure why. Maybe she wanted him to tell her himself. He'd avoided the subject when she'd brought it up, and maybe he didn't want to fight with her about something neither of them would change their minds about.

She shuffled forward and bit back a sigh of impatience when the sole postal clerk chatted loudly with the next in line, a woman with a daughter due to go into labor at any moment, and could Patsy (the clerk) guess what the daughter's rat bastard husband had done? Trying hard not to listen, Zoey told herself that the benefits of living in a small town far outweighed the drawbacks.

"This is taking forever, isn't it?"

Zoey turned to the voice behind her. The woman, probably in her mid-thirties but making a valiant effort to appear at least a decade younger, rolled her eyes.

There wasn't much else to say but to commiserate. "Seems like."

The woman stuck out a hand and gave her a broad smile. "Are you new in town?"

Her ripped skinny jeans were so tight on her thin frame that Zoey worried about the woman's circulation, while her hair, held back with a big clip, looked overly bleached and brittle.

After having her hand pumped enthusiastically, Zoey gave her a brief smile. "More or less."

"I've lived here my entire life. I know just about everybody." Her gaze focused on the nametag on Zoey's uniform. "And your name is Zoey Hardesty."

"Yep." Something was off about the woman. On the surface she appeared friendly, but there was a calculating gleam in her pale gray eyes in stark contrast to the open expression. Only one more person was ahead of Zoey in the line and she felt like offering her a twenty to let her take cuts.

"You're a forest ranger. Says US Forest Service, Department of Agriculture, right there on your shoulder patch."

Zoey returned her attention to the woman with an effort. "Um, no. A wildlife biologist."

"Pretty much the same thing, right? You wear the same uniform."

Some things weren't worth the bother of explaining.

"Hey, we should hang out sometime. Do you have a boyfriend? He could come, too."

Even for a small town, this woman was over the top.

The clerk called for the next in line. "My turn," Zoey said, trying to refrain from leaping for the counter to escape her new pal.

"Okay, I'll talk to you later, Zoey."

***

Zoey opened the door of Gio's Pizza and stepped inside. On the left was a glass barrier to the kitchen area, where a man with floury hands and a white apron tossed a round of pizza dough to spin in the air. She wondered if that was Gio. Several families sat in the booths along one wall for a weeknight dinner of pizza, or like the group at the table nearest her, calzones. A couple of older kids were hanging out in a partitioned area playing old-school video games that made beeping and buzzing noises. She didn't see Levi or his team. It hadn't occurred to her until she'd accepted Levi's invitation that she'd be spending the evening with a bunch of cops.

A little uncomfortable with that thought, she heard a loud chorus of laughter from a back room. She was crossing the dining area to investigate when Levi walked out of a hallway from the back. She gasped. He wore baseball pants and a sleeveless t-shirt that clung to his wide chest, and was all long-limbed and lean, his arms corded with well-defined muscles.

He must have gotten a haircut after their "interview." The sides were tight, and the thick, dark hair on top was shorter. He was the definition of eye candy.

His grin flashed and his eyes warmed when he caught sight of her, and she felt an unnerving surge of happiness from simply seeing him. Her heart banged around her chest, and she prayed she wasn't blushing.

As he approached, she didn't miss how his gaze traveled from her hair, over her breasts and hips, and down to her feet, taking in the dressy pair of flip-flops. With her hair held back from her face with a tortoiseshell clip, and a colorful skirt matched to a linen blouse, she knew she'd dressed for him, and from his expression he appreciated the effort.

"Too bad a hello kiss is off limits. I'll stick with I'm glad you're here."

There he was with his talk about kisses again, which made kissing him the only thing she could think about.

"You don't have to keep pointing out that we're not dating."

"Is that what I was doing?"

"Ah, yeah."

"Hm. Seems I've got kissing you on my mind. Guess that's my problem. I absolutely do want to go on a real date. But we'll save that for another time." He pointed to the back room. "We're through here."

When he turned, she saw his shirt had HLPD printed on the back in big block letters, as if she needed another reminder he was a cop. He led her down the hall to a room with picnic-style tables put together end to end in long rows. The Guns softball team took up half the space, most of them wearing shirts identical to Levi's.

He motioned her to a spot next to Emma Gallagher, who sat beside her husband, Brad. Logan Ross, and his wife, Maddy, sat across the table, and beyond them were Jack and Dory Morgan.

Zoey stepped over the bench and sat, Levi settling beside her.

"Hey, Zoey." Emma turned to face her.

"Hey back. Where are the kids?"

"Trish has them. The older two are staying for what they call a Gamma sleepover, but since I'm still nursing the baby, we'll pick her up. I'm glad Landon is lending a hand since Trish is also watching Mason and Keeley."

"That's brave of her to take on the brood so you all could have an evening out."

"I don't know what I would do without Trish. She's an awesome mother-in-law."

Brad leaned forward to look around his wife. "Hey, Zoey. Glad you're here. We need a team mascot and I thought of Lucy. She's gorgeous and an unusual breed so she'll get a lot of attention. What do you think?"

Emma turned to her husband. "Why a mascot? We've never had a mascot before."

"Blame the FD. Turns out the Hoses now have a mascot and they're bringing it to the game. A Dalmatian pup. They're planning to make a big deal of it. They want to bring a fire truck out on the field and let the dog ride along wearing a helmet. We can't let them get the crowd on their side because they have a puppy."

Levi made a dismissive noise. He leaned forward, his arm brushing against Zoey's and sending electric zings between them. "A Dalmatian? Those guys have no imagination."

"No kidding. What do you think, Zoey?" Brad asked.

Levi's hand found hers under the table and he gave her fingers a squeeze.

She was so wrapped up in the zings now traveling up her arms that she blanked for a long moment before she was able to answer Brad's question. "Ah, what would that involve?"

"You bring Lucy to the game on Saturday. We'll get her a bandana or something to wear. If you're good with it, we can take her out on the field before the game. There'll be a break for the seventh-inning stretch and we'll do some crowd events. I'll buy you both hot dogs and a beer."

Levi snorted. "Make that a tofu wiener, and Zoey might agree."

She elbowed Levi. "We'll decline the hot dog and beer. Otherwise, it sounds like fun. Lucy loves being the center of attention. She'll be a total ham."

A call came over the loudspeakers that an order was up. Brad rose to his feet and tapped Levi on the shoulder. "Help me carry the pizzas."

Logan also got up. "I'll get a couple pitchers of soda and water."

The minute the men were out of the room, Maddy leaned across the table, eyes bright. "Okay, spill. Are you and Levi dating?"

"No," she answered quickly.

Dory left her husband talking to someone farther down the table and scooted into the spot Logan had vacated. "I heard that. Why the heck not? That man looks at you like he's hungry enough to gobble you up in one big juicy bite."

"And earlier he was checking out the window to see if you'd arrived only about a dozen times," Maddy added. "I can tell when my brother has the hots for someone, and he's got it bad for you."

"It's not like that."

"Then I'll put it out there. If you don't like him, why are you here?"

Fair question.

"I do like him. We're friends. Okay, friends with sparks. We can't act on the sparks, though."

"Why not?" Dory asked. "Sparks are the fun part."

"Says the woman who ignored the sparks with that guy over there for years." Maddy pointed to Jack.

Zoey liked these women and figured honesty was the way to go here. "I like Levi, but I don't want to get into a relationship. And I don't date cops." She looked at the women around her and thought, *oh shit*. "Not that there's anything wrong with dating cops.

Obviously, you're all married to cops and must have dated them at some point." *God, she sounded so stupid right now.* "But it's not right for me."

"It wasn't right for Emma, either," Maddy said. "At least when she first met Brad."

"Really?" Zoey asked, turning to Emma.

Emma nodded. "True statement. I'd had bad experiences with police when I was younger and wanted nothing to do with him."

"What changed?" Zoey asked.

"I guess I did. Brad is," she grinned, "persistent. He made me see beyond the badge to the person who wore it."

"Break it up, ladies, pizza is here."

Brad set down what had to be a meat-lovers' pizza in front of Zoey while Dory scooted back down the bench to her husband. The sausage and what she thought might be ground beef was still bubbling, and the pepperoni had oily orange liquid seeping into the cheese. Levi stood behind her, motioning to someone farther down the table. "We'll switch you."

The meat-lovers' pizza was whisked away and was replaced with a vegetarian pie loaded with mushrooms, peppers, onions, and olives.

"You didn't have to do that."

"Did you want to stare at sausage and pepperoni?"

"Not really."

"So I moved it."

Loud voices came from the hall and what looked like a dozen men and women streamed into the room, most wearing t-shirts printed with HLFD. When they realized that the opposing team had had the same idea for post-practice pizza, there was a lot of good-natured laughing.

Eva rushed forward and Zoey rose and stepped over the bench to receive her hug before her friend turned and waved to the others from their table, many of whom had stood. "Hello, cousins and friends," she sang out in her cheerful voice.

Fists were bumped and hands shaken. Diego brushed Zoey's cheek with a casual kiss. "Good to see you, sweetheart." Levi stood behind her, and she bumped against him. Either he moved forward or she had moved back. In that crowded space she found herself standing with her back pressed against his chest, and it felt way too good.

Then Justin tugged her away from Levi and caught her in a hug before giving her a smacking kiss on the lips. "How's my girl?" The teasing gleam in his eyes told her he knew exactly what he was doing. She pinched him over his ribs. Hard. He leaned forward and whispered in her ear, "Easy, darling. I'm just having fun. I bet he doesn't know I'm gay."

Zoey felt a hand rest on her hip, and when Justin moved away, Levi pulled her closer. "What the hell was that about?" he growled.

"He's a friend."

"Casual friends don't kiss on the lips."

She was saved from responding by the arrival of a big black man whose shoulders looked wide enough to fill the doorway. Justin crossed the room to clap him on the shoulder as he pointed to the cops. "You all are warned. At practice today, my man Tank here hit three homers and he's got an arm like a cannon. Match Tank's hitting with Diego's base running, and you all won't be able to catch us."

"Your friend's trying to psych us out," Levi muttered.

"Is it working?"

"Hell no."

For the next hour, Zoey ate pizza and talked with her friends. While there was plenty of trash talk between the teams, it was obvious they got along well. She was surprised to find how much time had passed when the group began to break up. Who'd have thought she'd have so much fun with a bunch of cops and firefighters?

An hour later, stuffed from too much pizza, and with a box of leftovers on the passenger seat, Zoey turned into their driveway, Levi's motorcycle directly behind her. He followed her and came to a stop in front of her cottage, where the porch light gleamed with welcome.

She gathered her purse and the takeout box, and after locking her car, climbed the steps to where Levi stood in front of the door. He wore the reinforced motorcycle jacket unzipped and was pulling off his gloves to lay them on the small table. Lucy barked, then made her snuffling noises on the other side of the door.

"Everything as it should be?"

"Looks like."

She eyed him, not sure of his mood. "Thanks for checking out my porch for me. I'll see you later."

He didn't take the hint, instead widening his stance and crossing his arms over his chest. "So, Justin Trainer."

"What about him?"

"I got a gay sense from him that first night here, but not so much tonight."

"Justin's a good friend."

"That's it?"

"We were roommates for a while, if that matters."

"You're shitting me."

"Nope."

"How'd that happen?"

She shrugged. "I needed a place to stay when I first moved here. Justin's been living in the house he grew up in. He inherited it from his dad. It's a big place and he rents out a room. It's through him I met Eva and reconnected with Diego."

"You two ever hook up?"

"What is this, Levi? If I hooked up with Justin, it's absolutely none of your business."

A muscle jerked in his jaw. "Right. Because we're not dating."

"Even if we were, I don't see how Justin is an issue."

"Because you were standing right in front of me when he came up, grabbed you, and kissed you on the lips. I think he was staking a claim."

"Staking a claim like I'm a piece of property? Get real. Justin was jerking your chain."

"You even let Diego kiss you."

"Diego, who's happily married to your cousin and my friend, Eva."

He scowled, running his fingers through his hair.

"What's this about, Levi?"

"Really? You let two guys kiss you tonight and you won't go out on a real date with me because I'm a cop. Firemen must be on the approved list."

"I've kissed you too."

"And then you stomped on the brakes. You're judging me based on your experiences with two assholes who should never had been cops in the first place."

She took a deep breath. She prided herself on being open-minded and tolerant. Levi had done nothing to make her think he was anything but a good man. When she looked at him, she saw a guy who loved his family and community, and was a good person.

The raw emotion in his eyes pulled at something deep inside her. Blocking out the warning bells, she went with the feeling and grasped the front of his jacket to pull him down so she could reach his lips. He stood absolutely still for one long, pulsating minute until she was afraid she'd miscalculated. Then his mouth moved over hers, and he grasped her hips and yanked her to him.

When his lips moved against hers, her heart rate spiked. He smelled of sweat and hot male, and she gasped from the headiness of it. His tongue swept inside and ignited the liquid fire banked low in her belly.

Her hands flattened against his chest where his heart was thudding as wildly as hers as the kiss deepened, his arms squeezing tighter. He moved his mouth to her jaw, where his beard scratched her with a rasp. She angled her chin and his teeth tugged on her earlobe, making her shiver. He continued his exploration, warm lips nuzzling the sensitive skin where her neck met her shoulder. "Mm, you smell good," he murmured as he nibbled lightly, his teeth scraping against her skin.

"I was thinking the same about you."

He pulled back, his hands cupping the back of her neck, his thumbs stroking both sides of her jaw. He dipped his head to take her lips once again. She closed her eyes and saw stars when white lights flashed against her eyelids.

"What the hell?"

Levi pushed her onto the cushioned loveseat as headlights blinded her.

"Stay down." The order was issued sharply as Levi leapt off the porch. Inside the cottage, Lucy whined and scratched at the door. Same as the previous week, the driver slammed the car in reverse and backed onto the road, tearing away with tires squealing.

Levi raced to his bike.

"Did you see who it was?"

He unhooked his helmet and pulled it on. "Silver or light gray SUV with California plates. Get inside and lock the doors. Keep Lucy with you. Don't answer for anyone but me." He swung his leg over his motorcycle.

"Where are you going?"

"To see if I can catch up with the asshole." He pulled keys from his pocket and slammed down the face shield.

"Wait. What if this person is armed, or crazy?"

The motorcycle roared to life and disappeared down the driveway, its taillights fading as it sped down the road going in the same direction as the car.

Chapter Thirteen

Charissa loosened her grip on the steering wheel to wipe her sweaty palms against her jeans. The garage door clanked shut behind her and her breath shuddered. That had been too close. She'd taken a stupid risk and almost been caught. There was a part of her that wanted to be caught. If Levi caught her, then all his attention would be hers. She wanted to know what it would feel like to have those gorgeous blue eyes focused solely on her. If that happened, then maybe he'd really see her and he'd understand that they belonged together. Then Levi would tell her he'd harbored a secret love for years, and would grab her hand to kiss it as he dropped to one knee.

Oh heavens. The hand she'd imagined kissed flew to the ignition to turn off the engine. She'd left the car running in the closed garage. How could she be so careless? She was stressed. Zoey Hardesty was in the way and Charissa was worried. She needed to do something to keep Levi from doing as Brad had done, marrying the wrong woman.

Hurriedly, she exited the car holding her breath, and opened the side door of the single-car garage. She fanned the door a few times to get the carbon monoxide out, then shut and locked it before entering her tiny house through the kitchen door. She set down her purse and took a minute to admire the photo stuck to the refrigerator with a magnet. In it, she was standing next to Levi, his gaze adoringly on hers. She pressed her lips to his image as she did every day. She'd gotten several more pictures developed, and would add them to her special display.

With a sigh, she opened the fridge to pull out a bottle of wine. She tilted it to check the contents. How come there was only a quarter of the bottle left? It was one of the extra-large bottles and she'd found it on sale. She'd opened it only the night before and was pretty sure she'd only had two glasses, three tops. She must have opened it two nights ago, because drinking most of the bottle in one sitting wasn't healthy, however much she needed it to settle her nerves. She poured the pinot grigio into a glass and sat at the table.

Why wasn't Zoey Hardesty getting a clue? Charissa had seen her at the post office and made a stab at being friendly even while trying to find out if the stupid woman considered Levi her boyfriend. Damn the clerk for calling the next customer before Zoey could respond. Charissa thought the LookBook post on the city's community page would cause *something* to happen. Levi must have seen it. Why didn't he realize how inappropriate the hippie woman was for him? Apparently, subtlety wasn't going to get the point across. Charissa needed to be more direct. That's why she'd followed Levi after softball practice.

Sitting in her car in a corner of the parking lot of Gio's Pizza, she'd watched and waited. She could see through the back window of the restaurant all those police officers with their wives or girlfriends. There were even female cops, which she thought was stupid. That wasn't a proper job for a woman.

Levi had walked outside with Zoey, and Charissa had slid down in her seat, but neither of them had noticed her. Oh, how she had wanted to be the woman with Levi. She'd dress better than that slut, plus she was taller and better suited to be with Levi.

One day Charissa be the one sitting next to Levi. He'd want to hold hands because he wouldn't be able to bear not touching her. He'd steal kisses, and she'd have to pretend to shoo him away. Then she'd laugh and kiss him back. All the while, their friends would be looking on with a touch of envy at how close she and Levi were, how obviously in love.

Zoey and Levi had stood together next to the woman's hippie car, talking for several minutes. Something in their posture, the way they were standing a bit closer than people normally stood, the way Levi had reached out and touched her arm, had intensified the sick churning in Charissa's stomach.

She'd rooted around in her purse and pulled out the little white bottle and popped three of the pills in her mouth. Taking the prescribed single pill wasn't getting the job done. She had no idea how many she had already consumed that day. The water bottle in the cup holder had been in the car all afternoon and had been warm, but she'd used it to wash down the pills anyway, swallowing the tablets that were her only relief from the constant knot in her stomach.

Zoey had pulled out first, then Levi had followed her, looking like a sexy bad boy on that motorcycle. She hadn't needed to follow them because she knew where they lived. She'd waited five minutes, then had driven to their houses, turning off her headlights when she was close enough to creep up to the driveway. That's when she'd spied them on the porch and that bitch Zoey had yanked Levi close to kiss him like the slut she was. A roaring had started in Charissa's ears that had blocked out any other thoughts.

She'd slammed her car into gear, then floored it into the driveway, tires spinning in the gravel. It was satisfying how they'd jumped apart like they'd been caught doing something dirty. She'd had the insane urge to stomp on the gas pedal and ram the car into the porch, anything to disrupt that kiss. But she'd lost her nerve when Levi had jumped down the stairs and grabbed his helmet.

She'd sped down the road at breakneck speed, her breath coming in gulps, the single headlight of the motorcycle appearing in her rearview mirror. She'd turned onto the highway, cutting off a semi, grimacing when the angry driver laid on the horn. Desperation had her speeding up to pass another car. She'd driven recklessly, she knew that, but she'd been desperate to get away. As much as she wanted Levi's attention, she knew he wouldn't understand. Her street had appeared and she'd made the turn, hoping he was too far back to see, and sure enough, she'd lost him.

She drained her glass and picked up the bottle. Huh. It was already empty. She got up, holding the back of her chair when the room spun, then walked slowly to the cupboard where she carefully stored her bottles lying on their sides.

Everyone knew you laid wine on its side to keep the cork wet. When she and Levi were married they'd get one of those fancy wine racks she'd seen in a magazine. She picked out a bottle, Stella Rosa this time, and once uncorked, topped off her glass.

For her plans to come to fruition, Zoey Hardesty would have to be dealt with. Charissa had been plotting to marry into the Gallagher clan for years, taking little actions here and there, but being patient. She'd miscalculated when Brad had been more serious about Emmaline Kincaid than she had given him credit for.

Charissa wasn't going to make that same mistake with Levi.

He was hers, and she wasn't going to share.

***

Levi should have gone to the cabin and bed, gone to the brewpub and hung out, gone anywhere but where he was. He felt on edge, wired from the chase, worried about Zoey, and not able to get that kiss out of his head. Even knowing the odds were that he'd get a door slammed in his face, he knocked on the door.

He heard Lucy's bark and then her snuffling noises, then Zoey's quiet murmur.

"Zoey, it's me." His voice sounded hoarse.

She opened the door, Lucy at her side, and he swept her with a look. Men's boxer shorts, a yellow t-shirt with text that read "Shut Up and Kiss Me," and her wild black curls escaping from a ponytail. He didn't think he'd ever seen anything hotter.

Add the challenge in her expression and she was irresistible.

"Did you catch the car?"

"No. I tailed it to the highway, but the driver almost killed him or herself when he cut off a semi to get away." He ran a hand through his hair in frustration. "It's a light-colored SUV crossover. Not much help."

"Okay. Thanks for trying, Levi." Her end-of-conversation tone didn't match the hungry look in her eyes, but he was betting on the latter.

"You going to invite me in?"

The question hung in the air, both aware of what he was asking. Her gaze locked on his, the moment stretching as they silently took each other in, her internal battle evident in her turbulent dark eyes. Then she moved back to hold the door open wider. He stepped past her, and when she shut the door and turned the lock, he could feel the answering click like a physical opening of his heart.

He moved in and she met him halfway. His mouth crashed down on hers in a wild tangle of lips and tongue, his hands cruising over the curve of her hips, over her ass. He boosted her so their lips could more easily reach, hitching her up with her back against the door. His need was raw and powerful, urged on by the heat generated wherever they touched. With her hands in his hair and the blood roaring in his ears, a bomb could have gone off on the other side of the door and he wouldn't have noticed.

He wanted to feast but forced himself to slow down, to make sure she was with him. He moved a knee between her legs and let her rest on his thigh so he could free his hands. With both palms framing her face, he used his thumbs to brush along her cheekbones. Her eyes were open and aware, and the way she rubbed against his leg was making him crazy. He reined in the urge to take what was his, and asked, "You good with this?"

He saw the hesitation and thought that was the end, that by asking he'd given her the moment she'd needed to regain her senses. But then her hands went to his face to pull him down to her. "Oh yeah," she spoke the words against his lips.

Her sweet mouth went wild and met his in a kiss that ignited his blood. He boosted her once more, this time a little higher. She raised her legs to wrap them around his hips, pressing her heat against his rock-hard erection, and his blood roared in his ears. He should slow it down, savor their first time, but he couldn't get his actions to obey the orders from his brain.

Not that Zoey seemed to have any thoughts of slowing down. Her hands slid under his shirt to skim over the skin of his back, then tugged it up and over his head. "Oh yeah," she murmured again as she dipped her head to press her lips to his collarbone. She ran her hands through the hair on his chest, then ducked her head to use her tongue on his nipple.

He hissed out a breath. "Good god, woman."

"Like that, do you?"

"I like everything about you." He kissed the soft skin under her jaw, then scraped his teeth down the column of her neck.

She shifted her attention to his pants, trying to slide her hands under the back waistband to his ass. His belt blocked her, so she pushed her hands down between them and went to work to loosen it.

While she was busy with that, he pulled up her shirt, forcing her to raise her hands for a moment. Christ, she wasn't wearing a bra. He feasted his eyes on the bounty that were her plump, firm, rosy-tipped breasts. He wanted them in his mouth so badly he had to swallow before he started drooling like the dog. He boosted her higher.

Her hands went to his shoulders. "Wait, I had the buckle undone and was getting to the good stuff. I want—"

His mouth latched on to one perfect breast, taking it into his mouth with a hard pull, and felt her long, low moan vibrate through him. He tasted and savored, swirling with his tongue, and after a long minute, loosened the suction to give the other breast the same treatment.

He could have spent the entire night on her breasts alone, but eventually moved his lips to the luscious curve of her neck. He buried his face, breathing in the fresh scent of her hair. His hands had moved up her bare thighs to cup her ass under the boxer shorts.

Luckily, they were wide at the leg and gave him free access to the bare skin underneath. He nearly erupted in his pants when his fingers found no underwear, only moist warm flesh.

The next moan was his.

His thumb glided through her slicked folds as her breath caught, and when he slid two fingers into her, she let out a soft cry. He continued moving his hand, slowly at first, then picking up the intensity, working her until her breath came in uneven gasps even as she chanted his name over and over. Her head was tipped back, resting against the door. He accepted the invitation, and ran his tongue from her jaw to the sweet-smelling skin below her ear. He kept up the pumping rhythm while circling his thumb in time with the thrust of his fingers, and then she was coming apart against his hand with a sobbing cry.

She dropped her legs and her head tipped to rest against his shoulder. "Oh lord."

"You good?"

"Good? I'm amazing. Now it's time to make you feel amazing." She drew in a shaky, shuddering breath, then her hands were at his belt again, and this time he let her have at it. When she had his fly unbuttoned, she reached in to wrap her hands around him, pulling him out even as she stroked.

"Hmm, impressive." She grinned. That smile with her hand wrapped around his erection nearly had him losing it right there. "I don't suppose you have a condom with you?"

He couldn't hold back his answering smile. "As a matter of fact." He pulled out his wallet and retrieved the small packet, ripping it open with his teeth.

With protection in place, he lifted her, and when her legs went around his thighs, he lowered her to take him in as he thrust up. He caught her moan in his mouth as they moved together, setting a rhythm.

Her hands gripped his shoulders and he watched her watching him. The tone shifted from the playful to intense in a heartbeat. Her eyes were deep enough to drown in. The sensation of her surrounding him, welcoming him in even as he thrust deeper and harder, brought a response from him that was more than physical.

He held back, building the tension, feeling her need growing, matching his, until her eyes glazed and she shuddered around him. She rode out her orgasm with her face buried against his shoulder. He continued thrusting slow and deep, her lips warm against his neck as he picked up the pace, and he felt his own release building until the glory slammed through him, pushing him to climax with a hoarse roar.

Time stood still, their heated breaths the only sound he heard.

***

Slowly, Levi lowered Zoey until her feet hit the floor.

She grabbed his arms for balance. "Wow."

Rattled, like she was suffering from shell shock, she was unable to think beyond the intensity of the sensations that had flooded through her. Why couldn't mind-blowing sex with Levi be only mind-blowing sex? Why did her emotions leave her feeling so raw and exposed? She had the unsettling feeling that her heart was balancing on the edge of an unstable precipice and all it would take was a tiny nudge and it would fall with a crashing thud, never to be wholly hers again.

"Yeah, wow." Levi's voice was sounding a little breathless.

She avoided his searching gaze. "Who'd have thought?"

"You didn't think it would be hot between us?"

"I expected hot, but I never knew hot could be that…good." Zoey realized what she'd revealed and took a quick peek at Levi's face. Smug. Definitely smug. She looked around them. His pants were still hitched around his rear but the fly was unbuttoned and wide open in the most interesting way. Their shirts had been tossed aside and Lucy was lying on Levi's. Zoey still wore her boxers. He'd pushed them aside to gain access.

"Be right back." Levi took a few steps and went to the small guest bathroom. She gathered up her t-shirt and tugged it on. It was kind of like shutting the barn door after the horses had run off, but she needed a layer of protection. He was back a minute later with the fly still unbuttoned, but not enough to display the goods.

"I like that shirt."

She glanced down and bit her lip. No wonder he'd walked right through the door. "I hadn't even thought about it. Um, I'll get yours." She pushed Lucy with her foot so she could retrieve Levi's shirt. She spied her hair band that had somehow come loose and grabbed it, quickly pulling back her curls to some semblance of control.

"Do you want something to eat? I've got cookies or these brownie things. I could make tea, or coffee. You like coffee, so that's what I'll make." She should shut up and shut down the nerves that had her babbling like an idiot. Maybe she should gather an ounce of maturity and handle the post-coital moment with poise.

Levi caught her hand before she could move to the kitchen. "Zoey, look at me."

She wanted to look anywhere but at him, because she had a sinking feeling that looking at him would lead to kissing him, and kissing him would lead to doing what they'd been doing against the door, and doing that again would lead to more emotional intimacy, which scared the crap out of her.

She let herself be pulled to him. He framed her face with those wide palms and tipped her head up. "You're avoiding me."

"Pfft. You were *in* me not five minutes ago, so you can hardly say I'm avoiding you." But there was no avoiding him now. His bold blue gaze had fastened on her and wouldn't let her go.

"Maybe that was the easy part. Maybe acknowledging that we have something together that goes beyond hot sex is harder."

There was no hiding from the compassion practically radiating off him. She found herself confessing what she was most worried about. "You could hurt me, Levi. Really, really hurt me."

He lowered his forehead to hers and she found her hands linking with his. "We're both taking that risk, sweetheart. But if we don't take a chance, what we lose could be even bigger."

She drew in a shaky breath. "I like you, I really do. But I have issues. You might want to reconsider your interest in me. I'm a bad bet."

He put a finger to her lips. "Zoey Hardesty, will you go on a date with me?"

Why did that have her going all mushy inside?

"We've already had sex, don't you think we're a bit late for a first date?"

"No, we're not. Will you?"

She let out a huff of breath. "Okay, but this doesn't mean we're boyfriend and girlfriend, or any such nonsense. We hooked up, and we'll go on a date, but that's it."

Why did it feel like as soon as she took a stand, the ground began to crumble beneath her feet?

"One step at a time, sweetheart. One step at a time."

Chapter Fourteen

Levi entered the police station, taking his seat for morning roll call as Brad stepped behind the podium at the front of the room. Levi had woken up alone in his own bed. He was getting that Zoey had intimacy issues, but she hadn't kicked him out of her cottage until after they'd gone to *her* bed. The encore to what they'd done against the door had been equally as hot.

He could work with that.

He wasn't exactly sure where he wanted to end up with her. In the past few months he'd made major life changes, and he thought he was dealing with some issues that he hadn't really understood *were* issues. But he felt like he was breaking away from the hold some things in his past had over him. He'd stopped running and was dealing with them. He felt lighter somehow.

He made a mental note to call his partner from the Oakland PD. Maybe it was time and distance from the event, or maybe it was getting his head screwed on straight, but he was coming to terms with the decision he'd made.

Regardless, leaving OPD and joining the police department in his hometown had been the right move. Hands down, the best thing about moving home was finding Zoey. For the first time, he was thinking about a future that included someone else. If she had commitment issues, he was willing to let her set the pace. But that didn't mean he wasn't going to push when things needed pushing.

He'd left for work feeling pretty good about the situation. Lucy had still occupied her sunny spot, and even though he could easily maneuver around her with the motorcycle, he still tossed her the Eggo waffle he'd saved for her. He was partial to the buttermilk variety, and Lucy seemed to agree. On his ride in, he'd mulled over what had happened with the car coming up their driveway, then speeding away like a racecar driver. The driver hadn't been turning around on the street by accident. Whatever had been their intent, it hadn't been innocent, and that had him worried about Zoey's safety.

Waiting for Brad to start, he pulled out his phone and texted Zoey to find out if she'd made it safely to work.

His phone vibrated a few seconds later, and he opened the screen to a pic of Lucy riding shotgun in a Forest Service truck plus a thumbs-up emoji. Worked for him.

Levi had informed Brad first thing about the car and the driver's reckless effort to get away. Brad included that in the briefing and gave orders to increase patrols in the area around where Levi and Zoey lived. Once the meeting was over, Brad called Levi into his office, shutting the door behind them. Brad picked up a file folder from his desk and dropped it onto Levi's lap.

He opened the folder, the name Paul Clauson jumping out at him. He read the report, a sick feeling growing in his gut along with the rising anger. He looked across the desk where Brad sat. "Same fucking MO."

"Yeah. After you told me Zoey's story, I did some digging. The local sheriff's department let Clauson resign, so he went to Colorado, where he was hired by a small-town PD. From which, surprise, surprise, he took early retirement. I called, got someone who would talk to me. I suggested that it seemed suspicious Clauson would retire at a relatively young age when staying only a couple of years longer would have allowed him to increase his retirement substantially. The cop I spoke to was plenty pissed. He told me, off the record of course, that Clauson was allowed to leave after another officer accused him of raping a fifteen-year-old girl."

Levi thought if he ground his molars any harder they'd turn to dust. Zoey's claim that cops covered for other cops was ringing infuriatingly true. "Why didn't they prosecute?"

"The girl wouldn't corroborate the story, so no charges were filed." Brad shook his head. "Clearly, Clauson is a slick bastard. He picks his victims carefully, knows law enforcement, and uses all that to stay out of prison. His victims are almost always vulnerable women, and he knows the weaknesses of the system and plays it against them.

"That said, there was another teenage girl who accused him of assault, and this time he slipped up because it was a suburban teenager from a wealthy family on the way home from high school soccer practice. The girl got away from him much like Zoey had, and when there wasn't enough evidence for the DA to bring criminal charges, her parents sued the police department. They settled, and while the details are confidential, it must have cost them plenty. That's when the department pushed Clauson into retirement. They knew they had a predator cop in their department and didn't want any more negative publicity."

"That's chickenshit. They took the easy way out."

"Without a doubt. Do some digging, and find out where he is now."

Levi remained seated, and Brad raised a brow. "Something else?"

"Zoey and I are in a relationship."

Brad gave what Levi thought of as his *big brother* look, the same look he'd been getting all of his life. "Since I've got eyes in my head and saw you two together at Mom's barbecue and at the team pizza thing last night, I figured that out, bro."

"We're still kind of circling around exactly what being in a relationship means, but I'm leaning toward serious."

Brad grinned. "Good to know. I like Zoey. Watch out, or Mom will be talking weddings and babies." This time Brad laughed full out. "Gotcha. You've gone pale. You going to faint on me? Should I get smelling salts?"

"Fuck off. Mom's got her own wedding to plan so I think she'll leave me alone."

"Don't count on it. But seriously, Zoey will be good for you."

"She's already good for me. I wanted to be up front about it since you gave me her case."

"Do you want me to give it to Jack or Monica?"

"Hell no."

"Good. I trust you to do this right, Levi. Now go figure out where the fucker is hiding."

It didn't take long. Within the hour Levi was back at Brad's door.

"Clauson's back in Hangman's Loss." Levi all but spat out the words.

Seated behind his desk, Brad threw down the pen he'd been holding. "You're shitting me."

"He's in that older development on the other side of the lake called Alpine Meadows. He's unmarried, is late on his property taxes, and owns a Chevy Tahoe that's about a decade old. There have been a couple of complaints from a neighbor about, and I quote, 'very loud, very shitty country music.' No citations."

"Pay Clauson a visit and rattle his cage. Find out what he's been up to, what color his Chevy Tahoe is. You can use the noise complaints as a pretext." Brad frowned. "Damn it, I'd like to go with you but I've got a meeting with the mayor in an hour. Take Monica in case he gets testy."

"Testy? That's what they're calling it these days?"

"Yeah, that's what they're calling it. He may ratchet up to disagreeable or argumentative. Practice all the de-escalation techniques you have, because I don't want this visit to go sideways and become something bigger than it has to be."

Levi nodded. "I'll let you know how it goes."

***

Two hours later, Levi returned to the station, this time going in through the sally port. He kept a lid on his temper when he pulled the cuffed Clauson from the back of the cruiser, Officer Monica Valdez taking one arm, Levi the other.

Clauson had been uncooperative from the moment he'd opened his door, and had remained a pain in the ass. Walking in, he was resisting enough to show everyone he was pissed without going far enough to incite a physical response. "You sons of bitches take these cuffs off."

"Yeah, that's going to happen," Monica muttered.

They brought him through the door to the booking room. Since leaving law enforcement, Clauson appeared to have forsaken the trimming of body hair. What was left of the hair on his head grew long enough to be tied back with a rubber band into a scraggly ponytail, the beard creeping down his chest still held what looked like crumbs from his last meal, and his eyebrows and the hair sprouting out of his ears were bushy enough that Levi wondered if his hearing or vision was impeded. The tank top he wore revealed more hair on Clauson's back than Levi had on his chest.

The department wasn't big enough for a designated booking officer, so Levi did the honors.

"Full name?"

"Go fuck yourself."

"Right. Fuck Yourself is going right in that space, Paul 'Go Fuck Yourself' Clauson. Birthdate?"

"I'm not telling you my fucking birthdate. I'm not telling you anything. You got no reason to arrest me."

Levi pointed at his face. Adrenaline had initially masked the pain, but he was beginning to feel it. "See this?" He indicated the shiner high on his left cheek and edging toward the temple. "That's what got you here. You decided to buy yourself a shitload of trouble and now you have to live with it."

"If you hadn't gotten in my way, you wouldn't have gotten yourself punched."

"You were a cop. You know how this works."

"Yeah, I was a cop. So how can you do this to a brother, man?" He held up his cuffed hands. "You're a cop, I'm a cop. We got to stick together."

"Yeah, we have to stick together but you punched me in the face? Shut up and let me get this done."

Clauson didn't shut up. He complained about the mug shots, he complained about the fingerprints, his belligerence increasing as the process continued. "You know what? The police chief and I go way back, and I'm gonna have your job, asshole."

"You know him? We'll see how that plays." Levi picked up the phone and called Brad, then continued with processing.

A few minutes later, Brad strolled in.

"Your pal here says you two are buds, and that you're going to fire my ass."

"Hell, I just hired you. It's too much paperwork to fire you. Plus, Mom would be pissed."

Clauson looked from Levi to Brad, then back again. "You two assholes brothers? You look like asshole brothers."

"Your vocabulary range is astounding. Is that any way to talk to your friend the police chief?" Levi asked.

Clauson began coughing. "You got to uncuff me, I can't breathe."

Brad shook his head. "Here we go. You know what's next."

"I tell you. I can't breathe. I'm having chest pains."

"Bingo." Brad turned to Levi. "I'll call for an ambulance. Put him in a cell until they get here."

"You got to take me to the hospital. I think I'm having a heart attack." Clauson made his breathing more labored.

Ignoring the prisoner, Brad leaned in to get a closer look at Levi's face. "That's you not letting this go sideways?"

Since the part of his face that had connected with Clauson's fist hurt like a bitch, Levi could guess that it looked as bad as it felt. He walked Clauson to a cell, uncuffed him, and locked him in.

"You get me my warrant?"

Brad slapped an envelope on Levi's chest. "What set him off?"

"Me knocking on his door." Levi slid the warrant into a side pocket of his pants. "He was belligerent from the get-go, thought his 'fucking bitch-ass neighbor' had called the cops to complain about his crappy music, which we heard from the street. The neighbor appeared, yelling that finally someone was doing something about the douchebag. Clauson charged after the idiot neighbor and this happened." Levi pointed at his face.

"Neighbor hurt?"

"No. Wasn't touched. Monica and I will go back and search the place. I'll bring in any electronics, see if we can find evidence that he put up that post targeting Zoey."

"Our IT guy is supposed to be tracking that down from our end, but he's one guy and has a shitload of work."

"Now he's going to have even more."

Brad gave a curt nod as he headed for the door. "Put some ice on your face."

***

By the time Levi made it home that evening, his face throbbed, he had a headache that matched the pain pulse for pulse, and what he wanted most in the world was to down some pain meds and crawl into bed. He hadn't had time to get the icepack Brad had ordered, so maybe he'd get on that.

He rolled the motorcycle up to the cabin and set the kickstand. There was no sign of Zoey at the cottage. No Prius parked in front, no light in the window, no Lucy hanging out. He wanted to see

Zoey, figured that alone would make him feel better. But telling her that Clauson was back in the area and had been for nearly a year? That would ruin her night.

Since no one was around to hear, he allowed himself a groan as he pulled off his helmet, which put pressure on his battered face. Clauson had let himself go and probably weighed in at three hundred pounds. It felt like every one of those pounds had been packed into that ham fist. If Levi hadn't turned his head, diverted his attention for that short second to yell at the neighbor to get back in his house, Clauson would never have landed the sucker punch. He'd hit Levi, then moved like a bulldozer and tried to plow past them, but Levi and Monica had tackled him and now Clauson was sitting on his ass in a cell. Yeah, a cell. No heart attack. What a surprise.

Levi had a suspicion about what they'd find on the computer they'd picked up with the warrant. All the complainants against Clauson had been young, as in teenager young. A bit more digging had turned up another against him by a teenaged prostitute from earlier than when he'd assaulted Zoey. Levi figured the odds were they'd find child porn in Clauson's search history, if not stored on his hard drive.

While sorting through his keys to find the one for the cabin, Zoey's Prius turned into the driveway. He needed a few minutes to get himself together before facing her with the news about Clauson. It didn't look like he was going to get them.

She got out of her car, opening the back door to unbuckle the dog. Lucy let out a snuffling woof and loped toward him. Lucky for anyone Lucy considered a friend, Zoey had trained the bear dog not to jump. Levi reached down to scratch her big head when she stopped to sniff his pants. She did her leaning thing against him while Levi watched Zoey make her way up the driveway.

"You're one of her people now."

"Yeah?"

"Yeah. Leaning is how she shows her affection."

"At a hundred pounds that's a lot of affection."

Zoey turned her face up to his, her brows lowering into a frown. "What happened to you?"

"You don't want to know."

"I don't?"

"No." He sighed. "Let's go sit inside. I need a couple of aspirin and then I'll tell you."

She reached out to his shoulder and when she'd pulled him down to her level, she laid a kiss on his cheek below the bruise. "Have you had dinner?"

He'd always thought moms kissing their kids' hurts was silly, but now he'd have to rethink that. He shook his head, and even that hurt.

"Come over to my place then. I'll give you an icepack for that shiner and warm something from the freezer for dinner."

He found himself following her back down the driveway and into her house, where the colors and textures or whatever it was that made the space uniquely Zoey's immediately helped to relax him. With a hand on his arm, she propelled him to the couch. "Take your shirt and the vest off so you're comfortable, then you can sit, put your feet up if you like, and relax. I'll be back in a minute."

When Zoey went into the kitchen, Levi looked at the couch, thought what the hell, and did as she'd suggested. He peeled off his shirt and the vest, leaving on his white t-shirt. His head ached so badly that instead of sitting, he lay back on a soft pillow and, with his feet hanging off the end of the couch, closed his eyes. Lucy flopped down next to the couch and he dropped a hand to scratch her side. There was the sound of the refrigerator opening, the rattling of ice, and then water running.

The couch dipped and he opened his eyes to find Zoey sitting next to him, a glass of water in one hand and a white plastic bottle of ibuprofen in the other. "Sit up for a second." He pushed himself up and she shook out three tablets and handed him a glass of water. He downed the pills and lay down, closing his eyes. He needed to tell her about Clauson, but at the moment he was thankful she was holding off on the questions.

"Here," she murmured. She placed a cool icepack wrapped in a towel over the side of his face. Her fingers lifted his hair and she pressed a warm kiss to his forehead. "Rest for a minute."

Chapter Fifteen

Levi opened his eyes and frowned. He hadn't intended to fall asleep. The icepack had slid onto the pillow and he set it on the coffee table. He glanced around the room. Lucy had abandoned her spot by the couch and was doing her bearskin imitation splayed on her belly in front of the cold fireplace. Zoey sat at the little dining table tapping on the keyboard of a laptop. She'd changed into cropped stretchy pants and a tie-dye t-shirt. She had a wide green band around her head, he guessed to keep her hair out of her face. The most incredible smell of something baking made his stomach rumble, reminding him that lunch had been a long time ago. He pushed himself up and Zoey glanced over.

"Hey." She rose and crossed the room to sit beside him once again. "How are you feeling?"

"Better." And he was. The throbbing in his cheek had dulled, and the headache was all but gone. He snagged her wrist and, with his eyes on hers, brought it to his lips. Her hand smelled of soap. "Thanks."

"You looked like you could use some TLC." A light flush spread from her neck to her cheeks. It was kind of sweet that simply kissing her hand could fluster her.

"I guess I did."

The impulse was too strong to ignore. He leaned back against the cushion and tugged her down until she was leaning over his chest and pressed a kiss to her lips. He was becoming addicted. To her scent, to that flash of heat in her eyes, to the way he felt centered whenever he was around her. Her hand slipped to the back of his neck, and instead of keeping the kiss light as he'd intended, he took it deeper.

She opened her mouth, tongue tangling with his, the taste of her heating his blood and sending it spiraling straight south. Her response felt like a slow, smooth slide into heaven. He shifted until she lay fully on top of him, cradled between his legs, a position that brought her hot center into perfect alignment with his hard-on. She pushed herself up his body and he groaned.

"Jesus. You're making me crazy." He took her mouth again, then moved his lips over her chin, her collarbone, the flower-scented area below her left ear. Every bit of her tasted better than the last, and the breathy little sounds she made had him feeling like he could gobble her up in one big bite.

She wiggled until his erection was nestled more firmly where he wanted it despite the layers of clothing. It must have been where she wanted it too because she made a little hum of satisfaction.

His hand on her neck brought her lips back to his. Tongue, teeth, and the sweetness of Zoey made him want more. He flipped so she was under him. He braced himself with one arm while he skimmed his hand under her shirt, over the smooth skin of her belly, and found her gloriously braless. He cupped her breast, his thumb grazing over a nipple, and he caught her gasp with his lips. He had it in mind to tug her shirt up and off when a loud buzz from the kitchen broke the moment.

"What the hell is that?" he murmured, hand moving to the other breast, his lips now busy on the underside of her jaw.

"Timer." She pushed against him.

"Ignore it."

"Can't. Dinner will be ruined. And you'll really like dinner."

"You're killing me."

She kissed him and pushed up.

"Oh good lord." The words came out in a groan when she ground against him. He wasn't entirely sure it was an accident.

He reached for her but was grasping at nothing when she slid out of reach. Standing, she gave him a swift kiss on his chin and retreated to the kitchen. He took the icepack from the coffee table, debating whether to hold it to his crotch to cool things off or return it to his cheek. Deciding against either, he rolled off the couch to follow her. She twisted the old-fashioned timer in the shape of an egg and the buzzing stopped. With padded mitts she opened the oven to pull out a deep ceramic dish topped with a browned crust. It smelled amazing.

"What's that?"

"Chicken pot pie."

"Really? You made that?"

"Yep. I made two about a month ago and froze this one for a night like tonight. Feed Lucy while I cut up a watermelon to go with the pie, then you can see if it tastes as good as it looks and smells."

Thirty minutes later, Levi was swallowing the last bite of crust from the generous portion of pie Zoey had heaped on his plate. "That's the best damn thing I've eaten in a month, which says a lot because my mom brought me lasagna when I first moved back. This is better. I'm never buying a frozen chicken pot pie again now that I know how good it can be."

She took a sip of her wine and smiled. He loved how the gesture warmed her eyes. "Glad you liked it." Her expression turned thoughtful and maybe a little wistful. "I want to learn more about you being a cop. Tell me something you love about your job and something you hate about it."

He sat back in his chair. "Love about it? That's easy. I love making the world a safer place. Sometimes it's messy because there's always someone who gets caught up in other people's shit and it messes up their life. But taking a bad guy off the streets who's a danger to other people? That's what does it for me."

"What do you hate about it?"

He thought for a moment. "I hate when I'm in uniform and walk into the grocery store or wherever, and there's some lady with poor parenting skills. Her kid is giving her trouble, and she points to me and says, 'Look, there's a cop. He's going to arrest you and take you to jail if you don't behave.' And then you've got this poor little kid staring at you with big eyes, learning from his mom that cops take kids away from their parents."

"Geez. What do you say?"

"I carry badge stickers, and I get down to the kid's level and tell them I don't arrest children. Then I give them a sticker. And I usually tell the mom to cut it out." He shrugged. "Beyond that, there's not much else I can do." He turned his wine glass in his hand. "Same questions back at you about being a wildlife biologist."

She smiled. "The absolute best thing about my job is that I get to work outdoors and go to some of the most beautiful places in the world. Also, I have a hand in protecting plants and animals that are at risk. I also like the education aspect, like when I team up with rangers to do talks at the campgrounds. That never gets old."

"Anything you dislike?"

She shrugged. "Some of those talks include climate change. It's part of our job to educate the public about the impact a warming planet is having on ecosystems in the Sierras. But every now and then we'll have someone who wants to argue with us. They'll deny science, deny climate change, and accuse us of having some sort of political agenda. With my job, I see the impact of climate change every single day, but these people want to challenge me about it. You can't even have a conversation with them because they don't accept basic facts as facts. And I'll get off my soapbox now. Sorry."

He shook his head. "You have nothing to apologize about. You're doing exactly what you should be doing. And despite the naysayers, my bet is there are a lot of folks who listen to your talks and learn something valuable. Maybe they'll be motivated to step up and do their part."

"Hopefully."

He liked this, talking with Zoey, learning about her, seeing the gold in her eyes light up when she showed her passion for her work. She sipped her wine, and he found himself stalling, delaying when he'd have to crash the evening and bring up Clauson. "How's Charlie doing?"

There was that smile again. He was absolutely becoming addicted. "He started a new job in the computer center at his dorm. It's what he wants to do, but I worry because until people get to know him, sometimes they treat him like he's a freak."

"He has to learn to deal with that. You can't protect him all the time."

"I know that. But I also know how easily hurt he can get. I've always looked out for him and it's hard to turn that off." Zoey sipped again, gaze steady over the rim of her glass. She set it down carefully. "Are you going to tell me how you got the bruise on your cheek?"

He pushed his cleared plate back. He'd mention Clauson and the awful memories would return for Zoey. But she needed to know, and she was strong. She'd deal with it. "I arrested Paul Clauson today. He's been living in Hangman's Loss for the past ten months."

Her indrawn breath was quick and sharp, matched by shock. Then her expression hardened and her words came out in a snarl. "That bastard. That fucking bastard. I bet it was him who hit me.

Here I was not pursuing it because I thought it was an accident. That whoever had done it would lose their license and because of that maybe their job and they'd be homeless, but it was him. Did you arrest him? Did he punch you in the face? Did you punch him back?"

"I arrested him, and yeah, he punched me in the face, and being the guy wearing the uniform, I didn't punch him back." Levi pointed to the bruise. "This bought him the ticket to jail." Then he paused. "Clauson is going to make bail."

"I'm not afraid of that pervert. If he tries anything with me, I'll kick him in the balls like I should have done back then."

"Zoey, you stabbed him in the hand, and he's wearing that scar. I'd say you protected yourself admirably. But he's twice as big as you. I don't want you close enough to him to kick him in the balls. We got a warrant to search his house and found enough weapons to outfit a small army. Some of the guns are illegal to possess in California so we'll have more charges to add. We also confiscated his computer and we'll search that."

She set down her wine glass. "Do you think he's responsible for everything that's happened to me? The hit-and-run, messing up my porch, the pole dancer post?"

"We're looking into all that."

"Getting hit by a car aside, don't the other things seem kind of minor for him? I'm not saying Paul isn't capable of doing mean things, but they seem kind of low-key."

Which was something that had been bothering Levi, too. "A lot of the time that's how harassment starts." He raised her hand when she opened her mouth. "I know, we think things started for you with getting hit by a car, which is a giant step up from low-key. I'll be questioning him tomorrow once he's got his attorney lined up. At this point, your name hasn't been mentioned. He thinks we were at his house because of noise complaints from his neighbor."

"He liked country music, the twangy my-dog-up-and-died kind."

"That's what the neighbor reported. But I need anything else you might remember from since you moved back to town. Think back to anything that happened that maybe you dismissed at the time, that could have been Clauson targeting you."

Zoey shook her head. "There's nothing. I've told you everything."

He reached across the table to pick up her hand. "Once we question him, he'll know you're involved, and when he makes bail, he'll come out pissed."

"If he's been after me, he'll know that's why you were knocking on his door." Her fingers tensed around his. "You're afraid he'll come after me."

"The thought's crossed my mind. He's also pissed at the neighbor. We confiscated Clauson's weapons for the time being. That doesn't mean he doesn't have others stashed somewhere else."

She pulled her hand free. "I'll be careful."

"What's your schedule tomorrow?"

"I'm in the field. I'm partnered with a new guy. We're going out along Rock Creek to Little Lakes Valley. Lucy will be with us."

"Who all knows where you'll be?"

She shrugged. "People in my department."

He thought for a minute. "You'll take a Forest Service vehicle?"

"Yep."

"Okay. Check in with me when you can during the day."

She nodded. Levi picked up his dishes to take to the sink. Zoey followed, shadows darkening her eyes. She set down her dishes and he caught her hand, tugging her toward him. He took her other hand and brought them both up to his lips.

"You're not alone in this, Zoey. I've got your back. Brad does, too, and the rest of the department." He used his teeth to nip lightly at her knuckle. "Do you want me to stay with you tonight? I could sleep on the couch." He'd rather be in her bed with her, but if she wasn't ready for that, he'd suck it up.

She was already shaking her head. "Paul is in jail tonight, so if he's the one messing with me, I'll be safe. And I really hate the idea of changing how I live because some asshole wants to scare me."

"Bravado will only get you so far. Sometimes you need to rely on others. That's what I'm here for."

***

By the end of the week Zoey would be done with her current pika survey. Driving from the Forest Service office, she cranked up the air conditioning. Lucy rode in the backseat, panting despite the blast of cold air.

Today Zoey had partnered with another wildlife biologist, a recent college grad and new hire named Jorge Padilla. It had been nice to have someone to work with. Lucy had found another patch of snow and spent an hour enthusiastically digging and rolling in the cold stuff. Zoey had spotted a golden eagle plunging from the sky to capture a rabbit. She loved her job.

Because pika were poor body temperature regulators, the concern that climate change and warming temperatures would threaten the species made her current project imperative. In the talus slopes where she and Jorge had spent the day, they'd found the animals were doing what they usually did in the summer. Fecal pellets gave evidence that they were eating, and she'd documented drying vegetation that formed the hay piles the pika brought under the rocks to store for the winter. The mammals didn't hibernate, so they spent much of their summer preparing for the cold winter. She found it reassuring that at least at her current project location, the little mammal seemed to be doing fine.

She let Lucy out of the car and her baby immediately looked toward Levi's cabin. "Sorry, girl, your guy isn't home." She'd called Levi to check in as he'd requested, and he had passed on the news that they were trying to hold Clauson longer, but that he might make bail. That had cast a pall over what otherwise had been a good day. Levi had mentioned that he'd be at softball practice that evening and invited her and Lucy to come watch.

Zoey and Levi were at that in-between place. They'd hooked up, he'd asked her out on a date that had yet to be arranged, and he wanted her to check in with him during the day. Sure, that had been partly because of her evil stalker. But the check-in had gone both ways as he'd shared his day with her too. Being connected with someone like that was nice, but also a little unnerving. She had been doing fine on her own, not needing anyone, and with no one besides Lucy depending on her. Now she was feeling like half of a couple, and despite the obvious plus that the other half was Levi Gallagher, it made her a little itchy about where the whole relationship thing was going.

That itchiness was exacerbated even more because at odd times during the past few days, she'd found herself wondering what being in love felt like. She'd never been in love. She'd dated, had lived with the cheater who'd given her Lucy, but didn't think that had edged over into love.

She'd been more pissed than brokenhearted when she'd kicked him to the curb. Was there some sort of "I'm in love" checklist? Think about him all the time? Check. Heart rate speeds up when his name is mentioned? Check. Want to lick him like a popsicle at the most inappropriate times? Check.

How many checks before they tallied up to love? She could call Eva. This was exactly the kind of thing her friend would know the answer to. But Eva was a Gallagher cousin, and she worked with Maddy, so there was way too much risk of her friend spilling the beans. She might not intend to, but Eva liked to talk, and beans might be spilled nonetheless.

She wanted to watch the Guns' softball practice. She could tell herself that it would be fun, that it was smart to let Lucy become familiar with the stadium and the people before the game Saturday where her job as team mascot meant she'd have to be on her best behavior. But Zoey knew she was fooling herself. Watching your guy at practice was probably another box to be checked.

Back in high school, she'd gone to plenty of baseball games solely for the pleasure of watching Levi in motion. It didn't escape her notice that once again she was contemplating spending an evening hanging out with a bunch of cops.

She could blame Levi for that too. He was a good man. Her experiences with cops in the past had been horrible, and Paul was still an issue for her, but it did not seem right to put Levi anywhere in the same universe as that man. Levi, Brad, Logan, Jack, all of them were proof that not all cops, not even most cops, were power-tripping predators.

Lucy trotted up the steps to the porch.

Zoey squinted to try to identify the lump on her doormat in front of the door. She hadn't ordered anything and wasn't expecting a delivery. The dog bounded up and began sniffing the lump. "Lucy, no."

Zoey ran up the steps. Lucy looked at her with her "this looks yummy and I'm waiting for the magic word" look. Zoey snapped on the leash and pulled her dog down the steps and away from what looked like a pile of raw ground beef.

She tied Lucy securely to the rail and crossed the porch once again. She didn't know why she was moving so cautiously. It wasn't like the disgusting pile of raw meat could jump at her. She bent over to inspect it. It appeared the meat had been there for a while. It had turned a grayish color, and flies had found it, which meant there were likely already fly eggs deposited in it. She thought there were unusual dark specks in the meat, but she wasn't touching it to find out. She pulled her phone from her daypack and dialed Levi's number. He picked up immediately.

"Zoey."

"There's raw meat on my front doormat."

"Raw meat?"

"Yeah. Like hamburger. It's on a Styrofoam tray like you'd see in the grocery store meat section but without the plastic wrap."

"Did Lucy get into it?"

"No. She wanted to, but she was waiting for me to give her the okay signal." Dread settled like a lead weight on her chest. "Levi, it could be poisoned. Someone could have been trying to poison Lucy. Was Paul released on bail?"

"Yeah, about noon today, but I don't see how he could have pulled that off. We've been keeping an eye on him, and he went straight home and has stayed put. Regardless, we'll check this out. I'm on the other side of the lake, wrapping up a call. I'll get over there as soon as I can, but I'll have dispatch send over a unit to pick up the meat. We'll have it tested." He paused, his voice changing in tone. "If you think someone is still around, or if Lucy is giving any indication of that, get in your car and get out of there. In fact, you should leave now to be safe."

"I'm fine. If there was anyone here, Lucy would let me know."

A sigh carried through the phone. "Don't touch the meat, or anything else."

"Got it."

"I'll be there as soon as I can." His reassuring tone relieved some of the worry that was making her head ache.

With Lucy on the leash beside her, Zoey walked around her cottage, then around Levi's cabin for good measure, but didn't find anything else unusual. Only the pile of disgusting raw meat with a puddle that looked like blood forming around it.

An SUV with the Hangman's Loss PD insignia on the door and a light bar across the roof pulled into her driveway to park next to her Prius. She walked over as Jack Morgan stepped out. He was so tall, she barely came up to his shoulder. He always made her feel like a little kid standing next to him. He gave Lucy a good rub, then straightened to look at Zoey with his keen dark eyes. "Hey. Levi says you've got something to show me."

"There's raw meat in front of my door. Go on up and look. I don't want to take Lucy close enough that she could give in to temptation and grab a bite, so we're staying down here."

Jack went up the steps onto the porch. She watched him squat to examine the meat, waving a hand to shoo the flies. After a minute he rose to his feet to pull gloves and a large plastic bag from a cargo pocket. He bagged the meat, then placed it in his vehicle, returning to retrieve her doormat.

"You're taking my doormat, too?"

"Sorry, but yeah. The blood from the meat soaked into it, so I don't know if you'd want to keep it anyway. Right now it's evidence."

Another police SUV turned into the driveway to park next to Jack's. Levi stepped out and Lucy started prancing at the end of her leash when she spotted her favorite guy. Levi crossed to where they stood, and like Jack, leaned down to pet Lucy. His bold blue gaze locked on Zoey. "You okay?" The shiner high on Levi's cheekbone looked worse today than it had the evening before.

"I'm fine. I'm just glad Lucy didn't eat any of that meat."

"Jack, look away."

Without waiting to see if his instruction was followed, Levi lightly grasped the braid that held Zoey's hair back and bent his head. He kissed her, and they both seemed to need the connection because she could feel her tension ease at the same time Levi drew in a ragged breath. Lucy headbutted Levi's knee, then pushed herself between them, forcing him to let go.

Jack let out a short laugh. "That dog's like having kids, there's always someone else around when you want it to be only the two of you."

Levi stepped back, his gaze not leaving Zoey's face. She wasn't sure how or why things had changed between them, but the intensity level had certainly ratcheted up.

He pulled himself away to follow Jack, who opened the rear door of his cruiser. Levi took the evidence bag of meat, holding it up to examine the contents. He held out the bag and pointed. "See those?"

Zoey stepped closer to see what he was pointing at. "What?"

"Those things that look like green pellets? My bet is rat poison."

"Rat poison?" Zoey swallowed down the sudden roll of nausea. "Would that kill a big dog?"

"I don't know if it would kill her and it would depend on how much she ate, but it would make her sick. Lab test will tell us for sure what it is."

Jack pulled out his keys. "I'm going to get this to the station so we can log it and get it out to the lab before the end of the day." He cocked a brow at Levi. "You coming to practice tonight?"

"Yeah, I'll be there."

Jack nodded, then got in his SUV.

They watched Jack leave, then Levi turned toward her. "You want to come? I could impress you with my amazing skills with a ball."

She cast an uneasy look at her house. "I'll come for a bit. I think introducing Lucy to the team and letting her see what goes on there will make her more comfortable on Saturday."

"Hey, you okay?"

She shrugged. "I've never felt nervous about living here by myself, even though we're a little isolated. I'm not going to be able to let Lucy out off-leash any longer. There's no telling what this nutjob is planning next."

Chapter Sixteen

Zoey walked to the edge of the practice field, her dog plodding beside her on the leash. She recognized several of the players. Jack swung at balls spewing from a pitching machine, while Levi, Monica Valdez, and a couple of others fielded them. Logan practiced pitching to a player in catcher's gear on the far side of the field. Brad crossed from the dugout to greet them.

"Hey there." He rubbed Lucy's head, then held up a t-shirt he'd carried over. "Do you think our girl here could wear this?" It was one of the team's HLPD sleeveless practice t-shirts.

Zoey eyed the dimensions. "I'll have to modify it, but I can make it work." She rubbed the back of her neck, scanning the few people in the bleachers. Something was making her feel jittery.

Brad pulled a large navy bandana from his pocket. "How about this?"

"That's too small to fit around her neck, but if you have two, I can tie them together."

"I'll get you another one."

Levi loped over, his glove on one hand, a ball in the other. "Hey there. This Lucy's gear?"

Brad held up the t-shirt. "She'll rock this. Since the Hoses are bringing their dog out onto the field on a fire truck, I thought we could have Lucy riding in on a cruiser. We'll have the window down so she can hang her head out."

"She'll love that," Zoey said, even though she figured she'd have to ride in the cruiser too. The irony wasn't lost on her. She'd avoided the police for years, and she'd be riding in a police car to support them. Her social life was being taken over by all things law enforcement.

Levi tossed the ball and caught it and Lucy went on alert. She sat, her ears perked as she followed the movement of the ball.

"You want this, girl?" He tossed the ball and Lucy caught it neatly, looking at him with the ball in her mouth and her tail wagging.

"Lucy, drop."

At the order, Lucy set the ball neatly on Levi's foot, staring at it intently as if waiting for it to move.

"Did you teach her to fetch?" Brad asked.

"I didn't have to teach her a thing, she was a natural with it. If I didn't know better, I'd think she was part lab. Her favorite thing is the Frisbee, and it's even better if I throw it into the lake. It doesn't matter how cold it is, she'll run into the water to retrieve a Frisbee all day if I let her."

Levi picked up the ball. "Will she run off if you unleash her?" Zoey shook her head and unhooked the leash. Levi made sure Lucy was following his movements and winged the ball across the field. Lucy was off like a rocket, chasing down the ball, at the same time Jack hit one into left field. When Lucy saw that ball arcing toward her, she outran Monica and managed to get it in her mouth along with the first ball.

Levi let out a whoop. "Way to go, girl. Bring them back, baby."

"The balls are going to be all slobbery," Zoey told Brad.

"No worries, this is great. During a break in the game, we can have her fielding balls. Maybe get the FD's Dalmatian out there, too," Brad mused. "I'll have to work out the details, but the crowd will love it."

After getting Lucy to drop the balls, Zoey attached her leash and led her to the bleachers so the guys could get on with their practice. They had to go behind the home dugout to the opening in the chain link fence. As she passed through, she recognized the thin woman with the bleached hair from the post office walking hurriedly away from her toward the parking lot.

After practice, Zoey joined the team for dinner at a Mexican food place that had recently opened on Main Street. Waiting in line to order, she overheard Brad on his phone, saying something about Levi and Zoey like they were a unit. Was that how people were viewing them, like they were a couple? The itchiness turned into a spike of panic.

She started chewing on her lip as they moved up in the line. Several of the players, including Brad, opted to order their meal as takeout. Zoey sat next to Levi under an awning in the outdoor seating area while they waited for their order. Brad carried out two large bags and stopped at their table.

Levi raised a brow at the bags. "Your kids eat tacos?"

"Tacos are Owen's favorite food. He'd eat them for breakfast if we let him. Amaya is in a quesadilla phase."

"Good choices. Guess you're not joining us for a beer before heading home."

"Not tonight. Latest news update is that Amaya got a hold of a tube of her mother's lipstick and now both the cat and her brother are pink and everyone needs baths."

Levi tipped his head back in a full laugh. "Have fun, brother. Glad it's you and not me going home to that."

"Never a dull moment."

That evening as she readied herself for bed, Zoey found her mind refusing to settle. She brushed her teeth, used her facial cleanser, applied moisturizer, performing her nightly ritual, but found that the process didn't calm her like it usually did. She couldn't stop thinking about Levi. Levi telling Jack to look away so he could kiss her. Levi's delight in Lucy's ball-catching prowess. The strong column of his throat that had looked exceedingly bitable when he had laughed at his brother's parenting challenges.

Maybe they needed distance. It was all too tempting to slip into a life that included check-in calls, impromptu dinners, and mind-blowing sex in the evenings. Not that there'd been more than that one night of mind-blowing sex, but still. They were acting like a couple, people were viewing them as a couple, and she didn't know if she was ready for that. If she'd ever be ready for that.

She pulled down the covers and plumped her pillows against the headboard so she could lean back with the sheet over her knees. Once she was comfy, she picked up her phone and opened her favorites list. Seconds later the phone on the other end of the line was ringing.

"Hey, my girl."

"Hi, Mom. How's it going?"

As her mom talked, telling her about a student in her caseload, then about meeting Charlie's girlfriend, Zoey felt some of her disquiet ease.

She smiled at the description of Charlie's girlfriend. "A very nice girl," according to Dawn Hardesty, who also had a brother with autism.

"She seems to get Charlie," Dawn said. "Nothing fazes her. I met them for lunch and you know how he can be sometimes when there's a crowd, and she rolled with it. If I could create the perfect person for him, she'd be it. And he's over the moon about her."

"That makes me so happy. All your hard work with him has paid off."

"All *our* hard work. We three were a team. You worked as hard as I did to help Charlie become an adult who could cope with the world." Dawn paused. "You know, sometimes I think you had it the hardest."

"Me? You're kidding. Charlie had it the hardest. Or you, a teenage mom, then mom to a special needs child. If Charlie and I are productive, somewhat well-adjusted adults, that's due to you."

"Thanks, my girl. But I worried about you too. You worked so hard to help me, to help your brother, that sometimes I wished you could've been just a kid. I allowed that bastard Paul Clauson in our house. I will never forgive myself for that."

"He fooled everyone. He was working as a police officer and they didn't have a clue he was a pervert. Or maybe they did but ignored it. He was skilled in presenting the image people wanted to see. He's the one who did something wrong, Mom, not you."

"I'll always blame myself for poor judgment where he's concerned."

Zoey hesitated. Her mom wasn't going to like what she had to say. "Mom, Paul is back in Hangman's Loss." Dawn already knew about the hit-and-run, so Zoey filled her in on the rest of what had happened.

"That evil man. You come home, right now. Call your work and tell them you're taking a leave of absence, and you come home with Lucy until the police have this business figured out."

"I can't do that."

"Yes, you can. Or I'll go up there and finish up what you started when you stabbed that sorry excuse for a man. I'll do what that one woman did to another guy and cut off his dick, maybe his balls, too, and see how he likes life then."

Zoey laughed, she couldn't help it. It seemed like mama bear instincts didn't go away when your kids grew up. "I don't want to have to visit you in jail, Mom. But seriously, the police are on it. Do you remember the Gallagher family?"

"Of course I do. You had a crush on the youngest son."

"You knew that?"

"Moms know more than their kids give them credit for."

"Good to know. Brad Gallagher, who also is my landlord, is now chief of police, and he's taking my case seriously. In addition to the police investigation, he's having an alarm system installed here tomorrow." She plucked at the sheet on her lap. "You know the other house that's on this property, a little cabin? Levi is living there."

"Levi is the boy you liked?"

"He's definitely not a boy anymore. Um, he's a cop for the Hangman's Loss PD, too."

"Good. He lives close and he's a cop. He can help keep an eye out for you." Zoey was quiet, and moments later, Dawn asked, "Is he still as good-looking as he was back in high school?"

"Better. We're, um, kind of going out together. Nothing serious," she hurried to explain, "but, you know, hanging out sometimes."

"Do you want it to be serious?"

"I told you, he's a cop."

"So?"

"Geez, Mom. It's not like cops have been good to the Hardesty family."

"We've run into a few bad ones, for sure. But there are many more who risk their lives to protect people. You have to judge the person, not the uniform. If Levi Gallagher's a good person, he'll be a good cop."

It seemed so simple when her mom said it. Zoey lay in bed staring at the ceiling after saying good-bye. She didn't know why it surprised her that her mother didn't have the same issues with law enforcement Zoey did. She'd always felt her attitude about cops was reasonable and justified, but finding out that, despite what had happened in their past, her mom didn't hold those same views challenged her own presumptions.

***

Saturday morning dawned bright and sunny. The Guns and Hoses charity softball game was scheduled to begin at ten. At nine, Levi was knocking on the cottage door.

Zoey answered and gestured to her attire. "This is all your fault."

Levi took in her appearance, a grin spreading across his face. "You look cute. But what's my fault?"

"That I'm wearing police-issued gear. It feels wrong."

She hadn't been able to say no when Brad had presented her with the official game-day baseball jersey. It was white with blue sleeves, with HLPD GUNS written on the back, and a police badge on the front in the pocket area. In a nod to the temperatures forecast to be in the high eighties, Zoey had opted for denim cutoff shorts, which, if judging from Levi's extended perusal of her legs, might be a tad short.

He shrugged. "It's actually Brad's fault since he gave you the shirt, not me. And if you don't like it, change. No big deal."

"But it is a big deal. I could tell Brad thought I would like it. And I do, except when I get weird." She sighed. "I'm sorry. I'm making a big deal over nothing."

"Brad's not going to be hung up on a shirt. Change if you want, but if we're going to drive together, we need to leave soon."

Zoey picked up a daypack that held Lucy's shirt and bandana, and her to-go gear. With Lucy buckled into the back and Levi in the passenger seat, Zoey drove them over to the ball field.

Levi got Lucy out of the car and secured her leash while Zoey retrieved her daypack from the back. She swung down the hatch and nearly jumped out of her Chucks when she saw the woman standing directly behind her.

"Excuse me." Zoey took a cautious step back. It was the woman from the post office, and she looked awful. Her hair was pulled back in a tight bun that emphasized the thinness of her face, while her application of bright red lipstick hadn't been quite accurate, making her lips look too big and contrasting harshly with her pale skin. Her eyes were heavily made up, and when paired with the fake eyelashes, made her look more like she was going out to a nightclub than to a morning softball game.

"Are you okay?" Zoey asked.

The woman stared from Zoey to Levi.

"You drove here together."

Levi stepped forward with Lucy, angling his body in front of Zoey. "Charissa, can I call someone for you?"

"You remember my name? Do you remember me from that time in Oakland?"

Levi frowned. "Sure I do. Are you here to watch the ballgame?"

"Yes. I want to cheer for you."

"Ah, thank you. You sure you're okay?"

"I'm fine." She turned to follow a group of people making their way to the stands.

"What was that about?"

Levi looked thoughtful. "I'm not sure. She's someone who's always been around. I ran into her once at a gym in Oakland. She made a big deal about being from the same small town and meeting in the big city." He shrugged, but his gaze stayed sharp as he watched the woman's retreat.

A minivan pulled up beside them. Brad and Emma got out to unload their three kids and gear with practiced ease.

"Unca Levi! Unca Levi!" A little girl of about three with glossy black curls bounced up and down in her little white sandals. "Big dog, Unca Levi!"

"Lucy, sit." Levi gave the order, and when the little girl would have launched herself at the dog, he dropped to one knee to wrap his arm around his niece. "Hold on, Amaya. You have to make sure a dog is friendly." With Amaya's big green eyes wide, Levi showed her how to hold out her hand for Lucy to sniff. When Lucy licked her fingers, Amaya erupted in giggles.

Happy toddlers were the best thing in the world.

"Her name is Lucy." Levi smiled down at the enthralled child.

Amaya wrapped her arms around the dog's neck, then beamed up at her father. "Her name's Lucy."

"So I heard." Brad leaned down to lift up his daughter and set her on his shoulders. A dark-haired boy of about four or five stood beside Emma, who was securing a baby girl in a stroller that was packed full of what looked like every kid item that could possibly be needed.

Levi glanced inside the car as Brad pressed a button to slide the door closed. "You sure you didn't leave anything? It looks like you're hauling around enough gear to be ready for the apocalypse."

"Your day will come, brother, so don't get too smug. Let's go."

Zoey walked with Levi as Amaya asked with perfect pronunciation, "What's the apocalypse?"

Once they settled themselves in the bleachers where puffy white clouds provided some shade, Levi and Brad left for the Guns dugout. Zoey found Lucy's shirt, which she'd made into a cape since she hadn't been able to get the arm holes to work for the big dog. Wearing her cape, and with the bandana around her neck, Lucy was ready for the day.

Maddy and her twins joined them, and then Dory arrived with her son, Adrian, and a tiny girl with chubby cheeks in a stroller. Trish and Landon were there, plus Levi's other sister Jenny and her family. The entire group took up most of the first three rows. Zoey positioned herself at the end of the first row near the gate so she could bring Lucy out for her mascot duties when it was time. She was also saving a seat for Eva, who was currently working a shift at the concession stand.

People passing them to climb the steps to the seats higher in the bleachers stopped to pet Lucy, who wore a wide doggy grin and greeted them by raising her paw to shake. The announcer requested the mascots be brought onto the field, and Levi trotted from the dugout to open the gate for Lucy. A boy of about ten wearing a fireman's helmet and a Hoses t-shirt with "Tank Jr." on the back led out a Dalmatian puppy with a red bandana. The pup was at the gangly all-legs stage and tripped over itself walking out onto the field.

The dogs met at home plate and touched noses, then the pup started to dance around Lucy, who ignored him, more interested in the ball in Levi's hand.

Zoey smiled and held out her hand to the young boy. "Hi, I'm Zoey and this is Lucy. What's your name?"

"I'm Marcus. This is my dog. His name's Sparky."

Zoey glanced at Levi, half expecting him to roll his eyes at the predictable name. He didn't, instead reaching down to pet Sparky, who promptly rolled on his back for a tummy rub. The rest of the players trotted onto the field as they were introduced. Sparky scrambled to his feet and reached up to tug on the bandana around Lucy's neck. Lucy tolerated it for a minute, then opened her mouth in a wide yawn before lifting a big paw to knock Sparky to the ground and hold him there, which sent Marcus and the crowd into gales of laughter.

With the introductions over the game started. Zoey returned to her seat to find Eva there wearing a HLFD baseball cap and a red and white baseball jersey. While the rivalry between the teams may have been real, Zoey and Eva joined most of the crowd in cheering for both sides.

The contest was fun, especially because she got to watch Levi. That long, lean body stretching to catch a wild throw or swinging the bat to hit a ball over the head of the shortstop for a base hit was plain yummy. He moved with pure athletic grace, and she thought his enthusiasm reflected his sheer enjoyment in the game.

Enjoying the game, she was starting to understand the strategy of putting Monica Valdez at bat early in the lineup. Whenever she got on base, she challenged the pitcher and was a great base runner. Both she and Diego were fast and got the crowd excited when they stole bases. The crowd's enthusiasm peaked whenever Jack or Tank came up to bat, because both men seemed to hit home runs with effortless ease. Lucy followed the ball, and Zoey had a tight hold on the leash to keep the dog from bounding onto the field after the ball.

The woman Levi had called Charissa cheered wildly whenever he made a play or came up to bat. She'd removed the jacket she'd been wearing before the game, and now sported the Guns jersey, and while team members' jerseys weren't personalized with their names, hers was. Across the back "Gallagher" had been stenciled in black lettering.

Toward the end of the sixth inning, Zoey exited the bleachers to be ready for Levi to drive her and Lucy onto the field in an HLPD SUV. They rode behind the fire truck driven by Tank; Marcus was sitting in the front passenger seat with Sparky on the boy's lap, and the pup's head hung out the window.

The official vehicles were parked at the edge of the field, and Zoey and Marcus led the dogs to home plate. Brad and the fire chief shared the microphone as they worked the crowd. Levi brought out a bag of tennis balls. He hurled balls one after another onto the field and Lucy took off after them, Sparky doing his best to keep up. The puppy tripped over his feet, sprung up again, and had the crowd roaring when he began to bark his disappointment as Lucy chased down the balls. The big dog snagged three tennis balls and trotted back with them in her mouth, Sparky trailing behind her.

When it was time for the game to get under way again, Zoey clipped on Lucy's leash, whereupon she lay on her back, paws in the air, and refused to get up. Zoey cajoled, threatened, and tugged on the leash to no effect. Sparky sent Marcus into fits of laughter when the little dog imitated Lucy, rolling onto his back with his paws hanging.

"Come on, Lucy, time to go."

Lucy sucked up the attention. She closed her eyes, her tail swishing in the dirt.

"Hang on," Levi spoke in Zoey's ear. "I've got an idea." He trotted to the dugout, returning a minute later. He took the microphone from Brad. "Watch this, folks. Lucy, much like her owner, is after my own heart." The "aww" from the crowd had warmth creeping up Zoey's cheeks. She felt a little like a deer in the headlights. Levi held up the familiar red and yellow package for the audience to see. Lucy opened one eye when she heard the crinkling of plastic. "All I have to do is mention her favorite food, and Lucy will do anything. Watch this." He eyed Lucy, then spoke again into the microphone. "Slim Jim."

Lucy sprang to her feet, planted her rear to sit, her gaze riveted on Levi. Sparky must have figured something was up because he also jumped to his feet. Levi tore off a piece of Slim Jim, Lucy's gaze following every movement. He tossed it and she snagged it from midair. Levi made sure Sparky got some, then lured both dogs off the field to the audience's cheers.

Both teams came off the break with a competitive spirit, each determined to win. The score remained tied until the final half inning when Levi hit a double, and Jack followed it with his own double, allowing Levi to score the winning run. He crossed home plate to be met by a crush of his teammates, and then, instead of returning to the dugout, trotted to open the gate. With a flashing grin of triumph, he tilted Zoey's head back for a searing kiss to the accompanying cheer of the crowd.

With Zoey's hand in his, he led her and Lucy out onto the diamond, where both teams met to shake hands. Soon other family members and friends were spilling out onto the field.

Brad and the fire chief took the microphone to announce the dollar amount the fund-raiser had garnered to support local kids' programs. This brought a round of applause, plus hugs and high fives. When the crowd began to break up, Levi had to run to the dugout to get his sport bag. Zoey made her way to the parking lot with Lucy.

She stopped short when she saw her car. "SLUT" had been scrawled in big red letters with what looked like lipstick on the driver's window. She was starting to really hate that word.

Emma and her kids were coming toward the car. Zoey whipped out her phone and snapped a photo, then tugged off Lucy's bandana to wipe away the lettering. No way did the Gallagher children need to see that foul word.

With Lucy secure in the backseat, Zoey folded the bandana so the lipstick was on the inside and stashed it in the glove box. By the time she'd helped Emma get the kids buckled in, Brad and Levi were back and helped stow the gear.

The plan was for the Gallagher clan to meet up at Emma and Brad's lakeside home for an early evening barbecue. This gave Zoey a couple of hours to get home and put together the pasta salad she'd prepped, and for Levi to shower.

A barbecue would be fun, and she truly loved the Gallaghers, but she was starting to feel uncomfortable being constantly paired with Levi. He acted like they were a couple, other people saw them as a couple, and even in her own head she caught herself thinking in terms of her and Levi. And while she'd be damned if she'd allow herself to be intimidated, she was starting to think the choice of the word "slut" might have something to do with Levi.

What bothered her the most was that despite her efforts to limit their relationship, her feelings for him had deepened to something she wasn't sure she wanted to put a label on. Maybe she needed to ease back a bit, let things with Levi ride until she had a better handle on them.

Levi dropped into the passenger seat, twisting around to pet Lucy. "You're amazing, Luce. Taught little Sparky a thing or two."

Zoey drove out of the parking lot and onto the highway. She glanced at Levi, then away when his gaze met hers.

"What's going on?"

He was nothing if not perceptive. She picked up her phone off her lap and handed it to him, holding her thumb over the home button to unlock the screen. "Go to photos and look at the most recent picture."

He did as directed, then stared at the screen. "What the hell? This was today?"

"It was on my car when I came out after the game."

"You wiped it off? That was evidence."

"Yes, I wiped it off. Your brother's family was parked right next to me. I didn't want those kids to see that."

He grunted. "I can't blame you for that. What did you use to wipe it off with? Did you throw it away?"

"I used Lucy's bandana. It's in the glove box."

Levi retrieved the bandana, unfolding it to reveal the red smeared onto the fabric. He sniffed it. "Is this lipstick?"

"That's what I thought."

Carefully, he refolded it, setting the bandana on his knee. "We're going to figure this out. That's a promise."

Chapter Seventeen

Levi sat on Brad and Emma's deck and took a sip from a longneck bottle of beer. You couldn't ask for a better view. Hangman Lake reflected the orange and pink sunset, and the rough peaks of the Sierras rose like uneven teeth against the sky. At the other end of the deck, Brad wielded his spatula in front of an enormous built-in grill. On the lawn, Eva and Diego had corralled the kids into a game that looked like kiddie croquet.

The shooting he and his former partner had been involved in might have been what had pushed him to break away from his old life, but he wasn't sorry. He only wished the serenity of the scene would help quiet his unease. Zoey was pulling away from him. She'd come to the barbecue but appeared preoccupied and distant. Not that she didn't have reason to be worried, but there was something else going on with her.

He glanced across the deck to where she sat on a bench in what appeared to be an earnest conversation with Emma. Before that, she'd been buddied up with Eva and Diego. He absolutely didn't expect her to spend all afternoon with him, but the feeling she was avoiding him pissed him off. If there was a problem, she should tell him straight out. He didn't think it was solely worry over whoever was harassing her. She'd been dealing with that better than most people would, but he didn't know for sure because she wouldn't have a damn conversation with him.

Usually that would be okay. If a woman didn't want to be with him, he let her go without complaint. He wasn't a complicated guy, and he dealt with people by being straightforward. He sure as hell wasn't looking for drama in relationships. If a woman started pulling back, finding excuses not to spend time with him, playing games, it was time to move on.

When he lost interest, he was up front about it. That had been his modus operandi for the past decade. But damn it, this was different.

For starters, he didn't think Zoey was playing games so much as running scared. She didn't reveal much, but they had a connection, and he'd bet she felt it too. He drummed his fingers on his knee.

Okay, he *more* than liked Zoey. And wasn't that a jolt to the system. He was going to figure out who was bothering her, then they could talk it out. He wanted to know where he stood, to see if he was the only one with the uncomfortable feelings.

This harassment shit had to stop. He'd bagged the bandana with the lipstick on it and swung by the police station before the barbecue to log it as evidence. He had an idea about that lipstick, and there was no time like the present to bring his brother in on it.

He wasn't able to get Brad away from the others because as soon as Levi rose to his feet, Emma stepped onto the deck with the proclamation that everyone was to come inside and grab a plate. Resisting the need to run his theory by his brother, Levi walked into the kitchen.

Emma had all the food arranged as a buffet on the kitchen counter. Levi spotted Zoey and edged in line behind her. She wore a tank top and skirt that emphasized her curvy figure, and her black curls had escaped from a long ponytail that trailed down her back, exposing the nape of her neck. Amaya seemed to have decided Zoey was her current favorite person and was propped on Zoey's hip.

She cast him a sideways glance when she noticed him behind her. "Hey."

"Hey back."

"Unca Levi."

"That's right, kid. Best uncle in the world is here."

Zoey moved along the counter. He stacked his hamburger with lettuce, tomato, and onion, adding a splash of ketchup, while she piled her plate with what he considered sides: pasta salad, balled melon, baked beans, deviled eggs. She'd set her plate down to add her selections, but now she was having trouble managing her plate, napkins, utensils, and a kid.

"I want a quesadilla," Amaya announced.

"Hmm, doesn't look like quesadilla is on the menu tonight," Zoey said. "How about a hot dog."

"Don't like hot dogs."

"Yeah, me either. I like pasta salad. I bet you do, too."

Amaya seemed to give this idea undue consideration before nodding her head regally like the princess she was. "I like pasta."

"Good girl. I'll share mine with you."

"Let me get that for you." Levi reached around Zoey to snag her plate, leaving her no choice but to follow him out on the deck. He set both their plates down at the outdoor table. He wanted to sit with her and figured this was the best way to ensure that happened.

"I sit with Unca Levi."

"You bet. I'll get us some drinks and we'll sit together." He looked at Zoey. "What can I get you?"

She gave him a look that said she knew she was being maneuvered, but spoke in an even tone. "Water, please."

He returned a minute later with water for all three of them. They ate, and Levi couldn't help noticing that while she responded to Amaya's chatter, Zoey didn't say much to him. The animation that had always made her appear so vibrant had dulled.

"I have to pee." Amaya gave Zoey an expectant look.

"Do you need me to go with you?"

Emma demonstrated super-sharp mom hearing because she rose from her spot farther down the table to take her daughter by the hand. "She's pretty good but we don't want to risk an accident. Come on, angel."

With the little girl gone, Zoey fiddled with her fork. She hadn't eaten much.

"Hey, you okay?"

She glanced at him, then away, and Levi could have sworn there was a gleam of tears in her eyes. Then she pushed up from the table, gathered up her plate and cup, and rushed into the house. Levi was about to go after her when Brad also got up from the table and gave a head jerk to his brother.

Levi glanced into the house, then followed Brad off the deck and down the slope that ended at the lakeshore. Levi turned to his brother. "What's going on?"

"Owner of the self-storage in Bishop came through with the list of people they're leasing units to."

"Let me guess, Paul Clauson is on that list."

"You'd be guessing right. I'm working on a warrant, but the judge doesn't like to be bothered on the weekend. I'll call to give him a push, but he's got an ego I'll have to dance around."

Levi shook his head. "Helping to put a bad guy behind bars isn't enough of an incentive to get him off his ass?"

"Hasn't been in all the years I've known him, and I've known him for a few. He'll use a power play at every opportunity. Regardless, we'll have it by Monday at the latest."

Levi nodded. "I've got another angle. You know Charissa Winslow?"

"Yeah. She's a clerk over in the city services office."

"How would you describe her?"

Brad raised an eyebrow but went along with Levi's questioning. "A strange woman. Way too thin. I've wondered if she's anorexic. Doesn't look healthy. She was at the game today."

"Did you notice the jersey she was wearing?" When Brad shook his head, Levi continued. "It was the Guns jersey, but she'd printed 'Gallagher' on the back. And she made a big deal whenever I made a play or got a hit."

"Think she has a thing for you?"

"If she does, it's an unhealthy thing. I ran into her once at a gym I belonged to in Oakland. It seemed odd at the time that she'd be there. And she always seems to be wherever we are. It could have been her last week watching us at Mom's from the other side of the arroyo. Could be she's targeting Zoey because she's jealous of our relationship."

He told Brad about the word scrawled in lipstick on Zoey's car. "We saw her before the game. She looked off, maybe on something. She made a comment about Zoey and me arriving together and was wearing lipstick about that color. Add the use of the word 'slut' on the car and the LookBook post, and there's a pattern."

Brad bent his head in thought, then met Levi's gaze. "I'm not saying you're wrong, but it's all circumstantial. Get me more so we have a basis for a search warrant."

***

Levi arrived home to find Zoey's cottage dark. They'd driven to Brad's separately at Zoey's request. She'd told him she needed more time to put together her pasta salad. Now he thought that was a bullshit ploy to keep them apart.

Levi and Brad had made a quick trip to the police station to do a background check on Charissa Winslow. They hadn't found much other than that her mother had died two years previous and that she lived in the house her mother had owned.

Zoey had left the party before he'd returned, and now he didn't know where she was. He could text her, but that would make him look like he was checking up on her, and since he didn't know what was going on in her head, he didn't want her to get the wrong idea.

He prowled around the cabin, feeling out of sorts. He hated brooding. He decided that since he hadn't done it yet, he'd hang his big-ass TV and hook it up to the cable and Internet. He killed a half hour doing that. Once done, he turned on ESPN, got a beer from the fridge, and went to the window for the millionth time since he'd gotten home. He still wasn't used to how dark it got at night, how it made him feel like he was alone in the universe. Which sounded pathetic.

He settled onto the couch and took another pull on his beer, trying to focus on the game on the screen. Didn't look like the Giants were playing any better than they had the year before. The newly installed security light at the front of his house came on, followed by a knock. He set down the bottle and used the remote to mute the TV. He opened the door and felt his heart land at his feet with a thud.

There she was. Spiraling locks of hair, beautiful brown eyes, and an expression on her face that made him want to grin and kiss her at the same time. He rubbed a heel over his chest to ease the ache.

"Hey."

"I was doing fine, you know."

Funny how he knew exactly what she was talking about. "Yeah, well, so was I."

"I didn't want to feel like this."

His aching heart gave a solid lurch. Finally, an acknowledgment. "I agree. It sucks. But we have to deal with it." He paused. "Where's Lucy?"

"See?" She pointed a finger at him, stepping forward with a little wobble to jab him in the chest. "That's exactly what I'm talking about. I don't want to care about you any more than I already do, then wham-o, you ask me about my dog and my stupid heart gets all mushy. She's in the house, by the way, probably sound asleep."

He frowned when "sound asleep" came out more like "shound asheep." He glanced past her. There was no Prius parked in front of her cottage. "You been drinking?"

"That, mister," which sounded like "mishter," "is none of your business. But Eva had this really amazing hard cider, and Diego says I'm a lightweight."

"Okay." Which told him who she'd been with. He stepped back. "You want to come in?"

She strode past him, nose in the air. She wore pink stretchy pants with a red college sweatshirt and green Chucks on her feet. The colors clashed and he figured he was a goner if he thought she looked even cuter because of it. She gestured to the silent TV where a reporter was interviewing the Giants' pitcher. "See. There's another reason we're noncompatible. You like sports. Sports are stupid. A bunch of overpaid jocks getting overpaid for chasing around a stupid ball."

"I think you mean *in*compatible, and you said overpaid twice."

She blinked at him. "Did not."

Figuring it was wise to let that go, he asked her, "How did you get home?"

"Justin brought me. He said I was in no condition to drive, which is totally untrue. I only let him drive me home because he was making such a big deal about it. Then he said you and me should talk, because talking is what grown-ups do. Pfft." She fluttered her hand in dismissal of Justin's advice. "I'm not drunk."

Levi decided Justin wasn't such a bad guy, after all. "Honey, you're toasted."

"A lot you know. Do you have toast?"

He stared at her. "You want toast?"

"Yes, please, with strawberry jam. I'll sit here." She gestured grandly to the couch.

Concluding that he'd had about the strangest conversation ever, Levi left her sitting on the couch watching the muted TV and went to the kitchen to make toast. Since she liked tea, he put water on to heat while he hunted up the bags his mom had brought over. A few minutes later he was carrying a steaming mug and a plate piled with strawberry jam-topped toast into the living room, stopping when he spotted Zoey, head on a cushion, feet curled under her, fast asleep. Well, hell.

He set the mug on the coffee table, then sat beside it. He took a bite of toast, chewing as he considered what to do with her. In the end, he tugged off the Chucks and dragged a blanket off his bed to drape over her. Turning off the TV, he went to his room, stripped down to his boxers, and crawled into bed.

***

Levi came slowly to consciousness feeling warm skin pressed against his. The dark curls tickling his nose told him he wasn't dreaming. He opened his eyes to the quiet light of early morning. Zoey was curled around him, legs entwined in his, arm circling his waist, her head nestled on his shoulder. Good fortune was certainly smiling on him. All he wanted to do was turn into her and do as nature was screaming for him to do, but consent had been drummed into his head with a metaphorical hammer. He figured an ice-cold shower was in order and shifted away. She tightened her arm and had him going still when he felt warm lips brush his chest. Lifting his hand, he finger-combed the explosion of black hair back from her face to find heavy-lidded eyes open and aware.

"Good morning." Her voice sounded husky, and he decided right then he'd never heard a sexier sound.

"Good morning back." He ran his fingers through her hair again, the flower scent surrounding him. "When did you decide to join me?"

"A couple of hours ago. I used the bathroom, got a drink of water, and peeked in here. I had to decide whether I would be taking advantage if I joined you."

"Side note, take advantage any damn time you please."

Her smile fluttered even as her hand began to slide through the hair on his chest. "It was nice to fall asleep lying next to you."

"I think you can tell how I feel about that." His erection was throbbing where it rested under her thigh. Her hand drifted in its exploration of his chest, moving along his pecs and across his ribs.

He tugged off the sweatshirt she still wore, freeing him to do his own exploring. He unclipped her bra, then buried his face between her breasts, using his thumb to tease a nipple before following the movement with his mouth. He groaned when she wrapped her hand around his erection and thrust into her hold. "Hell yeah, baby, keep doing that."

She did better than that. Shimmying down his body, she gave him a sultry look as she took him in her mouth. He couldn't help the involuntary jerk, but she didn't release her hold, only pulling him farther in. "Holy Jesus, you're good at that."

He lay back, never losing sight of her while he let her work her magic, the pleasure pulsating through him, until he was on the brink of losing control. She released him and he reached for her, tugging her pants down and off, then turning her onto her back. It was his turn to use his mouth, licking her, loving her, building the tension until she was panting his name.

She pulled on his hair. "I want you in me. Now."

He fumbled with the drawer in the bedside table, found a condom, and rolled it on. He moved his body over hers and thrust forward, the emotions he'd been battling swelling to nearly overwhelming intensity.

She wrapped her legs around his ass, raising her hips to pull him in deeper. They moved together, perfectly synchronized, reaching higher. He held back his release, pushing into her harder and faster until she convulsed around him, crying out her climax. He followed seconds later with a hoarse shout.

He rolled until she lay sprawled on top of him. His hand drifted down her back and over her rounded ass. He'd nearly dozed off when she stirred.

"I need to let Lucy out."

"I'll do it."

"No, I will."

There was something in her tone that had alarm bells ringing. When she would have rolled off him, he caught her face between his palms. "Are we good now?"

"I don't know."

He expected an affirmation that they had moved past whatever had been bugging her. "What don't you know?"

"You're a good guy, Levi. It's me who has commitment issues."

"Save the 'it's not you, it's me' crap." It took a monumental effort to push the irritation aside. "Spend the day with me."

"What?"

"Remember we were going on a date. I'd been aiming for next weekend, but I'm on duty then. Come out with me today."

"Where to?"

"Yosemite. We can be there in less than an hour. We'll have brunch at the lodge, and there's a place in the village where we can rent electric bikes. I've been wanting to try them out, and riding around the valley might be pretty cool."

"That sounds really nice." She chewed her lip. "We wouldn't be able to take Lucy. Let me call Eva. She and Diego have a fenced yard and have doggy sat for me in the past."

"Great. While you call Eva, I'll let Lucy out."

***

Zoey climbed a contour line over the talus slope looking for fresh hay piles that were evidence of the pika preparing for the winter. A sound came from above her, and she glanced up to see the furry creature that looked like a small rabbit but without the ears perched on a flat rock calling out its warning. She documented the sighting, moving farther along the contour line, where she found two hay piles and recorded their contents. Climbing over the rocks wasn't Lucy's favorite activity, so she'd stayed in the meadow below the talus and was currently sprawled in the shade of a grouping of pine trees.

Her survey finally complete, Zoey made her way off the rocks. She joined Lucy, where she retrieved her portable dog water dish from the doggie pack and filled it with water from her thermos. They shared a PBJ, then Zoey took a swig of water before stowing their gear and rising to her feet. "Let's go, girl. We'll get back early. We did good work for a Monday."

They took the path back down the mountain to where she'd left the Forest Service vehicle. There was a bathroom, well, a vault toilet to be precise, at the trailhead that she'd make use of before the drive back to the field office.

Since she'd started her day early, she'd be done by three. She had chores to do around her house, and since her fridge currently lacked even the most basic food to sustain life, stopping at the grocery store to restock was a must. She could give Lucy a bath. And if she kept busy enough, maybe she'd stop thinking about Levi.

Saturday evening she'd shown up on his doorstep tipsy. Okay, a little drunk. Two days later, shame still brought a flush to her cheeks. She hadn't been trashed. If she had, then maybe she wouldn't remember that she'd about admitted her feelings for him.

Waking up on his couch early Sunday morning had been insult to injury. Then, instead of leaving, as any sane woman would have, she'd joined him in bed, which led to great sex. Then, before she could marshal her defenses, she agreed to spend the entire day with him. A wonderful day in gorgeous Yosemite with a guy who made her heart trip with something as simple as a smile.

Levi made her feel too much.

She was ten seconds away from falling in love with him. She needed distance, that was all.

When she was with him, all she could think about were the sparks that ignited whenever they touched. Or how much she liked his eyes, especially when the blue burned hotter when they kissed. Or how amazing sex with Levi rocked her world.

She needed the breathing space to think rationally about their relationship.

She used stepping-stones to cross a creek, and with only a hundred yards to go, she followed the trail from the shade beside a creek into the open, Lucy about ten yards ahead of her. A loud crack split the air. The rifle fire had her dropping to a crouch amidst the brush. Another shot rang out, echoing against the rock face on the far side of the valley.

Zoey grabbed the whistle she'd trained Lucy to respond to and blew to give the shrill call. When Lucy bounded to her side, she grabbed her collar and attached the leash. Mid-June was too early for hunting season, so that meant poachers who were recklessly endangering hikers and anyone else enjoying the outdoors. She wasn't a ranger or game warden. She had no law enforcement authority and didn't carry a gun. Going after illegal hunters wasn't an option. But that didn't mean she couldn't inform the authorities.

The trailhead was about fifty feet away. She edged out of the shadows, then began to run across the last thirty feet, Lucy in front of her. Another shot rang out. This time the bullet ricocheted off a boulder only a few behind her and Zoey's heart slammed into her throat. Either the poacher had really bad eyesight and had mistaken her and Lucy for wild game, or he had a completely different kind of game in mind.

They made it to the bathroom, Zoey bringing Lucy behind the concrete block structure for protection. She crouched down, her arm around the big dog's neck, heart beating a frantic tattoo in her chest.

Grabbing the satellite phone from her belt, she keyed in the numbers and waited for her call to be picked up. It was routed to a California Highway Patrol dispatcher and she tried to speak calmly despite feeling like she was going to hyperventilate. She recounted what had happened, her name and job title, and her location. The dispatcher told her to wait someplace safe until help arrived.

Zoey took that time to scan the parking area. Her Forest Service truck was the only vehicle in the lot. She peeked her head around the corner of the bathroom, looking in the direction the shots had come from. The brush-covered slope behind her was topped by a rocky ridge, which provided plenty of hiding places. She waited and was rewarded several minutes later when movement caught her eye. She dug out her binoculars, brought them to her eyes, and adjusted the focus.

A dark figure separated from a clump of boulders, and for a brief moment was silhouetted against the bright sky of early afternoon. She couldn't tell if the person was male or female. But she saw a rifle held in one hand.

She watched for another minute, then, counting on there being only one shooter, rose to her feet and whispered, "C'mon, Lucy."

Adrenaline surged as she dug in her side pocket for her keys even as she raced for the truck with Lucy. Zoey opened the driver's door and her baby hopped in ahead of her. Fearing a bullet could rip through her at any moment, she buckled Lucy in before jamming the key into the starter. The engine roared to life and Zoey was steering out of the dirt parking area, tires churning up dust, even as she pulled on her seatbelt.

She had an idea where the shooter was heading. The trail from the ridge sloped down to another trail, about a mile back, that had forked off the one she'd been on. The trail met a creek at the bottom of the slope, and from there crossed the road to continue onto a small lake.

Zoey wanted to get to that crossing before the shooter. Driving as fast as she dared on the dirt road, she dodged the worst of the ruts and subsidence until finally reaching the paved section. Now able to go faster, she sped around the curve of the mountain, Lucy bracing her front legs against the motion. There it was: the sign marking the trail crossing and a turnout big enough for one vehicle. The vehicle that was parked there was a smallish, silver Ford SUV.

Zoey hit the brakes and brought the truck to a fast stop. She rolled down her window, but before she could use her cell phone to snap a picture of the license plate, a shot rang out. She let out a startled yelp and threw down her phone while stomping on the accelerator.

Another rifle crack, this time followed by the solid thud of impact on metal. The truck had been hit. She spun around a curve in the road and without braking took a quick survey. No blood from her or Lucy, no blown tires, no exploding gas tanks.

She was good.

Chapter Eighteen

"You did what? What the hell were you thinking?" Levi stood with hands on hips, looking way too official in his uniform, eyes blazing.

"I slowed down to get a picture of the license plate."

The twin blazes burned hotter. "You should have gotten out of there as fast as you could. What if you'd been hit? What if Lucy had been hit? Would it have been worth getting the picture then?"

"Lucy and I are fine." Zoey decided now wasn't the best time to bring up that her truck had a bullet hole in its side. Instead of returning to the Forest Service office and picking up her car, she'd driven straight to the Hangman's Loss police department.

They stood in Brad's office where he leaned back against a cabinet that held a coffeemaker, his arms crossed over his chest, his gaze moving back and forth between Levi and Zoey like he was watching a ping-pong match. Lucy had decided all the action had worn her out and lay stretched at Brad's feet, her rumbling snores filling the air.

"You took a careless risk," Levi growled.

Zoey was getting a little tired of being chastised like she was incapable of rational thought. She stepped up to Levi, her own eyes narrowed. "I absolutely was not careless. I'm not a careless person. Someone was shooting at me and I didn't want them to get away with it. I also don't want to worry every time I step outside of my home that there is some crazy person waiting for me with a rifle. So, yeah, I calculated that I could get a photo to help identify the person before the shooter could make it to the road."

Levi tipped back his head, closing his eyes as he seemed to be willing himself to calm down. He leveled his gaze on her again. "Fine, it's done. The Forest Service has jurisdiction in the location where the shots were fired, but we will investigate because it's part of an open case. Do you have any idea of the type of weapon used?"

She shook her head. "Too far away. I can't give you a description other than it was a rifle. I don't know guns so I don't think I'd be able to tell you anything about it even if I held it in my hand."

"Damn. Okay. Send Brad and me the photo of the plate and we'll run it."

"I didn't get the photo."

"What? You said you slowed to take a picture."

Zoey eyed him cautiously. He was probably going to go totally crazy about the next part. "Um, you could probably get some evidence from my truck."

"Meaning?"

"There's a bullet hole at the back of my truck. I slowed, rolled down my window, then I heard more two shots. One hit my truck and I floored it. That's why I didn't get a picture."

Levi clenched his fists, the muscle in his jaw working overtime, but he didn't say a word. Brad moved to his desk and picked up the phone. "Monica, can you meet me in the parking lot?" He thanked her, then hung up.

"Monica and I will look at the hit to the truck."

Brad paused on his way out the door, glancing from Levi to Zoey like he was afraid they'd come to blows. "Glad you're safe, Zoey. You two going to be okay if I step out?"

"We're fine," Levi growled. Again.

Zoey wasn't so sure, but Brad must have trusted his brother because he disappeared down the hall.

The minute he was gone, Levi went to the door and shut it. Turning back, slowly, he stalked toward Zoey, making her think of a blue-eyed cougar on the prowl. He stopped in front of her, grasped her by her elbows, and hefted her onto tiptoes as he brought his lips down on hers.

There was nothing tentative about this kiss. Anger, hunger, and possession tangled together, signifying something deeper. Her lips parted and he took the kiss deeper and hotter. She felt a shudder run through his body, and an answering trembling in hers, then his hands loosened as his lips gentled.

She broke the kiss and settled back on her heels, reaching up to place a hand on his cheek. "It's okay." She wasn't sure who she was reassuring, herself or Levi. "I'm safe. Lucy is safe. We're fine."

"I'm not. You could have been killed."

She shook her head and repeated, "I'm fine."

A quick rapping sounded on the door before it was pushed open. Monica popped her head through the door. "I recovered a round."

"Where did it hit the truck?" Levi asked.

"The rear. It passed through the fender above the back tire well and lodged in the bed liner on the other side. I'm going to send the slug to the lab."

Levi nodded, then Brad entered the room, a couple sheets of paper in his hand. He nodded to Zoey. "Got a call from Logan. Sheriff's deputies went up the trail where you say the shots came from and recovered shell casings. They're thirty-thirty center fire."

"Really?" Levi raised a brow.

"Why is that surprising?"

Brad turned to her. "Thirty-thirty rifles were fairly common for deer hunting in the first half of the twentieth century, but they're not used that often anymore."

"Does that make it easier or more difficult to catch the shooter?"

Brad shrugged. "That'll depend." He looked to his brother. "Warrant finally came through to search Clauson's self-storage unit. Let's go see what we find."

***

Zoey maneuvered her Prius into a parking space on Main Street, a half block down from Hangman's Best Café and Bakery, the closest spot she could find. Maddy's business operated as a popular gathering place for the town and did a steady breakfast and lunch business. Zoey had left Lucy at the cottage, then returned to town to pick up dog food.

She pushed open the door of the café and was greeted by the mouthwatering smells of cinnamon and coffee. Maddy stood behind the counter, her sunny smile shifting to a look of concern when she saw Zoey. "Honey, are you okay?"

"I'm fine. The small-town grapevine beats social media, hands down, for spreading news. Are you closing?"

"Soon. We close at three, so we still have twenty minutes. I'll take your order, then I want to know what happened today. What can I get for you?"

"I texted Eva and she said you still haven't sold out of your delicious broccoli cheddar soup. I'd like a tub of that to take home." Zoey perused the bins of fresh-baked bread. "I'll also take a small round of the French to go with it."

"You got it."

Eva stepped through the swinging door. "Hey, there, bestie. I thought I heard your voice." She fisted her hands on her hips. "I had to hear you'd been *shot* at today from Maddy. Something you neglected to mention in your text."

"I kinda figured better to deliver that news face-to-face."

"True, so you're forgiven."

"You both go sit at a booth." Maddy gestured to the dining room. "I'll get us all tea and a pastry we can split between us, on the house. I want to hear what happened too."

Zoey was happy to comply. She was leaning back against a cushioned seat and sipping citrus chamomile tea while Maddy used a knife to divide up a French apple tart. For the first time since the shooting she felt the tension ease in her shoulders.

Eva looked at her expectantly. "Spill."

With another sip of tea to fortify her, Zoey related the details of the incident that was already taking on a surreal quality. She concluded with Levi's response at the police station.

"Oh, I love hot and bothered boyfriend kisses," Eva sighed.

"Levi is not exactly my boyfriend. I'm not sure what we are, but boyfriend and girlfriend scares me, so we're not using that."

Maddy pushed a small plate with apple tart in front of each of them. "I get what you're saying, but be honest with him. Levi has had a rough time since the shooting in Oakland, and he deserves that you be up front with him if you can't return his feelings."

"He hasn't told me about the shooting in Oakland."

"You might have heard about it in the news. That's what led to him coming back home."

Zoey stared at Maddy, a sinking sensation in her stomach. "I've asked what led him to leave the Oakland PD, and even mentioned I'd heard about a shooting, but he deflected and told me he wanted to come home to be close to family."

Maddy shrugged. "Family was a big part of his decision, but the rest is his story to tell, so ask him about it. He's still dealing with what happened and I worry about him."

Zoey nodded, her mind spinning.

Eva set down her tea mug. "I'm so glad you're safe. It sounds like Levi and Brad are following all leads. They'll figure out who's been threatening you."

"I hope so. This whole thing scares the pants off me."

Twenty minutes later, Zoey returned home, carrying the cute paper bag from the café. She didn't like feeling wary as she approached the cottage. None of her porch furniture had been overturned, there was no disgusting meat dumped in front of her door, and while it would have made her feel more secure if Levi's motorcycle were parked in front of his cabin, she shouldn't bank her safety on him.

She took a bracing breath and told herself she was holding it together. Except for when thoughts of what could have happened on that mountainside slipped through. She closed the door and keyed in the disarm code on the new alarm system, another unhappy reminder of the danger she faced.

Lucy greeted her with a tail wag. "So glad you're safe, big girl," she told Lucy as she gave her a rub. The dog followed her into the kitchen where the soup went into the refrigerator to be heated later. Zoey pulled out a bottle of Chablis, uncorked it, went to pour, but had to set down the bottle when her hand shook so badly it rattled against the wineglass.

She gripped the countertop. Delayed reaction, that's all. Who wouldn't be frazzled after what had happened? It wasn't every day that she got shot at, and then on top of that to learn the guy she was kind of in a relationship with had been involved in a serious police shooting and he hadn't told her.

Her iPad was on the counter. Curiosity overrode her good sense and had her typing out search parameters. A long list of articles came up. She tapped on one, read it to the end, then the next. After two articles, she was sick to her stomach, and clicked off the tablet.

Mind reeling, she dug out her softest flannel pajamas, found her fuzzy socks, and took them to the bathroom. She'd planned to take a quick shower, but instead opted for something she rarely did, twisting the taps to fill the tub with hot water.

After dumping in lavender bath salts she'd had for years and had used only once, she caught her hair up in a messy bun, undressed, and stepped into the tub. She slid into the frothy water, and with her head tipped back against the edge of the tub, closed her eyes as the heat and fragrance engulfed her.

Images and sounds echoed through her mind. The crack of gunfire, the realization the bullets were meant for her, racing for cover while waiting for the shot that would find its target and rip through her body or Lucy's.

She wondered how the young black man Levi had shot had felt. She should have known better than to get involved with someone in law enforcement. Her chest felt constricted and her breath started coming in gulps.

Zoey brought her trembling hands to her face. Her throat tightened and the tears she hated refused to be held back, so she let them come. She was safe now. She needed to remember that. When someone had shot at her, she'd gotten herself out of the situation, and despite what Levi had said, had been smart about it.

Getting out of a relationship with Levi with her heart intact was an entirely different matter. Her shoulders shook and she pressed a washcloth to her eyes. When the sobs finally petered out, she splashed water over her face, then leaned her head back against the rim of the tub again.

The crying jag had exhausted her, but maybe letting go for even those few minutes was cathartic, because by the time the water had cooled and she'd drained the tub, then took a quick shower to rinse, she felt calmer and better able to cope with whatever came next.

She was scooping dog food into Lucy's dish when she heard a knock on the door. Levi. Dread formed a knot of tension in the middle of her chest. She had no idea how to deal with the chaotic emotions he dragged from her.

She'd been worried she might be falling in love with him, but now heaped on top of that was the keen disappointment he'd been involved in a shooting he'd told her nothing about, even after she'd asked.

Love hurt, and she wanted nothing to do with it.

A loud rapping sounded again. She set the dog dish on the floor, said "crickets" to the expectant Lucy, and, despite her confidence that it was Levi, peeked through the curtains over the front windows before unlatching the deadbolt and opening the door.

He stood in the glow of the porch light wearing a dark flannel shirt open over a white t-shirt. He had the brooding scowl down perfect.

"Hey."

His gaze searched her face and his brows came down in a frown. "You've been crying."

She could never accuse him of being oblivious. She hitched a shoulder.

"Can I come in?"

She paused, then pulled the door open wider.

He walked in, and when he raised a hand as if to touch her, she stepped back.

He dropped his hand. "What's going on?"

"Honestly? I don't know. I'm a mess. I'll let you know when I figure it out."

"You're not a mess. You're dealing with a lot, so cut yourself some slack."

And here he was acting all understanding.

With another shrug, because that was about all she could come up with, she turned to the kitchen where she put the kettle on to heat water for tea and set the container from the café in the microwave. She retrieved two bowls from the cupboard. Lucy rested her chin on the counter.

Zoey glanced at the dog dish. It looked like it had been sucked clean by a vacuum. "Out, Lucy." Zoey pointed to the living room. "Go lie down." When Lucy trudged to her spot in front of the fireplace, Zoey turned to Levi. "I'm heating soup, which I'll share with you, but it doesn't mean anything."

"What the hell's that supposed to mean?"

"I don't want you reading anything into it."

There was that hand through the hair thing that he did whenever he was agitated. He'd be an awful poker player. "Jesus, Zoey. I have no idea where I stand with you, and I'm not a playing games kind of guy."

"Are you a shooting an unarmed black man kind of guy?" She slapped a hand over her mouth. She hadn't meant to say that. She'd meant to ask him what had happened, to let him explain.

He jerked back, then his face went carefully blank. "What do you think you know about it?"

"Not what you told me, because I've asked you why you left Oakland, and you didn't share anything about a shooting."

"And you've jumped to conclusions."

"Which I wouldn't have done if you'd told me yourself. What happened?"

"It sounds like you've already got that figured out. Who told you about it?"

"Maddy, but she didn't explain what happened. She said I should talk to you."

He narrowed his gaze. "But that's not what you did. You search it online? Did you read reports about me shooting an unarmed man and decide I was guilty of murder? These things are tried in the court of social media, truth be damned." The words came out in a staccato burst of sound.

"If you had told me, I wouldn't have had to search online."

"So there's nothing more to be said, is there?" His eyes turned an ice blue. "I came by to tell you that we searched Clauson's self-storage unit in Bishop this afternoon."

Zoey wrapped her arms around herself as a chill skittered down her spine. She tried to focus on Levi's words, and not that she'd made a big mistake. "And?"

"He'd been there ahead of us. The security camera from Saturday morning showed him carrying out two long guns in cases."

"So it was him shooting at me today."

"Could have been. Did he ever spout off, vow revenge against you, complain that you'd ruined his life, or some such crap?" He might have been any cop requesting information in a dispassionate tone, emotional distance clearly marked.

"Not to me, but you can talk with my mom. He might have said something to her. If he did, she didn't pass it on to me. Are you going to arrest him again?"

"When we find him. He wasn't at his house and is in violation of the conditions of his bond. Do you remember if he had friends he hung out with when he lived here, someone who might give him a place to hide out?"

She shook her head. "From what I remember, his friends were all cops."

"Can you stay with someone else tonight? If it was Clauson who shot at you, he failed, and he'll try again." She saw the brief flash of emotion, but it was gone before she could identify it. A muscle in his jaw tightened.

She was already shaking her head. "I'm fine. I have Lucy, plus a new alarm system."

"Which won't do jack shit to stop a man with a gun from kicking in the door and shooting the dog and then you. Clauson knows every cop in the county will be after him. He's either on the run or determined to finish his mission before he's arrested or dead." Levi's expression turned even more grim. "I'll sleep on your couch."

"You will not. I don't want you in my house."

"Too bad. I'm staying. We're both going to have to suck it up until this is over. I'll make you a deal. I'll stay until we stop whoever is stalking you, then I'll find another place to live so we won't have to see each other every time one of us steps outside."

Chapter Nineteen

Levi watched Zoey turn the Prius around and head down the driveway to the road, Lucy a bulky shadow in the backseat. He didn't know when he'd ever been in a shittier mood. They'd spent the evening and morning ignoring each other. He didn't like being pissed off, but he was angry with Zoey for buying into the bullshit spewed in the cesspool on the Internet, and for not getting his side of the story about the shooting first. It didn't make him any less angry that he knew good and well she'd asked him what had happened. Twice. If he'd been up front with her, she might have gotten the facts from him and not gone looking online. But he'd wanted her to trust him first before he told her the details of what happened, and why he left the Oakland PD.

Of the twenty words they'd said to each other this morning, he'd extracted a promise that she wouldn't go out in the field today, that she would work from her office, and she'd alert her coworkers to be on the look-out for anyone acting suspiciously.

Levi went to his cabin, where he put on his motorcycle gear, grabbed his go bag to strap to the rack, and headed for his bike. Once at the department, he changed into his uniform and sat through morning roll call, where Brad gave an update on the Hardesty case. While he listened, Levi mulled over what had been bugging him since the shooting the day before. He joined Brad in the break room after roll call.

"I don't think it was Clauson shooting at Zoey."

"Why's that?" Brad asked.

"For starters, Clauson is trained law enforcement. She and Lucy were out in the open. He'd have hit them."

"Could be he only wanted to scare her. What else you got?"

"The shooter had to hike up a steep trail with a lot of switchbacks to get upslope from Zoey." Levi shrugged. "Clauson's at least a hundred pounds overweight, and the trail is at the eight-thousand-foot elevation mark. That's a tough hike if you're not in shape."

Brad nodded. "Agreed, but not impossible. Anything else?"

"Yeah. Clauson never mentioned Zoey when we arrested him. He assumed we were there because his neighbor had complained about the music." Levi rubbed his temple where a headache had settled. "There was child porn on his laptop, but no evidence that he'd put up that post targeting Zoey." He shrugged. "The post, writing 'slut' in lipstick on her car window, the poisoned meat—rat poison, by the way, the labs came back—feels female to me."

"You're thinking Charissa Winslow."

"I am. I don't have anything concrete, but a bunch of small things are adding up. And I think she's harassing Zoey because she thinks Zoey and I are together."

"You're not?"

"I don't know what the hell we are right now, except not talking."

Brad shook his head. "Don't blow it. You're good together."

"What makes you think I'm the one blowing it?"

"Work it out. I'll send Jack to talk to Charissa, see if she admits to anything."

"Can we get a warrant to search her house?"

"Looking for what?"

"Rat poison, lipstick that matches what was on Zoey's car. Those would prove the stalking charge."

Brad nodded. "Okay, I'll see about getting the warrant. While we're waiting, I want you to focus on finding Clauson. I've got a bad feeling about him."

Levi nodded. "We've got the child porn on his laptop, so he knows he's done. If he's not on the run, and I don't think he is, he knows this will end with him in prison, or dead. Either way, my bet is he'll go out with a big bang as his way of telling the world to fuck off."

***

Levi spent the morning doing the same kind of police work he'd done as a detective in Oakland. Lot of legwork. Since Logan Ross was a deputy with the sheriff's department, Levi tapped him to ask around for anyone who remembered Clauson and might have heard from him in the last year. It had taken a couple hours, but Logan had reported back that a couple of old-timers remembered Clauson and said he'd been friends with the then sheriff. The consensus was that Clauson had seemed decent enough on the surface but had raised red flags after a few incidents involving female minors. No surprises there.

Levi leaned back in his seat at his desk as he sipped coffee. He couldn't get past his gut instinct that was telling him that it wasn't Clauson harassing Zoey. He tried to think back over everything he remembered about Charissa Winslow. Which wasn't a whole lot. She always seemed to be around, but on the fringes of his life in Hangman's Loss going back to when he was a teenager. He frowned, turning over an idea, then pulled out his phone and opened his favorites list.

"Hello, my boy."

"Hi, Mom. I'm doing an investigation and think you might have some helpful information."

"Me? What could I help you with?"

"Tell me everything you know about Charissa Winslow."

He heard her sigh. "That poor woman. Is she in trouble?"

"Not sure. Why is she a 'poor woman'?"

"Rough upbringing. Really rough early on. The father, I don't recall his name, Bruce or Bill, abused both her and Darleen, her mother. Darleen wouldn't leave him. I talked to her once, and she gave that pathetic 'but I love him' argument while her face was covered in bruises. I guess you'd say the problem solved itself because he got himself killed in a knife fight at a biker bar in Big Pine. Darleen had some family, but they were as poorly off as she was. My nonprofit helped her get on her feet and find a job, then helped her find a program that provided down payment assistance so she could buy a house. I think things settled down after that. Darleen passed away a year or so ago."

"What about Charissa?"

"Charissa is one of those women who always seems to be trying too hard to find her place. It's like at the baseball game Saturday. Everyone is there to support the teams, but she goes one step too far. Did you see that her jersey had 'Gallagher' printed on the back?"

"Zoey noticed it, but I get what you mean. Anything else?"

"She still lives in the house she shared with Darleen and she has a job as a clerk for the city. She seems brittle, like if you touched her she'd shatter in a million pieces."

"Okay, Mom. This helps. Thanks."

After disconnecting the call, Levi did a search on the computer and found Charissa's address, then mentally traced how one would get to that location from his house. He'd chased a car that evening but had lost it when the driver had nearly caused an accident by cutting off a semi. The car had traveled in the general direction of Charissa's house. Another search came up with her vehicle information. Ford Escape, silver, eight years old. It fit the vehicle he'd chased that night, and matched the description of the car Zoey had seen parked along the road when she'd been shot at.

Brad walked into the bullpen. "IT says the post about Zoey originated from a city computer located in the office Charissa works in. She called in sick today, so Jack hasn't spoken to her."

"We get a warrant to search her place?"

"Yeah, just came in. Let's go. Hopefully she'll be there and we'll bring her in for questioning."

Levi rode shotgun as Brad drove to Charissa Winslow's home. They parked in the street in front of a small home with an overgrown yard. Jack pulled up behind them in his cruiser. Brad and Jack went to the front door while Levi opened a side gate and went around the back of the house. Like the front, the tiny backyard was choked with weeds, the fence Charissa shared with a neighbor missing slats.

The sound of the backdoor opening had Levi putting a hand on his sidearm until Jack poked his head through. "She's not home. But, man, you gotta see this."

Levi entered the house and followed Jack down a short hallway to a tiny bedroom where Brad stood, scanning what looked like a hundred photos arranged on bulletin boards or picture frames around the room. Every one of them containing Levi's image. He surveyed the array. He recognized one from when he'd been out during the holidays. There were several of him at Maddy's café, even some of him checking out the bananas at the grocery store.

"Holy shit."

Brad pointed at a long-distance image taken of the family barbecue in their mom's backyard. "It was her across the arroyo. We'll look for those binoculars and see if they're missing a lens cap." He shook his head. "You called it, brother. She's got it bad for you. Sick bad, and she sees Zoey as a threat."

There were candles arranged around a trio of photos that looked enough like a shrine that Levi's stomach rolled. Printed on computer paper, the center image showed Levi in the parking lot of Gio's Pizza.

"Look at this." He pointed. "I'm wearing the practice jersey. This was that evening Zoey joined us after practice for pizza. We'd left together, and I was talking with her. The photo has been altered to take out Zoey and add Charissa and make it look like it's her I'm talking to. Charissa must have been there."

He peered more closely. "From the angle, she was probably at the far end of the parking lot, maybe sitting in her car. That was the evening when a car drove into the driveway and I gave pursuit. I'm betting that was her."

Jack picked up a card from a stack, holding the cream-colored cardstock by the edges. "You getting married and not telling me, bud?"

Levi looked at words printed in gold lettering with a curly script announcing the marriage of Levi James Gallagher to Charissa Louise Winslow. "Oh shit."

"The wedding is only a month out. I don't know if I can make it on such short notice."

Levi's, "Shut up, Jack," had the other man laughing.

Brad opened the closet door with a gloved hand and revealed a row of hanging dresses, all with sheer plastic covers. Each dress had a tag attached to the hanger. He lifted one, peered at it, then the next in the row. "Fuck."

Levi moved to peer into the closet while Brad pulled out his phone. One of the dresses was billowy and white and was obviously a wedding dress. The others were a kind of filmy material, all in the same pinkish color. He picked up a tag. "Maddy" had been scrawled in spidery writing. The next dress was tagged for Jenny, and one for Emma. "What the hell?"

"Bridesmaids' dresses," Jack said. "You gonna have good food at the reception? I'll only go if you'll have good food. And if you allow kids. I'm not going if my kids aren't invited."

"You're a riot, Morgan."

"I've put out an APB for Charissa Winslow," Brad announced. "We need to log all this as evidence. Jack, search the rest of the house, see if there's more."

Levi moved to the doorway. "I'm going to Zoey's office. I'm not leaving her side until Charissa and Clauson are found."

Brad handed Levi the keys to the police cruiser. "I'd do the same if she was my girl. Will she cooperate?"

"Zoey's not liking me right now, and probably she'll accuse me of bullying cop authority, but she'll have to suck it up."

***

Levi set his phone in the holder on the console as he drove and called Zoey. After several rings, it went to voicemail. He had no way of knowing if she didn't pick up because she was pissed at him, or she wasn't available. The tone sounded, and Levi spoke, "Zoey, stay at your office. I'm on my way there. Call me when you get this message."

He disconnected, the worry that had been nagging at him all morning intensifying by about a hundred-fold. What they'd found in Charissa's house put her in the red zone on the bat-shit crazy scale. Add Clauson to the mix, and the feeling of impending danger was magnified.

The Forest Service office's front lobby was decorated with framed photos of area wildlife, and two men with backpacking gear were speaking with a uniformed ranger at the counter.

Not willing to wait, Levi skirted the counter and strode through a doorway that opened to a wide office space. He circled the room so he could look in each of the cubicles. No Zoey. He approached a woman wearing civilian clothing who was standing at a copy machine. "I'm looking for Zoey Hardesty. You know where she is?"

"She left a little while ago." He stifled a groan when the woman batted her eyes. "Can I help you, officer?" She did a flip thing with her hair, never breaking eye contact.

Ignoring the flirtation, he asked, "Do you know where she might have gone? It's important."

"I'll take you to her boss, he might know." Leaving her copies in the machine, she crooked her finger to beckon Levi to follow her.

The boss was more helpful, informing Levi that Zoey had left twenty minutes earlier to take Lucy home before a scheduled meeting with a California Fish and Wildlife biologist in Bishop later that afternoon.

Figuring he might catch her, Levi got in the cruiser and used lights and sirens to race the five miles home.

Damn it. She wasn't there. He parked and got out. He knocked on her door, expecting to hear Lucy on the other side, but there was nothing. Zoey must have stopped somewhere and he'd beat her home. He crossed the driveway. He still had the spare key for the cottage from when the security company had installed alarms. He'd get the key from the cabin, take a peek inside Zoey's house, see if maybe Lucy was there but snoozing, then figure out his next step.

He was standing on his stoop, key in the lock, when a voice spoke from behind him.

"Hello, Levi."

He turned slowly. Crazy-eyed with bleached blonde hair and lipstick too bright for her pale complexion, and what looked like a .30-30 resting in the crook of her arm, Charissa Winslow had her index finger on the trigger, and the muzzle of her rifle pointed at him center mass. Shit.

"Charissa, what's going on?"

"Everything's ready. All our friends will be there."

"Be where?" Keeping his voice calm, he turned to face her.

"You know, silly. At our wedding. A Gallagher wedding will be the social event of the summer."

"Ah, I'm sure it will be. Hang on a sec." He raised his hand slowly to the mic at his shoulder. He depressed the button, but when he would have spoken Charissa gestured with the gun.

"No," she screeched. "You're going to call for backup. Put that down."

Levi released the mic. Dispatch would have already heard Charissa. "No problem. Why don't you give me that gun so we can have a conversation? You can fill me in on the wedding plans."

Her smile bloomed across her face, showing small, even teeth. "Have you done your vows yet? I'm memorizing mine."

"No, I need to get to that. Maybe you can help me."

"I'd love to help you."

"Great. Give me the gun, Charissa."

She was going to do it. He could see the decision on her face. Then a gunshot ripped through the air with a loud report, hitting the side of the cabin. Charissa screamed and dropped to the ground, hands covering her ears, the rifle flying out of her hands.

In one motion, Levi pushed the door open and grabbed her under the shoulders. She continued her high-pitched, keening cry as he hauled her inside. Another shot rang out, this one splintering wood in the doorframe before he could slam the door shut.

"Shots fired, civilian down, injuries undetermined." Mic in hand, Levi rattled off his address. "Shots came from high ground across the road. Approach with caution."

Charissa lay curled on the floor.

Levi dropped to his knees. "You hit?"

She didn't answer, but at least the screaming had wound down to whimpering. There was no blood visible. "Charissa, are you hurt?"

She stopped whimpering to look at him. "You saved my life. I love you."

Shaking his head, Levi rose to his feet. He peeked out his front window, scanning the slope on the other side of the road, searching for the shooter's location. Then he saw it, a man wearing a red shirt and dark pants and holding a rifle, moving almost nonchalantly from behind a tree.

At that moment, Zoey's Prius turned into the driveway. The clutch of panic nearly stopped his heart. He battled it back so he could think clearly. Zoey's life depended on it.

He whipped his head around. "Is that thirty-thirty fully loaded?" he demanded.

Charissa stared at him blankly.

"Stay inside." With no time to waste, he rushed out the door, grabbing the rifle off the ground by its strap and slinging it across his back even as he took off for the front of the cottage.

He pulled out his service weapon and shot off six rounds in quick succession. Zoey parked next to the police vehicle and opened the door to step out. "Get in front of the cruiser, Zoey. Leave the dog and get to cover. There's a shooter across the street."

Zoey stared at him for a split second, eyes wide, then ignoring his command opened the back door of her car.

Across the street, an empty meadow sloped upward to a ridge. Levi caught a flash of red between pine trees and, shooting in that direction, emptied his Glock as he ran. He wasn't likely to hit Clauson, but he'd keep him pinned down. Levi grabbed Zoey around the waist and pulled her with him for cover in front of the cruiser.

She squirmed in his hold. "I won't leave Lucy." More shots rang out and the rear window of the police vehicle shattered. Sirens sounded in the distance. He let go of Zoey and grabbed his mic, telling the responding officers to cut the sirens and giving them a more precise location for the shooter.

He turned to Zoey. No cowering on the ground for her, she crouched in front of the cruiser, leaning forward to look around the side.

Levi grabbed her by the belt and yanked her back. "Oh no you don't."

"I'm getting Lucy."

"Stay. I'll get her."

"You shoot to distract Paul, I'll get her."

"No." He pulled her around to face him. "I mean it, Zoey, stay under cover. I need to count on you following orders."

Her nod was reluctant, but it was there. He turned to peer around the front end of the cruiser to scan the slope.

"Be careful, Levi."

Clauson was taking cover behind a trio of tall trees whose trunks provided him protection, and through which his red clothing was visible. Levi holstered his handgun and brought the rifle from behind his back. He worked the lever action on the .30-30, brought it to his shoulder, drew a bead, and fired. Loaded. That nutjob could've killed him. He repeated the action twice, aiming for the red, then ditched the rifle. After reloading his Glock, he took a deep breath and stepped out from cover, firing as he circled the Prius. He dove into the backseat to unbuckle Lucy and grab her leash.

Pulling the big dog behind him, he rounded the front of the car. He thought he'd done it, that he was in the clear, until shots rent the air once again. A bullet whistled over his head. Another crack of sound and he felt something punch him under his right shoulder. The force slammed him to the ground like he'd been hit by a mortar shell.

He lay on his back, staring at the deep blue Sierra sky, gasping as he struggled to breathe.

Chapter Twenty

Terror gripped Zoey when Levi reeled back and slammed into the ground. Sharp reports of gunfire split the air, there was a return volley, then silence. She prayed that meant the cavalry had arrived.

She took a quick peek, saw no one was pointing guns at them, then, heart racing, darted from the cover of the cruiser to grab Levi by his Kevlar vest. Digging in her heels, she used all her strength to pull him. Even while gasping for breath, he kicked back with his feet to help. He still held the leash in his fist and Lucy did her part by pulling along with Zoey.

Levi lay on his back in the dirt, heaving for breath. Zoey pulled open his shirt with hands that were shaking. She expected at any second to see ripped flesh and blood, but there, high on the right side of his chest, a plug of metal lay embedded in the heavy plating of his body armor.

"It hit your vest. The bullet hit your vest. I don't think it went through, but I need to check." Lucy stuck her nose in Levi's face and Zoey pushed her away.

Zoey ripped apart the Velcro. He wore a navy t-shirt beneath the vest. She pulled up where the plate had been hit, nearly passing out with relief that the bullet hadn't penetrated the Kevlar. "There's no blood. The vest stopped the bullet."

Levi sucked in a shallow breath. She bent over him, a hand on his cheek. "Deep breath, Levi. Deep breath."

Eyes on hers, he sucked in air, held it, then let it out. After repeating the process, he seemed to breathe more normally. Word came over the radio at his belt that the suspect was in custody. A vehicle roared up the driveway, kicking up a cloud of dust, followed by a car door slamming. "Levi?"

Zoey stood and waved. Brad covered the distance at a dead run.

"He was hit in the vest, but I don't think it went through."

Levi had pushed himself up to lean against the bumper. Brad dropped to his knees and undid the Velcro to pull the body armor completely off. "Where's the pain?"

"Shoulder. Sent me head over ass, knocked the wind out of me. Doesn't hurt too bad."

"It'll hurt like the devil as soon as adrenaline stops pumping."

"Clauson?"

"Surrendered as soon as we engaged." Brad pulled a radio from his belt. "Hangman One, here. Beth, send an ambulance."

"Already on its way, Chief."

Even as the dispatcher spoke, the wail of a siren could be heard in the distance.

"Send two," Levi said.

Brad passed on the order, gaze traveling over Zoey. "You hurt?"

She shook her head. Levi spoke. "Charissa's in my cabin." He nodded to the rifle on the ground. "Had that deer rifle pointed at me and started talking about our wedding." His voice sounded strained. "Shots fired. She hit the ground, screaming like a banshee. No blood so I don't think she was hit."

More vehicles pulled into the driveway. Brad rose to his feet when Monica approached. He motioned to her and moved toward the cabin.

Levi put a hand on the bumper to brace himself and rose to his feet. He leaned heavily against the cruiser.

"You should lie down, Levi," Zoey told him.

He shook his head but didn't say anything. The sound of the siren stopped at the end of their driveway. Lucy leaned against Zoey, and she dropped down to put an arm around the dog's neck, as much for Zoey's comfort as Lucy's.

The next several minutes passed in a blur.

The ambulance crew rushed to Levi with their kits. Pulling Lucy out of the way, Zoey sucked in a horrified breath when the EMT cut off Levi's t-shirt to reveal an angry, red welt below his shoulder, the surrounding area turning a deep red.

A second ambulance crew arrived and was directed to the cabin. A gurney was rolled up, and despite his protests, the crew loaded Levi onto it. She followed the gurney to the back of the ambulance where he was pushed inside. His gaze met hers for a brief moment, then they shut the doors and, with lights on and siren wailing, took him away.

***

Zoey sat on her sofa, staring out the window at the darkening sky, Lucy at her feet. Her baby had kept close to her since the commotion. The entire area around her cottage, including her car and Levi's cabin, had been designated as a crime scene and encircled in yellow tape. Zoey had been allowed to stay in her cabin, but with strict orders not to cross into the quarantine zone.

She should get up, feed Lucy, get herself something to eat for dinner, but all she could do was stare out the window and think about how close that bullet had come to killing Levi. The doctors at the hospital had wanted to keep him overnight, but he'd resisted and had been released with the proviso that if any problems arose, he was to come straight back.

Not that she knew this from Levi, because Zoey hadn't heard from him. Eva had called and filled her in, letting her know Levi was at his mom's house. Zoey was sure it eased Trish's mind to tend to her son for the night.

After Levi had been whisked away in the ambulance, Monica Valdez had taken Zoey's statement, and informed her she would need to come to the police station the next day. Then Zoey had retreated to her little cottage while the police had continued their business. A half hour ago an officer had knocked on her door to inform her that they would return to finish processing the scene in the morning.

She'd wanted to go to the hospital but didn't think he'd want her there. The last thing he needed was for her to make him angry, especially after he'd been shot getting her dog to safety.

For hours she sat on her sofa and replayed every conversation they'd had, and relived every kiss and touch they'd shared. He'd been kind, patient, and loving. She hadn't taken Emma's advice. Zoey never really looked beyond the uniform to the man. She'd been a fool. And the price was losing Levi.

She forced herself to get up and go to the kitchen. She fed Lucy, poured a glass of iced tea, and when she sat at her dining table, she put her head on her crossed arms and let the tears come.

***

The soft knock on the kitchen door roused her. Wiping her eyes, she flipped on the back light. Levi stood in faded jeans and flannel shirt. The sight of him made her heart stop. She opened the door, holding Lucy back by her collar.

"You've been crying again."

"Yeah." She sighed. "I'm not a crier, but you wouldn't know it from the past week." She stepped back, and he entered carrying a plastic bag. "How are you feeling?"

"Like someone hit me with a baseball bat." He started to shrug, then winced.

"Are you in pain?"

"It's better if I don't move my arm." They were standing in her kitchen, and despite being relieved he was there, she felt awkward and stupid.

"Why were you crying?"

She shooed Lucy out of the kitchen and turned to open the freezer. "Everything adding up, I guess. I have some veggie patties in here, if you want burgers." She glanced at him. "Have you eaten?"

He nodded. "Mom fed me and sent spaghetti for you." He waved the bag at her and set it on the counter. "It's still warm. Want to tell me what's really going on?"

"I'm hungry. I haven't eaten since noon. It's been a stressful day."

He gave a laugh, then sucked in a breath. "I can't laugh, it hurts. Stressful is an understatement."

He moved to the table and lowered himself into one of the chairs. Zoey filled a plate from the container Trish had sent, then moved to sit next to Levi. But when she picked up her fork, she only toyed with the food on her plate.

"Zoey, no more hiding."

She pushed the plate back, and for the first time really looked at him. His face was lined with fatigue. He held his body in a way that told her he was in pain. And his entire being was focused on her.

She nodded. This was it. Go big or go home. "You were my high school crush."

"What?"

"You want honesty, there it is."

"You liked me in high school?"

She nodded. "Took me a long time to get over it. Then you moved in next door to me and it all came back."

"You still have a crush on me?"

She shook her head. "Your turn. I gave you something, now you give me something."

He caught her hand in his. "I love you."

She put her other hand to her heart. "Really?" she whispered.

He brought the tips of her fingers to his lips and pressed a kiss to them. "Your turn."

Trembling, frightened, elated, breathless, she forced herself to bare her heart. "I love you too."

A huge grin split his face, and he pulled her closer, then groaned. "God, I want to hold you, but I think it would kill me."

"Don't move, I'll kiss you." She bent forward so she wouldn't put pressure on his shoulder, and gently pressed her lips to his. All the fears and worries of the past weeks lifted to be replaced by the warm glow that loving Levi brought. He made her feel full of light.

He moved his left hand to cup her neck and hold her there, his forehead resting against hers. "Is it too soon to say I want to spend my life with you?"

She shook her head. "Nope," she rasped as she lowered her lips to his once again and felt like all the pieces of life's puzzle had settled into place.

***

Sitting on the sofa, Zoey was leaning against Levi's uninjured side. She'd lit a fire, and Lucy lay sprawled before it. He reached down to remove his shoes and gave a pained moan.

"Let me do that." Zoey slid off the couch and unlaced his shoes and then pulled them off. "Do you have pain meds?"

He nodded. "I'll take them before bed. I wouldn't have been able to drive if I'd taken them earlier." He pressed a kiss to her forehead when she returned to his side.

She laced her fingers through his. "What happened with Charissa?"

He told her what they'd found in Charissa's house. "It's creepy. She's been taking pictures of me for over a year. Stalked me for a time in Oakland, then around the Loss. She targeted you after seeing us together that night we had dinner on your porch with Eva and the guys. I don't think she understands she was doing something wrong." He gave Zoey a sideway glance. "When Brad and Monica went into my cabin? They found her in my bed. Naked."

"Geez. She's sick. Let's hope she gets the help she needs."

"The wedding dresses, the photos? If that was all, I'd be fine with a mental hospital. But deputies recovered shell casings on the mountain where you were shot yesterday. I'm positive we'll get a ballistics match to Charissa's rifle. Jack found an open box of rat poison in her garage. She committed serious crimes that could have killed you or Lucy."

"I guess they'll figure out how to deal with her before there's a trial."

The fire snapped behind the screen, sending a shower of sparks up the chimney.

"What about Paul?"

Levi picked up her hand to rub his thumb across her palm, spreading warmth around her heart. "Brad had six guys up there and had Clauson flanked. He knew he was done. They exchanged a few shots, then he threw down his rifle and put his hands up. He's going for the best plea deal he can get. He's already admitted everything. He said you weren't on his radar, didn't even know you were back in town. Sick bastard said you're too old for him. He was after me, not you."

"Then it wasn't him who did the hit-and-run? It wouldn't have been Charissa."

"Could be he's telling the truth, but I'm not taking his word for it. I'll continue investigating who hit you. They shouldn't be on the road."

She closed her hand around his and brought it to her lips. "I love you. Thank you for looking out for me."

He rested his head on hers, then said in a rough voice, "I need to tell you what happened in Oakland. I didn't before because of your experiences with cops. I didn't want you to judge me, especially when I felt so damn bad about it."

She nodded.

After a long moment, he said, "I shot a man. It was deemed a 'good shoot' by the department, meaning I was within the law to kill him. But that doesn't make me feel any better about it. There should have been another way to deal with it. A kid is dead."

"Why did you shoot him?"

"He'd had a gun, was noncompliant. I waited too long to pull the trigger, and my partner was shot. He tossed the gun before I shot him, turned out it had jammed. My partner was down, I'd taken a half second to look at her and didn't see him toss the gun. All the media cared about was that another white cop had shot another unarmed black man."

"You feel guilty."

"Hell yeah, I feel guilty. I put a bullet through a nineteen-year-old kid. I didn't want to shoot him, waited too long for him to comply, and he shot my partner, who had to take a disability retirement because of it. She actually thanked me, sent me a postcard from a Mediterranean cruise she's on." He stared into the fireplace." I did whatever I could not to shoot that kid, but ultimately it's what happened."

The agony in his expression had Zoey sitting up so she could face him. "I guess I'd worry more if you didn't feel guilty. You're a good man, because you care. I'm lucky to be loved by you."

He snorted. "I'm the lucky one, here. The shooting was horrible, but the one good thing to come out of it was it pushed me to make the break I'd been contemplating but hadn't acted on. If I hadn't come home, I might never have found you."

Epilogue

Levi thought he'd be nervous. God knew this was a big step. But since the granddaddy of all big steps had already happened, this one would be a piece of cake. Instead of being nervous, sheer happiness made him feel like the most fortunate man alive. He was exactly where he wanted to be.

Across from him, Brad looked sharp in his tux. He raised a brow. "You good to go? Not getting cold feet, are you?"

"Hell no, I'm not getting cold feet. I'm ready for this." Trish smiled at him from the front pew, Landon next to her. On the other side of the aisle Dawn sat with Charlie, still geeky-looking in his dark-framed glasses, holding hands with his girlfriend, Beth.

Levi looked out across the church at the people of Hangman's Loss. Jack and Dory, Logan and Maddy, all the people who'd helped to shape him into the man he'd become.

The processional began with Eva and Diego walking arm and arm down the aisle to take their places as the only attendants. Amaya toddled up the center aisle waving what Emma had called a ribbon wand in her hand. Owen followed with a satin pillow holding the rings, then came Keely and Mason carrying a cloth banner between them that read "Here Comes the Bride."

The music changed and there she was. His heart. His future. He didn't know the first thing about wedding dresses but this one suited Zoey perfectly. She'd gone with a braided hairstyle that incorporated a crown of flowers to match the ones she carried. As she walked down the aisle, she kept her eyes on his until coming to a stop in front of him. He took her hand and they faced forward.

The minister said his part, then it was Levi's turn. With Zoey's hands in his, he gazed into her eyes as he vowed his love and said the words that committed him to her forever. He held her gaze as she gave her vows to love and cherish him for the rest of their lives.

Then the minister spoke the words that sealed their union: "I now pronounce you husband and wife."

Levi dipped his head to kiss his bride, his hand at her waist touching the baby bump.

ABOUT THE AUTHOR

National Readers' Choice Award winner for her novel, *Solitary Man*, Diane Benefiel has been an avid reader all her life. She enjoys a wide range of genres, from westerns to fantasy to mysteries, but romance has always been a favorite. She writes what she loves best to read – emotional, heart-gripping romantic suspense novels. She likes writing romantic suspense because she can put the hero and heroine in all sorts of predicaments that they have to work together to overcome.

A native Southern Californian, Diane enjoys nothing better than summer. For a high school history teacher, summer means a break from teenagers, and summer allows her to spend her early mornings immersed in her current writing project. With both kids living out of the house, in addition to writing, she enjoys camping and gardening with her husband.

Diane loves hearing from her readers.

Website: dianebenefiel.com
Twitter: twitter.com/dianebenefiel
Instagram: diane_benefiel
Pinterest: diane_benefiel
Facebook: facebook.com/DianeBenefielRomance
BookBub: bookbub.com/authors/diane-benefiel
Goodreads: goodreads.com/author/show/8075321.Diane_Benefiel
Newsletter: https://landing.mailerlite.com/webforms/landing/n1i2u8

www.BOROUGHSPUBLISHINGGROUP.com

If you enjoyed this book, please write a review. Our authors appreciate the feedback, and it helps future readers find books they love. We welcome your comments and invite you to send them to info@boroughspublishinggroup.com. Follow us on Facebook, Twitter and Instagram, and be sure to sign up for our newsletter for surprises and new releases from your favorite authors.

Are you an aspiring writer? Check out www.boroughspublishinggroup.com/submit and see if we can help you make your dreams come true.

www.ingramcontent.com/pod-product-compliance
Lightning Source LLC
Chambersburg PA
CBHW022108170626
46808CB00002B/645